WICKED
Beginnings

l. a. cotton

Published by Delesty Books

First Paperback Edition
Copyright © 2017 L A cotton
All rights reserved.
ISBN: 9781549759598

Edited by Andrea M Long
Cover Designed by Lianne Cotton
Images licensed from Adobe Stock and Shutterstock

Dedication

Samantha.
For everything.
Thank you.

Also By L A Cotton

Chapter One

I flashed the customs officer a reluctant smile as he scanned my mugshot, silently saying a prayer he found a valid reason to rescind my visa and put an end to this living nightmare. But my plea went unanswered when he ushered me through with a lackluster wave. One that said he enjoyed his job about as much as I was excited to be in his country.

Dad was already at the luggage belt waiting for our worldly belongings to appear. "All set?" he asked, barely able to contain his relief at being back on American soil. I offered him a polite smile from behind the safety of my sunglasses. Large enough to cover half my face, they hid a multitude of sins.

"Your Uncle Gentry should be waiting in arrivals."

Excellent.

Not.

Dad paused, searching my eyes, and then let out a heavy sigh. *Giant sunglasses, one, Dad, zero.* "It'll be okay, you know, Lo. Gentry is family. He can't wait to see you again. I know it's a big change, but we'll make a good life for ourselves here, sweetheart, you'll see." He reached for my shoulder but I slunk away, unwilling to do the whole father-daughter thing in the middle of LAX airport.

If Dad was offended, he didn't show it as he turned to face the luggage belt, hands jammed deep in his trouser pockets, heavily creased from our sixteen-hour journey.

I wanted to be more enthused, I really did. But up and leaving your home and moving halfway across the world wasn't something I could just 'get over'. Not to mention the stress of the long-haul journey.

Uncle Gentry might have been family, but how could you really call someone you'd met once—for a brief stint last summer—family? Sure, he was Dad's brother, but since the events of the last seven months he was no one to me. A distant relative I'd met once and now I would be living with him and his wife, Rebecca; and their four children.

The Stone-Princes.

I wanted to give them a chance—they'd been nice enough last year when we'd visited and all—but I just couldn't find it in me to care. Not when, sometimes, just getting through each day was a mammoth task.

"I think this is the last one." Dad's voice cut through my thoughts and I looked up to find him behind a trolley piled high with our luggage. The last remnants of our life in England. What couldn't be packed into a suitcase, had been sold on eBay or donated to the local charity shop. Lucky for me, I'd managed to condense most of my bedroom into the two suitcases Dad allocated me for the move.

"All set?"

I gave him a tight-lipped nod and followed him toward the arrival lounge, and to our new life.

~

"Robert, Eloise, over here." A tall man with eyes identical to Dad's waved us over with a warm smile. Dressed in black trousers and a sage-green polo shirt that hugged broad shoulders, his sandy hair from last summer was now peppered with grey. He was a taller, fitter version of Dad, even if he was four years older.

"Gentry, it's good to see you." Dad took his hand, clapping him on the back with his other. I let them have their moment while I watched the other travellers search for their families in the awaiting crowd, anything to take my mind off how busy the place was. A young girl launched herself into the arms of a teary-eyed couple, letting them envelop her in a parent sandwich. It was impossible not to smile at their reunion, but as the corners of my mouth lifted my chest constricted, sucking the air clean from my lungs.

"Lo... Eloise." A hand landed on my arm and I jerked back to my father. "Sorry," he added. "I didn't mean to startle you. Your Uncle Gentry would like to say hello."

I swallowed down the lump in my throat, pushed the glasses up my face and rested them on my head. "Hello," I said holding out my hand, but Gentry laughed, knocking away my arm and wrapping me into a bear hug.

"It's really good to see you again, Eloise." He held me tight while my arms hung limply at my sides. "I'm so sorry for your loss."

My body tensed and I clamped my eyes tight, counting down from ten. At zero, I inhaled deeply, forced them open, and stepped out of his hold. "Thank you." The words still choked me, even after seven months.

"Right, well then, shall we?" Gentry took control of the trolley and motioned to the huge exit doors. And just like that we were welcomed into his family.

Only, it occurred to me, he was the only one here.

~

3

Dad and Gentry sat upfront in his sleek black Range Rover while I watched California whizz by from the back seat. I'd only visited the States once before, but I'd forgotten how different it was from our home back in Surrey, England. *Old home*, I reminded myself.

"Kyle and Summer can't wait to see you again. He's stoked to have you starting junior year with him. Macey too. And I'm sure Maverick will make you feel very welcome."

How wonderful, I inwardly groaned, letting my head fall against the cool tinted glass. As if being a Brit in an American high school wouldn't be hard enough, I was going to be paraded around like a freak show.

Gentry continued, apparently unaware of my lack of excitement about starting a new school. "Rebecca made the arrangements. You'll meet with the Principal first thing on Monday."

And not only would I be the British freak show, I had to endure two more years of high school, whereas back in the UK, I would have been in my final year at college. But Dad and my new school had decided it would be better for me to stay back a year and sit all the classes I needed to get the high school diploma. Something about making it easier to apply for colleges. Although part of me wondered if my behaviour of late had anything to do with his decision.

Fuck. My. Life.

"Isn't that great, Lo?" Dad covered for my silence and I managed to grumble out something about being excited to see them again.

I wasn't.

Life will do that to you though. Rip out your heart and leave it bleeding all over the floor, then expect you to pick up the pieces and get on with it. I got on with it, but I was only going through the motions.

Like right now, being in a new country. There was no

crackle of excitement in the air. No seed of anticipation blossoming in my chest at the endless possibilities and adventures that could await me.

I was numb.

A hollow pit of nothingness carved deep in my stomach.

The sea glistened in the summer sun. It was beautiful, and, in another life, I would have appreciated it, but right now I just couldn't. And as the 4x4 sped past a sign welcoming us to Wicked Bay, I shuddered. I'd been here once before, it should have felt familiar. But all I could remember was a pair of intense eyes, the colour of dark chocolate interspersed with flecks of gold, and a wicked smile that could charm even the most impressionable young girls.

Shaking the unwelcome thoughts out of my head, I observed the big detached houses flanking us on either side. All unique with fancy brickwork, sloping driveways and perfectly pruned lawns, the whole place looked like something out of The OC. Uncle Gentry drove to the end of the street before turning off onto a road steeped with tall billowing trees. I shifted into the centre of the backseat, watching with morbid fascination as he rolled to a stop, parking next to a fancy sports car. I'd forgotten just how big their house was.

"Welcome home," he said with a strange note of hesitation in his voice. As my eyes swept over the mini-mansion in front of me, the joke—and his sudden change in mood—was lost on me.

We climbed out and I stood awkwardly outside the house while Dad and Gentry fetched our luggage. No one mentioned the lack of a welcoming party for our arrival, so I didn't bring it up. It wasn't like I was in any rush to do awkward introductions either.

"So, you'll be in the pool house." Gentry opened the

door and motioned for me to go ahead, but I hung back, waiting for him to pass. "Now, I know there's only one bedroom, but we've replaced the old couch with a sofa bed. I hope that's okay?"

"Gentry, it's more than enough. The agent left a message. The work should be finished soon. They anticipate it being wrapped up in a month. A couple at the most."

He gripped my father's shoulder. "There's no rush, Robert. We're excited to have you both here."

He kept saying that, but I couldn't work out if it was for our benefit, or his.

Dad nodded and motioned for his brother to lead the way. I traipsed after them, through the house that resembled a small mansion. It really was something else. We passed the deep staircase which led to a balcony, and what I knew to be at least five bedrooms positioned down the long hallway. The kitchen was just as I remembered, spacious and modern with a centre island and six black leather stools tucked neatly underneath. Sparkly dark counters lined the walls housing various gadgets, all of which looked brand new.

"Lo?"

My eyes snapped to Dad and Gentry. They had stopped by the French doors, both smiling at me, and I realised I was gawking. "Even though I've been here, it's like seeing it again for first time." The words tumbled out before I could stop them and Gentry let out a smooth chuckle.

"I'll be sure to tell Loretta you were impressed. Honestly, I don't know what we'd do without that woman."

"Loretta, right," I grumbled with a shake of my head. They had a housekeeper. I'd forgotten about that.

This wasn't life. At least, it wasn't my life. Sure, Dad did okay. We'd lived in a nice house in the country and money had never been an issue, but this was... well, this was going to take some getting used to.

Gentry helped us get situated in the pool house and then left us to unpack. It was more of a small self-contained apartment overlooking the amazing pool in the beautifully landscaped gardens. It was all so annoyingly perfect, I wanted to hate it.

Dad insisted I take the bedroom. He started at Stone and Associates on Monday and expected to be working long hours to get up to speed with the family business. Which meant I would be spending a lot of time alone, or with my new family. The ones who were so excited to see me again they still hadn't bothered to show up yet.

I'd just finished unpacking one of my cases into the small closet, when Dad poked his head around the doorframe. "Gentry made us something to eat."

"Great."

His eyes scanned the room, and he smiled. "It's already starting to look like home."

I cocked my eyebrow at him in disbelief. Surely, he knew it was going to take more than a few strategically placed photo frames and sentimental keepsakes to feel homely? But instead of starting an argument I said, "Come on, I'm starving." I ducked under his arm and headed for the house.

We found Gentry placing a bowl onto the island. "It's not much. Loretta took a personal day, but she'll be back tomorrow."

"It's fine, right, Lo?" Dad flashed me a reassuring smile, and I said a polite thank you, helping myself to some salad.

"They'll be here soon." Uncle Gentry checked his watch again. "Rebecca can't wait to see you both."

He kept saying that, but we'd been here at least an hour and still hadn't caught so much as a glimpse of his wife and their children. Dad gave a strained laugh, and I kept my head low, shoving the green leaves around my plate.

"They promised," Gentry grumbled under his breath so quietly he was probably unaware he'd actually said it out loud.

"Sorry, I'm sorry." A woman breezed into the room, arms wide as she made a beeline for her husband. "I got held up."

"It's fine," Gentry said, standing to greet his wife. "You're here now. Come and say hello to Robert and Lo."

"Oh my." She glanced in my direction and her eyes widened. "Eloise, what a beautiful young lady you've become."

I blushed wanting the ground to open and swallow me because if she thought I was beautiful it made her Aphrodite. "Thank you, it's nice to see you again."

"Rebecca." Dad rose from his stool. "It's good to see you again." He wrapped her into an awkward hug that had me stifling a laugh.

"Are they with you?" Gentry looked to the door.

"They're not here?"

Gentry and his wife shared a strange look, but Rebecca's smile widened as she launched into a game of twenty questions. *How was our flight? Did we need anything? Was the pool house okay?* Dad was halfway through his not so funny story about the layover in Reykjavik when a door banged somewhere in the house and the sound of chatter filled the air.

"Thank God," Gentry grumbled and I was about to ask what he meant when a familiar face bounded into the room. Kyle, with his father's good looks and same sandy hair, grinned in my direction. "Cous, looking good."

Heat crept into my cheeks and I offered him a small wave. His sister, Summer, the youngest of the Stone-

Prince children, and a perfect mix of Rebecca and her father, edged forward offering a small smile. "It's nice to see you both again."

"You too, Summer," Dad said. "I know Lo is looking forward to spending time with you all."

"Yeah," I grumbled in earnest.

Gentry shared a look with his son and Kyle shrugged as a tall willowy girl entered the room. I hadn't met her last summer—she and her brother were visiting their dad—but I knew her to be Macey, Rebecca's daughter. The resemblance between them was startling, but from my limited knowledge on the Prince daughter, she was the polar opposite of her mother. Macey didn't speak, offering me a tight-lipped smile. I gave her the benefit of the doubt, because if she felt even an ounce of the awkwardness coursing through me, I got it.

"Macey," Rebecca scolded. "Please say hello to your Uncle Robert, and Eloise."

"Hello." Her flat tone matched her expression, and I received her message loud and clear—we wouldn't be BFF's anytime soon.

I shot Dad a discreet look but he didn't seem to share my concern, smiling reassuringly just as Uncle Gentry said, "And this giant here, is Maverick."

My head lifted watching as another person entered the room. I did a double take, my eyes widening with surprise, and then something much, much worse. My stomach sank and then plummeted into the tips of my toes.

It couldn't be.

There was absolutely no way this could be happening.

My fingers curled around the edge of the stool as I tried to stay upright all while I was unable to tear my gaze away from a face I thought I'd never see again.

A face I didn't want to see again.

Dark hair curled at the ends giving way to an angular jaw and a perfect nose set between two of the most intense and unfathomable eyes I'd ever seen. Eyes I'd almost lost myself in once before.

Fuck.

No one seemed to notice my shock as Gentry clapped a hand around his stepson's shoulder, jolting me back into the room. The eldest Stone-Prince flinched, and I saw the tension between them. Felt it descend over the room. We all did. It radiated from Maverick like a wall of blistering heat. Then his eyes narrowed on me, and I saw the realisation flash across his face. His glare turned icy cold … unresponsive, and I balked. I wanted the floor to open and swallow me whole and if that failed, I'd settle for spontaneous combustion. Anything to escape this nightmare.

How could this be happening?

How?

"Hi." His voice turned my blood cold. He shirked out of his stepfather's hold and folded his arms over his chest, standing to his full height. Uncle Gentry wasn't wrong, he was a giant. Easily six two—and about three inches taller than last summer—there was nothing boy about him. My eyes scanned the length of his body, lean muscle stacked on more lean muscle. When I reached his face, his lips twitched as if he knew I'd been checking him out.

Shit.

What the hell was I doing?

Maverick Prince might not have been my blood cousin, but he was family. He was also the boy I almost gave myself to on a warm summer's eve at a beach party last summer.

Double fuck.

I risked peeking up at him through my lashes. His hardened gaze was still trained on me, but his smirk slid away replaced with a look of disgust. My stomach clenched violently as my grip on the stool tightened until the blood drained from my knuckles.

How on earth had this happened? How had I spent hours talking to a boy on a beach and not known *who* he was?

How had I not realised? And how had he not put two and two together?

He remembered, and from the looks of it, he wasn't too happy about it either.

This wasn't good—not good at all.

The chink of metal against glass broke our stand-off, and I focused on Uncle Gentry as he cleared his throat. "Now everyone's present, I'd just like to say how happy we are to have you both here." He smiled warmly at me and moved to Dad, squeezing his shoulder. "Our home is yours for as long as you need it. Robert, Eloise, welcome to the family."

My eyes shuttered, and I inhaled a sharp breath. When I plucked up the courage to open them again, Maverick was gone.

I'd thought moving to Wicked Bay was the worst thing that could happen to me, but I was about to find out, it was only the beginning.

Chapter Two

"Are you nervous, kiddo?"

I shot Dad a terse glare. With no sunglasses to protect him from my 'are you for real' face this time, his head shook with laughter. "Too much?"

"Just a little." I helped myself to another bagel, picking off a tiny chunk with my fingers. "And I'm not sure nervous sums up how I feel about all of this."

Since realising just who Maverick Prince was, I'd felt nothing but a tight knot in my stomach. I popped the pastry flakes into my mouth and glanced around the kitchen. It was almost seven-thirty and no one else had surfaced yet. I'd wanted to eat in the pool house, but after a strained weekend Dad insisted we eat with the rest of the *family*.

"It'll get easier. It's just new, for all of us." He gave me a pointed look, one that told me he'd also picked up on the serious vibes between Uncle Gentry and Maverick.

After the less than stellar introductions on Friday, Macey disappeared after her brother. It was clear he wasn't the boy I'd gotten to know that night last summer, but then maybe he was. Maybe the Maverick I'd spent hours talking to was an illusion? An attempt to seduce the awkward, shy girl. But that made no sense either.

Whatever.

It was done. And everything that had happened since then put that night into perspective.

Maverick Prince was no one to me. He might have been family, but that didn't mean I had to interact with him.

Ever.

Kyle and Summer had stuck around for a while but eventually went off to do their own thing, and I retreated to the pool house. In two days, it had fast become my sanctuary, and I only left if necessary. Unfortunately, for me, the first day at a new school required leaving my room and facing reality.

"Ahh, Robert, Miss Eloise; good morning, it's so good to see you again." A short plump woman hurried into the kitchen, arms full of bags. "I'm Loretta, remember, si? The housekeeper."

"As if we could forget your cooking," Dad said around a wide smile.

"Oh." Her crow-lined eyes widened in my direction. "So pretty, Miss Eloise, I see what Gentry meant now."

My ears perked up, and I arched an eyebrow at Dad. He shrugged, continuing to eat his French toast.

"Where is everyone?" *Good question*, I thought to myself, relieved I wasn't the only person who wondered. "It's back to school today, no?"

"Loretta, thank God, we've missed you." Rebecca breezed into the kitchen like a Greek goddess. The woman didn't walk, she glided on air. "Robert, Eloise, you're up. Excellent." She air-kissed Dad and squeezed my arm on the way to the coffee maker. "Nervous, honey?"

It was my turn to shrug. "Not really." *Liar.*

"You'll be fine. You'll have Summer and Kyle, and I'm sure Macey will help you get settled."

I very much doubted that. But whatever. I didn't need

or want their help if they didn't want to give it. It was just school; how hard could it be?

"Is Kyle—"

"Is Kyle what?" He breezed into the room looking as fresh as a daisy and I had to wonder where they all were. Was there another kitchen they hung out in before joining us, because they sure didn't look like people who had just climbed out of bed. Two coffees in, I was still slouched over my plate trying to kick-start my body into action.

"Are you giving Summer and Eloise a ride into school?"

"No can do, Momma P, first day back and I have to make a good impression with Coach."

Rebecca's eyes narrowed with a hint of frustration and I stifled a laugh. "Kyle, what have I told you?"

He pulled open the refrigerator and stuck his head inside. It was one of those huge American types with a built-in ice dispenser. When he reappeared, juice in hand, he grinned. "I think you said, 'please don't call me Momma P'."

"So..." Hand planted on her hip she glowered at him, and I stifled a snigger again. Kyle had an air of a cocky boy who didn't care much for the rules. I liked it. He reminded me a lot of my brother. My chest tightened, and I swallowed over the pastry stuck in my throat.

"My bad. You're right it isn't very appropriate." He tilted his face up as if deep in thought. "Got it." He snapped his finger in the air. "Step Momster."

Her mouth fell open, and he shot me an amused wink before disappearing. Rebecca yelled after him, but he'd already gone. She let out a heavy sigh. "That boy will send me to an early grave."

"He's all Gentry," Dad said not looking up from the papers scattered over the island top.

"And don't I know it. I suppose I should thank my

lucky stars he hasn't charmed his way into some girl's bed and gotten her pregnant yet."

"Darling, I thought we agreed to give him a break." Gentry appeared at his wife's side and hooking an arm around her waist he pulled her against him. She giggled like a schoolgirl and leaned up to kiss him, and my bagel threatened to make a reappearance.

"He's unruly, Gentry."

"Oh, he's just testing the waters. He's a junior now. Remember what we were like at that age, Robert?"

"Daughter present," I choked out and everyone laughed.

"Can you drop Summer and Eloise off at school? Kyle had to go in early."

Deep lines creased Gentry's face. "No can do. Robert and I need to leave shortly too. There's a breakfast meeting we can't miss."

Rebecca leaned in to him, lowering her voice. "Well, I can't take them. I'm meeting Cheri to discuss the fall event."

Summer appeared in the doorway looking every bit the American dream. Long honey-blonde hair framed a heart shaped face, giving way to big blue eyes. Ugh. I needed serious time to look that good. "Morning," she said, taking a seat at the island and helping herself to breakfast.

"Hey," I replied trying to figure her out. She was quieter than the other Stone-Prince children.

"Are Macey and Maverick still around?" Gentry asked Summer, and she gave him a small nod. "Then it's settled, they can take them," he said.

"Gentry, I'm not sure..."

"What's up?" Maverick entered the kitchen, and the mood changed immediately. Even Dad straightened beside me. I watched the eldest Prince move around the room from under my lashes. His body was lithe, the basketball jersey hung loose until he twisted and turned revealing lean and defined muscle. The boy I met last summer had filled out in all the right places. My stomach fluttered in an act of betrayal and I felt a little lightheaded.

Damn him.

He couldn't have shrunk or contracted a bad case of teenage acne?

"Maverick," Gentry leaned back on the counter. "You'll give your sister and Lo a ride to school this morning." It wasn't a request.

"We can't." Macey appeared, her expression as cold as it had been Friday. "We have a thing."

"Macey, please," Rebecca hissed low, but not enough we all didn't hear it.

"We can walk, it's not too far." Summer gave me a tight-lipped smile, and I wondered what she knew that I didn't.

"Maverick." Gentry's tone was final and something crackled in the air. I glanced from my uncle to his stepson and back again wondering who would be crowned winner in battle of the wills.

To our surprise, Maverick conceded. "Fine. We leave at eight-fifteen."

He didn't look at me. Didn't address me directly, but I felt his animosity all the way down to my bones, and I realised whatever I thought had existed between us that night was a fantasy. Macey grumbled something under her breath, grabbed a glass of juice, and stomped out of the room. I went back to deconstructing my bagel. He left too; I knew because the tension rippling in the air evaporated, and Rebecca and Uncle Gentry went back to chatting with Dad about his first day at Stone and Associates while Summer and I sat in easy silence. And we pretended none of that just happened.

~

"You're not wearing that?" Macey looked me up and down and I bristled, standing a little taller.

"Well, I hadn't planned on changing when we got there," I shot back with a scowl to rival her own. Maverick appeared and for a second I was sure I heard him snigger, but when I met his eyes, his expression matched his sister's.

What the hell was his problem? It was a year ago— thirteen months to be exact. It wasn't like it was that big of a deal, anyway. I was surprised he could even remember. He was the one who left me cold and alone on the beach. Not the other way around.

"I think she looks nice," Summer came to my defence, and I was about to offer her my thanks when Macey snapped, "We're going to be late, let's go."

Following Summer into the back of Maverick's sleek black Audi, I glanced down at my outfit, hating she'd made me second guess myself. I'd never cared before about what I wore, I wasn't about to start now. As far as I was concerned, I looked good in the skinny jeans, black vest top, and my favourite zebra print Converse.

"I like your tattoo, Eloise."

"Thanks." I gave Summer a small smile, feeling the familiar pinch of grief around my heart.

"Mom and Dad would kill me if I ever came home with a tattoo."

"Because you're fifteen, Sum," Macey said, her voice a lot less growly. But that quickly changed when she turned to us and swept her severe gaze over my arm. "You might want to cover that up at school."

I answered by sliding my glasses down my face and turning my head to the window. It had been a spur-of-the-moment thing getting the floral sleeve. I'd had one too many drinks and Chris, my on-off boyfriend at the time, had been all too willing to ink my virgin skin. Dad almost shit a brick but there wasn't much he could do about it, and eventually he shelved it with the rest of my bad decision-making moments. Losing your wife and son in the same accident that almost took your daughter's life did that to a man. And for the last three months, it had been my get out of jail free card, but I had a feeling I was all out of excuses now. California was our fresh start. Dad's attempt at piecing back together what was left of our family. I was to attend Wicked Bay high school, play nice with Dad's family, and decide what I wanted to do with my life.

If only it were that easy.

Even with the top down, ten minutes inside the car with the Prince siblings, was ten too many. They chatted in low whispers while Summer and I sat in the back in awkward silence. Part of me had hoped they would show me around when we arrived, but that dream evaporated when my eyes had landed on *him* in the kitchen on Friday. During conversations I overheard last summer, I'd picked up on some tension between Rebecca's kids and Uncle Gentry. But that was common for most blended families, wasn't it? Still, something seemed off.

A stream of kids filtered into the parking lot as Maverick pulled into a bay. He cut the engine and climbed out not sparing us—or me—a second glance. Summer seemed immune to their surly attitudes. "I can show you where the office is," she said as we got out of the car. Heeding Macey's words, I pulled the cardigan out of my bag and slipped it on.

A group of boys approached Maverick, laughing and fist bumping, and I realised it was the first time I'd seen him crack a smile since I arrived. But that wasn't what caught my attention. It was the way all the other kids watched their group, as if a celebrity had just turned up on campus. Conversations paused. Heads turned. A mix of envy and awe painted on their faces. Longing on most of the girls. Even the group Macey made a beeline for, seemed more interested in her brother and his friends, whispering and pointing, all dreamy-eyed and breathless. Part of me wondered if it was the reason her scowl remained firmly in place.

Either way, neither of them said goodbye.

Refusing to show any signs of weakness, I hitched my bag up my shoulder and followed Summer toward the building. But a voice stopped me in my tracks.

"London, wait up."

I turned slowly, glaring at Maverick through my glasses. He glanced around at his friends who were watching with a mix of curiosity and amusement. "Don't get lost," he laughed, the corners of his mouth pulled into a cocky smirk, and I clenched my fists at my sides trying to curb my anger.

Screw it.

Screw him.

Maybe he thought I was the same shy meek girl from last summer. An easy target. Someone to toy with, to laugh about with his friends. But that girl was long gone. I lifted my hand and flipped him the bird. A couple of the guy's mouths dropped open and one elbowed Maverick in the ribs, but he didn't laugh. He didn't flinch as he tilted his head to the side and rubbed his jaw, his cold, assessing gaze narrowed right on me, as if he was trying to figure me out.

Trying to figure out my weaknesses.

I didn't stick around to find out if he had.

~

After a brief meeting with the Principal, I hurried to my first class, praying I wasn't going to be made to stand up and introduce myself. But when I slipped inside the room, it was much worse.

"Cous, over here." Kyle beckoned me over to his table

at the back of the room, and I groaned to myself. For the love of God. Did these boys not know how to use someone's name?

I waved him off, not wanting to make a scene, but he pounded on his desk, jumped up from his seat and announced, "Everyone, this is my cousin, Eloise from England. Eloise, this is everyone."

Most of the class cheered, but a couple of girls rolled their eyes at me as if they thought I wasn't worthy of Kyle's grand gesture. I wanted to agree, instead I ducked my head and veered around the tables to get to him. "Really? You had to do that?" I hissed, dropping onto the chair behind the empty desk beside him.

"Come on, Cous, we're family. Mi casa es su casa." Kyle grinned and oddly, I found myself grinning back. The boy was annoying as hell, but he meant well and I liked him. He made it so easy, unlike his two more hostile stepsiblings.

"So, how'd your meeting with Principal D go? Let me see your schedule." He held out his hand, and I passed the sheet of paper I'd left the Principal's office with. "AP English, ouch. But you're in Physical Ed. with Mr. DeLuca, nice. I'm in that class. History and Math, too."

Five classes with Kyle? I didn't know whether to be relieved or afraid for my life. But having someone was better than no one. And Kyle seemed like a good person to have in your corner.

"And Macey's in your English and Bio class." He flashed me a knowing smirk and I shook my head. "Yo, guys, this is my cousin, Eloise."

"Lo," I corrected, smiling at the two guys watching our exchange. They introduced themselves just as the teacher arrived and called time on the morning chaos. I settled my eyes up front. I would have to work my arse off to keep up, but at least I had Kyle to help me. Then one of his friends whispered, "So Kyle, are we partying with Maverick tonight or what?"

And just like that I became alone again.

Chapter Three

L unch was interesting. They'd given me a pre-loaded card in my registration pack which you added dollars to and then used like a credit card. At my old school, you just handed over your money and went on your way. But as the day wore on, I began to realise this wasn't just any old school. Most of the kids wore designer labels, and I'd spied more than one brand new sports car in the car lot. Even the school building was state of the art. All hi-gloss, glass, and chrome furnishings.

"Hmm, here." I handed the woman my card and waited for her to do her thing. When she was done, I picked up my tray and scanned the room. It was a huge lofty space with floor to ceiling windows down one side, opening out onto a patio with picnic benches. The sound of teenage chatter and laughter echoed off the walls, but one voice stood out.

"Cous, saved you a seat."

I wanted to be pissed at Kyle's overbearingness, but I couldn't deny the flicker of relief in my chest knowing I wouldn't have to fight my way through the crush to find an empty table. A chorus of hellos greeted me as I slid in beside him.

"How was chem?"

"Is it ever anything besides dull?" I replied, and he cracked a wide grin, slinging his arm over my shoulder.

"I knew we were related 'cause I fucking hate science too."

"Except reproductive class, am I right?" A guy with shaggy brown hair laughed but Kyle slapped him around the head.

"Dude, ladies present." He grinned but then joined the other boys in a debate about who was hooking up with who.

"Hey, I'm Laurie, we met last summer." A pretty girl across from me leaned over, grabbing my arm. "I like your tat." The start of the floral pattern was peeking out underneath from where I'd rolled up my sleeves.

"I remember." I did, vaguely. "And thanks." I tugged the material back down.

"Want to get out of here?" She glanced around conspiratorially and I wondered who she was looking for. When her gaze rested on Kyle, I wondered if I really wanted to know.

"Sure."

Her face lit up. "Awesome. Come on."

I said a quick goodbye to Kyle, not giving him a chance to make a scene, grabbed my sandwich and hurried after Laurie. Like me, she wore jeans and a t-shirt. A stark contrast to all the flowy skirts, summer dresses, and cropped pants.

"So, Kyle said you've moved here permanently?" she said as we made our way out of the huge sliding doors. I nodded slipping my glasses over my eyes. There was something in the way she said his name. A mixture of longing and irritation that only came from knowing someone well, *too* well.

"Let me guess, ex?"

"Something like that," she murmured cutting across

the grass to a smaller building. We disappeared around the side and I could see it was the Gym, and behind, the sports track. A group of kids were huddled by the bleachers.

"Laurie, what's up?" The guy spoke to my new friend, but his eyes lingered on me. "Who's your friend?"

"This is Lo Stone, Kyle's cousin from England. She just moved here."

"Lo, nice," the guy said. "I'm Devon."

I scanned the rest of the small group, and Laurie introduced me to Autumn and Liam. They didn't hit me with twenty questions or pass any judgement on my outfit or accent, like most of the kids in my morning classes. It was refreshing.

"Want a smoke?" Liam asked me after a few minutes.

"I'm good, thanks."

"Hey," Laurie said. "Show them your arm. Autumn, you have to check this out."

I peeled back the sleeve, rolling it up my arm. Autumn leaned in close. "Holy crap, that's awesome."

"Right?"

"I'm so freakin' jealous. My parents would die if I did that."

I flinched at her words but stuffed down my emotions. Now was not the time to go postal. "My dad wasn't so happy with me when he found out."

"Oh, shit," Devon laughed and soon we were all laughing. It felt good. Strange, but good.

"So, what's it like?"

"What's what like?" I said.

"Oh, come on, you know, living with them. The Stone-Princes." His voice was nasal, mocking, and Liam stifled a laugh.

"Devon, don't." Laurie warned, and I wondered who she was protecting. Me, herself, or Kyle.

He threw up his hands. "I mean no harm. But she has

insider access. I'd love to know what makes Prince tick. That guy is..." Devon raked a hand through his hair but changed the subject after receiving another death stare. "So, Lo, do you like to party?"

Did I like to party?

It was a loaded question. I liked to get drunk or high, and forget, yeah. But something told me these kids partied on a whole other level. One I wasn't sure I was ready for.

"No, I like to stay home and study." I flashed Devon an amused smirk, disguising the ball of nerves knotted in my stomach.

"Touché, Stone, Touché. Well, there'll be a thing at the Bay tonight. A bonfire, barbecue, that kind of thing. The annual back to school gathering. You should come. Everyone will be there."

Everyone?

I remembered the Bay, the local beach. As if I could forget. It was a popular summer hangout. But if Maverick and Macey would be there, I wasn't sure I wanted to go.

Something snapped.

What the hell was I saying? Screw them and their shitty attitudes. I hadn't done anything to deserve their hostility, and just because they wanted nothing to do with me, didn't mean I had to sit and fester in the pool house. Besides, maybe it was better this way.

"Sounds good," I said earning me a little shriek of approval from Laurie as she looped her arm through mine. "This will be so much fun. Oh, you should totally come to my house first and we can get ready together."

That was how I found myself sitting in her bedroom, six hours later. Dad wasn't home by the time I'd left. I'd texted him to let him know I would be hanging out with a new friend. He seemed pleased, or relieved. Either way, he wanted me to embrace my new life and told me to be home by eleven. He'd already programmed the house's number into my new phone along with Rebecca, Gentry and Kyle's numbers. Speaking of Kyle, my phone vibrated. As soon as he found out I was going to the party with Laurie, he'd been giving me shit.

Kyle: Traitor.

Lo: You love me really.

Kyle: Yeah, I do, Cous. See you at the Bay.

It bleeped again.

Kyle: And behave.

I frowned. What the hell did that mean? Had Dad asked him to look out for me? Was this some kind of father-cousin tag team?

"Let me guess, Kyle?" Laurie eyed me through the free-standing mirror and I nodded.

"Geez, he's so overprotective. It's why I called it off, you know? I felt like I couldn't breathe. You're going to have your hands full with them."

Didn't I know it?

"Summer is cool," Laurie went on. "She's quiet and doesn't like the limelight. Kyle thrives on it. He's even worse since he made the varsity football team. Macey is the same bitch she's always been, and in case you hadn't already noticed, Maverick is ... well, let's just say no one knows what has gotten into that guy over the last year."

So, I wasn't the only one who'd noticed his mood change.

"Do you..." I hesitated. Did I really want to understand him? He sure as hell didn't deserve it. "Know him?"

She shrugged, dragging the straightening iron through her honey-blonde hair. "Not really. I mean, I dated Kyle throughout tenth grade and I hung out at the house occasionally, but Maverick keeps his group small. No outsiders. And I don't know if you noticed, but there's some major tension between them and your uncle."

"Oh, I've noticed. What is that?"

"Nobody really knows. I figured it was because Mrs. Prince left their dad, married your uncle, and they had a baby together, but that was years ago. This is something recent, it has to be. Or maybe it's stuff with his dad. I've heard he can be pretty intense."

She wasn't wrong. Surely, they didn't resent Gentry for something that happened over fifteen years ago? They were just children themselves.

"Macey is a grade A bitch. Watch your back with her." Laurie switched off the iron and added some gloss to her lips, smacking them together before pouting into the mirror. "I think Devon likes you."

"He's a guy, I bet he likes anything with a vagina."

She sniggered and spun around to face me. "I knew we'd hit it off. Welcome to Wicked Bay, Eloise Stone. Time to show you how we party."

~

The beach swarmed with people. Some I recognised from school. Most, I didn't. I stuck close to Laurie as she guided us through the chaos, the familiar rush of panic threatening to consume me. But, surprisingly, the feel of the sea air brushing my skin grounded me. Autumn waved us over from where she stood with Devon and another guy. "You made it," she beamed, hugging Laurie while I stood awkwardly taking in the scene before me.

There was a huge bonfire in the middle of the small horseshoe bay. Flames flickered high in the dusky sky, throwing out more heat than necessary given the temperature was still well into the eighties. Glad I'd left my cardigan back at the pool house, I wore a sleeveless t-shirt and a pair of cut-off jeans. People stared at my tattoo openly, but so what? It was a part of me. A permanent reminder. I wouldn't hide it away like some dirty secret.

Someone came up beside me and I turned to find Devon grinning down at me. "Drink?"

"Sure." I replied. One wouldn't hurt. Maybe two would take the edge off and help me relax, but I wouldn't have any more. I'd been there one too many times and promised Dad I'd not slip back into old habits. Even I knew getting wasted and making a fool of myself on the first day of school wasn't the greatest idea. No matter how tempting the idea was.

Devon disappeared into the crowd with his friend, and I moved closer to Laurie and Autumn while they chatted about things that meant nothing to me. Until Autumn said, "Kyle, two o'clock."

"I don't care," Laurie huffed in an overdramatic sigh, silently telling us she cared probably a little too much.

"Yeah, right." Autumn glanced at me and we shared a knowing look.

"You won't care he's talking to Melissa Tanske then?"

Laurie's head whipped around only to elicit a grumble of disapproval when she realised Autumn was baiting her.

"Just admit it, you still want him."

"Do not." She folded her arms over her chest defiantly.

"Is it always this crazy?" I changed the subject. Kyle only took me to one party last summer, but it had been nothing like this. I quickly pushed the thought out of my head, not wanting to go there.

"Not always. First party back is something else, but after tonight people do their own thing unless it's game night."

"Game night?"

"Yeah football season kicks off soon and then come winter, it'll all be about the Wicked Bay Wreckers."

I stared at them blankly, earning me a sigh. "You do know who your cousins are, right?" Laurie said.

When I didn't answer, she blew out an exasperated breath. "You are far too cool for your own good. Wicked Bay thrives on two games: football and basketball. See those guys." Laurie pointed to a group of boys over by the bonfire, all big and ripped. "That's the football team. Kyle is tipped to captain the team next year."

"Football, got it."

"And those." She swung her arm around to another group hanging out by the volleyball net. They were taller and leaner, but every bit as gorgeous. "They are half of the Wicked Bay Wreckers."

Oh.

My eyes found him first. Maverick Prince in all his shirtless glory as he lunged for the ball, fist clenched out in front of him. I ran my slick hands across my jean shorts. Jesus, it should have been illegal for my step cousin to look so hot. I mean, he'd been gorgeous last summer, but he was different then. Even though he'd left me feeling cheap and confused in a darkened corner of the beach, he'd been nice to me.

Kind.

I'd sensed a vulnerability about him. It was the reason I talked to him in the first place. But something told me nice and Maverick Prince weren't words that belonged together anymore.

A hand clapped me on the shoulder and female laughter pulled me back into the present. "Don't worry, we've all been there. Once you get used to seeing him like that, life can resume. Soak it up, store that shit in your Jill till, and move on."

"Jill till?"

She exploded with laughter. "You know, spank bank?"

"What? No! That's gross, he's like family." *Or something.*

Laurie sniggered again. "You should see your face. It's a completely normal reaction. It's like he was crafted from Adonis himself. But trust me when I say that what's on the outside is far more beautiful than what's on the inside with him. Look, enjoy, but don't fall for the illusion."

"Laurie, I'm not—"

"Not what?" Devon reappeared with bottles of beer balanced precariously in his hands. "A little help?"

We relieved him of the drinks and fell into easy conversation. He lingered a little too close for comfort, but I needed the distraction. Now I knew where *he* was, my eyes insisted on trying to search him out, and I couldn't risk getting caught. Not in front of Devon and Laurie.

"So, Lo, how you are liking it in Wicked Bay so far?"

"It's okay, I guess. I haven't really..." My spine tingled, the hairs along the back of my neck electrifying. I shook off the sensation, inhaling a steadying breath. "Had much time to explore yet."

"Well, if you need a tour guide, just shout." Devon was talking, his lips were moving, but I couldn't respond, too paralysed by the person burning holes in the back of my head. I glanced over my shoulder slowly. Sure enough, Maverick was watching me. His eyes dark and emotionless.

Seriously? He couldn't be that hung up on that night. It wasn't like I was the one who left him feeling dejected and unwanted. I held his gaze, refusing to be intimidated. He broke away first, when a petite brunette strolled up to him, commanding his attention.

"So, what do you think?" Devon watched me with eager eyes, but I had no idea what he'd just said. "Hmm, sounds good." I smiled wondering what I'd just agreed too.

When the sun disappeared on the horizon, the party really broke out into full swing. Someone turned up the volume on a docking station and music filled the warm air. Laurie and Devon introduced me to some more people, and we formed our own little gathering by a smaller bonfire. Devon came and went, and I was grateful for the space. Whilst not uncomfortable, I wasn't entirely at ease being here either. I watched Kyle make a fool of himself but realised it was his front. He was the joker. And people loved him for it. I tried to avoid looking in Maverick's direction, choosing to sit with my back to his group. And it worked, for the most part.

"Hey, do you mind if I bail?" Laurie whispered to me, clutching her cell phone to her as if it was her lifeline. I'd noticed her texting someone for most of the night. Funny, because I'd also spotted Kyle with his nose buried in his phone more than once.

"Where are you going?" I said unable to hide the accusation in my voice.

"Nowhere." Her gaze flickered to Autumn.

"Your secret is safe with me."

She grinned and left me. They were discreet. She wound her way through the crowd completely ignoring Kyle. He waited a few minutes then slipped out of the party after her.

"Where'd Laurie go?" Devon dropped down beside me offering me another beer but I declined.

"Hmm, she said she had a thing."

"Okay. It's getting late. What time do you need to be..." he stopped, something over my shoulder holding his attention. I didn't need to turn around to see what...

or *who* it was.

"London, let's go," Maverick's voice was so cold a chill rippled through me.

"London, who's London?" Devon glanced between us. "What is he talking about?"

"Don't worry about it, Devon," I said not wanting to cause a bigger scene than Maverick was already making.

"Say goodnight to your boyfriend, I'll be at the car."

Boyfriend? What the…? Red hot fury sizzled through my veins but Maverick was already moving, cutting through the crowd of people, most of whom were watching us. I squeezed my eyes shut, pinching the bridge of my nose.

"Lo, what just happened?"

When I opened them again, Devon was looking at me like a wounded puppy.

"Your guess is as good as mine," I murmured getting to my feet, and he followed me up.

"You don't have to go with him, I can give you a ride back."

I eyed the beer in his hand. He was more than above the legal limit. "Do me a favour, yeah? Don't get behind the wheel tonight. I kind of like hanging out with you."

He stood a little taller wearing a goofy grin. "Yeah?"

"Yeah. I'll catch you tomorrow at school. Promise me, no driving." I gave him a pointed look, and he nodded. "Scouts honor."

I smiled and went after Maverick.

Chapter *Four*

"What the hell is your problem?" I marched up to Maverick as he stood next to the Audi, his arms folded over his chest, jaw clenched tight. His eyes widened a fraction, as if my outburst surprised him, but he narrowed them quickly. "Get in the car, London."

"Stop calling me that! It's not my name. My name is Eloise. Or Lo. Not. London."

He looked bored. It only infuriated me all the more, and I got right in his face, craning my neck up to meet his ruthless gaze. "You might get to boss around the rest of your friends and family, but newsflash, tosser, I am neither of those things."

He cocked his eyebrows, a momentary flash of amusement in his eyes. "Tosser?"

"Yes, you know idiot... jerk... dickhead."

"You think I'm a tosser?" His voice was smooth with a hint of annoyance.

I annoyed him?

Good.

"Well, you are, aren't you?" It was my turn to arch my eyebrow.

"Get in the fucking car, *London*." It came out a low

growl.

Aargh. I wanted to scream or punch his pretty little face, but I did none of those things. I wouldn't give him the satisfaction.

Maverick slipped out from between me and the car and went around to the driver's side, and I got into the back seat. The further away from him the better. But as if the universe hadn't had enough fun at my expense, the passenger door opened and Macey ducked inside.

"What's she doing here?" She flicked her head in my direction with a sneer, but otherwise ignored me.

"Devon Lions was hanging around her. I fucking hate that guy."

I sat a little straighter. He hated Devon? Interesting. He had been nothing but nice to me.

"You hate everyone." Macey sank back into the seat and the car purred to life. "I need sleep. Practice starts back up tomorrow and I am so not ready."

My phone vibrated, and I slid it out of my pocket.

Kyle: Sorry I bailed. Get a ride with Maverick.

Lo: Traitor. I hate you!

Kyle: Love you too, Cous.

A couple of classes with Kyle, and I'd somehow already fallen into friendly banter with him. But he made it so easy whereas these two moody sods made it impossible. Then it occurred to me, maybe I was here because Kyle arranged it? He lost serious brownie points if that was the case. No wonder Maverick was pissed at having to play babysitter. When I glanced back up, his eyes were on me in the rear-view mirror. "New boyfriend?"

"Fuck you."

Macey barked a laugh. "Who knew the princess had claws."

I winced at her mocking tone, and we rode the rest of the way in thick silence. The second Maverick pulled into the Stone-Prince's driveway, I was out of there. He didn't follow. Macey got out of the car, leaning back in to say something. Whatever it was, she didn't look happy, her usual scowl even more menacing. She slammed the door, and the car roared out of the drive and disappeared.

"Where's he going?"

She shouldered past me. "None of your fucking business."

I watched her go. She had a runway worthy body, all long legs and slender curves. Her hair was the same dark tone of Maverick's, and it hung to her shoulders in an angular bob. She was strikingly beautiful, but her eyes screamed *don't mess with me or I will eat you alive*. I didn't want to get in her way—or Maverick's—but I was here and we had to find a way to co-exist.

After going to the kitchen to grab a drink and snack, I went to the pool house. Dad still wasn't home, and I had noticed Gentry's car wasn't in the driveway. What time did they work until around here? Back home a late finish was around eight. It was almost eleven. Still, I sent my dad a quick text letting him know I was home, and went to my room. Stripping out of my clothes, I pulled on my favourite Oxford University t-shirt letting its familiarity seep into my skin. It had belonged to my brother, Elliot. I'd stolen it one weekend after visiting him during his freshmen year. I had quite a collection. Now I lay on the bed imagining what he'd make of all this. He would have given Maverick a piece of his mind. Macey too, if he hadn't tried to sleep with her first. I swiped the tears falling with the pad of my thumb. I couldn't think about Elliot without feeling swamped with grief.

Which is why I rarely let myself remember.

~

"Morning, sweetheart. How was your first day?" Dad was already up, fiddling with the puce tie hanging loose around his neck.

"It was fine," I said. "Here." I went to him and took the material, folding it into the perfect knot, stepping back to survey my handiwork.

"Thanks. You'd think after all these years, I'd know how to get it right. But your..." He didn't finish. Sometimes it was easier to not talk about the things that once meant the most to you.

"I know, Dad. Late night? I didn't hear you come in." I smoothed my hair into a ponytail and stretched my arms in front of me working out the kinks from the restless night's sleep I'd had.

"Gentry organised drinks with the team. One became two and, well, you know how that one goes." I heard the accusation in his voice but his expression wasn't scathing. We'd had that argument enough times.

"And yet here you are, looking as fresh as a daisy."

He came over to me and dropped a kiss on my head. "Oh, trust me, on the inside I'm dying. The party was good? You got home okay?"

I pressed my lips together and nodded, feeling the taste of bitterness on my tongue.

"Oh no," Dad chuckled. "What's that face for?"

"Nothing."

"Lo?"

"You could've warned me about them." I leaned back against the counter of our small kitchenette.

"Who?" He feigned ignorance.

"Oh, come on, Dad. Maverick and Macey. What's their deal?"

"You caught that, huh? Gentry mentioned there was

some tension, but I didn't expect it to be this bad. They're being nice to you though, right? Because if they're not I can—"

"No, no, it's fine. I can handle them. Besides, what they lack in personality, Kyle makes up for in droves."

"The kid has zest, that's for sure."

A comfortable silence settled between us as we carried on getting ready. When I grabbed my bag off the floor, Dad held the door open for me, and I slipped underneath his arm as we made our way to the main house.

"Did the agent give you a date, yet?"

"She's working on it. There was a delay with the final paperwork. Hopefully we'll be in our own place soon enough." His eyes darted around. "It's not so bad here, is it?"

I shrugged my shoulders. "It's alright, I just don't think I'll feel settled until we're in the new house, you know?"

Dad paused when he reached the kitchen door and turned back to me. "I know it's been a big upheaval, but I know we can be happy here, kiddo. If you just give it a chance."

"I know, Dad. I'll try." Though I couldn't make any promises. We'd left so much behind it felt wrong being here, but maybe with time, things would get easier. His eyes lingered on me, and I saw doubt there.

"Guess what?" I grinned, wanting to reassure him I could do this.

"What?" He opened the door, and we entered the kitchen.

"I made a friend. Three, in fact."

"Wow, three, and were these friends girls or boys?"

I punched his arm playfully, but froze when my eyes landed on the two figures sitting at the island.

"Something smells good," Dad said seemingly

oblivious to the tension.

Macey shoved her plate away and rose from her stool. "We ate all the pancakes."

Well, okay then.

"Maverick?" She barked, and I half expected him to jump to attention. But he didn't.

"I'll meet you at the car," he said coolly, and her expression slipped for a second as she murmured 'whatever' under her breath, before spinning on her heels and marching out of the room.

"There's fresh coffee in the pot." Maverick spoke again and Dad searched for cups. I was too confused to move. He was being amicable now? This was new.

"So, Maverick, Gentry tells me you're captain of the Wreckers? I hear you're tipped to do great things this season?"

I slipped onto the stool opposite the eldest Stone-Prince son and peeked at him through my lashes. He shovelled another spoonful of cereal into his mouth and washed it down with juice. "We have a good shot at the championship, yeah."

"Maybe you can get us some tickets? I'd love to come and watch you play. Back in school I used to play myself."

I felt his heated glare on the top of my head as I stared at my empty plate. What was happening right now?

"The season doesn't start for another couple of months, but I'll see what I can do."

Dad pushed a cup of coffee in front of me and I smiled, my eyes sliding to Maverick's as he watched the interaction.

"Good morning. Please tell me there's coffee." Gentry shuffled toward the counter with his head in his hands.

"Still suffer after a skinful, brother?" Dad chuckled beside me but I was too busy watching Maverick. His body was rigid, his hand gripping the spoon so tight the colour had drained from his knuckles. He didn't say a word as he got up and stalked out of the room. Gentry didn't acknowledge his behaviour, and neither did Dad, they were too busy joking about the night before.

"Hey." Kyle poked his head around the door. "Ready to go?"

"Yes." I downed the rest of my coffee and said goodbye to Dad, relieved Kyle planned to give me a ride into school instead of forcing me on Maverick and Macey again.

"Let me shout for Summer again and then we'll head out. Dad, Uncle Robert." He tipped his head in a salute and disappeared again.

"Don't wait up tonight, Lo. It could be a late one again. Do you need any money?"

I waved Dad off, ignoring the prickle of annoyance I felt. He'd slipped into this new life so easily it was hard to believe he had been away for so long. I wasn't sure I'd ever feel so at home here.

When I got outside, Summer was already standing by Kyle's bright yellow jeep. She lifted her hand in a small wave and I was about to say hello when I noticed the buds jammed in her ears. The Jeep bleeped and Kyle appeared, keys dangling in his hand. "Shall we?"

I hovered waiting to see what Summer would do, but she slipped into the back without protest so I took shotgun.

"How'd you like the party last night?" Kyle eased the Jeep out of the drive and pulled onto the street.

"Shouldn't I be asking you that?" I struggled to hide the amusement in my voice.

Kyle's face transformed into a cocky smile and he flicked open a pair of sunglasses with one hand, sliding them over his face. "Rule number one, I never kiss and tell." His smirk softened. "Did you get home okay?"

"I survived."

A throaty laugh rumbled from his chest. "I'm sorry about that, Rick can be... well, I'm sure you've realized he has a giant stick up his ass. Macey too, but once you get to know them they're not so bad."

I pressed my lips together. He had no idea I already knew what a dick Maverick could be. And I couldn't imagine a world where Macey was anything but a mean bitch. She wore it too comfortably, like a second skin.

"Laurie is good people. Stick with her and you'll be okay."

"I like her, she seems cool."

Kyle glanced at me over his glasses, and waggled his eyebrows. "I like her too."

I rolled my eyes. "You're so gross."

"Welcome to the family."

Less than ten minutes later, Kyle pulled into the school, found a parking spot, and we all bailed out. "Listen," he said. "I have practice after school. Can you two manage to get home without getting into trouble?"

"Seriously, Kyle," Summer huffed. It was the most I'd heard her speak. "You act like I'm a baby. It's bad enough with Maverick, I don't need this shit from you too." She stomped off with Kyle gaping after her.

"Whoa, baby sis grew up."

"What just happened?" I asked watching Summer as she approached a shaggy-haired boy and disappeared inside the building with him.

"I'm as clueless as you." He rubbed his jaw. "But *that* isn't good."

"What? The boy?"

"If she's dating, Rick will—"

"Oh, my God, what is wrong with the two of you? She's fifteen, of course she's going to date."

"Lo, cous." He slung his arm around my shoulder and guided me to the door. "You have so much to learn. This will be fun."

Fun?

There was no time to ask as a crowd of girls and boys descended on Kyle Stone, class clown and incessant joker.

"I'll catch you later." I ducked out of his hold and disappeared down the hallway. Laurie was waiting next to my locker.

"I see you've experienced the Kyle effect," she said with a hint of sarcasm. I didn't understand what was going on with the two of them but the girl had it bad.

"It's an actual thing? And here's me thinking he just liked the sound of his own voice."

She smiled, but it didn't quite reach her eyes. "I'm sorry I bailed last night, it was a shitty move."

"Hey, no apology needed. I got to ride with Maverick and Macey which was…" I searched for the right word, but she beat me to it.

"Life altering."

"Something like that."

"Come on." Laurie linked her arm through mine. "Autumn and Devon are waiting with Liam. I swear he can't do anything before his morning smoke." She yanked me in the direction of the door at the end of the corridor.

And I realised Dad was right, maybe it could be that simple. Maybe all I had to do was want it bad enough and life in Wicked Bay would work itself out.

Maybe.

Chapter *Five*

The rest of the week passed without too much drama. Summer didn't have any more outbursts, Dad was MIA most nights, and I rode to school with Kyle. Laurie and Autumn treated me like one of their oldest friends, and I avoided Maverick and Macey as much as possible. Which was pretty easy given their complete lack of interest in me.

But something was missing, and I felt restless. It was like living a split life. The kids at Wicked Bay High got the mysterious girl from England who smiled at the right times and laughed when someone cracked a joke. Then behind the closed doors of the pool house I became withdrawn and sombre. Dad's absence didn't help. He was the only person I had to talk to about anything here. Laurie had good friend potential, but it was still new. She didn't know me—didn't know about what I'd left behind in England. Dad was the only person who understood, and his answer was to bury the pain and throw himself into work leaving me to fend for myself. He might as well have thrown me to the wolves.

So, I did what any seventeen-year-old with a shed load of emotional baggage did. I pulled on my favourite outfit, smudged some gloss over my lips, and headed to another party.

"You look hot," Laurie smiled as I ducked inside her car.

"Thanks. So, remind me whose party this is."

"JB Holloway's, the football captain; and his sister, Caitlin. She's a junior with us."

She was? I must have missed that memo when Laurie was giving me the who's who of Wicked Bay High.

"Right, and the team will be there?"

"Yeah, it's like their pre-season party. The Holloways are rich, their house is like a freakin' palace. Seriously, the pool, ugh. I told my dad we needed something that size in our life and he told me to keep on dreaming..." She kept going but I tuned out. I was only here because it beat spending another night in the pool house alone.

When her car rolled to a stop, I immediately saw what Laurie had been talking about. The two-storey house resembled a mansion with imposing alabaster pillars and a second-tier wraparound balcony. Holy crap. It was like something straight out of a magazine minus the streams of kids coming and going. Just when I thought it couldn't get any more extravagant here, it did.

"Come on, let's find the others."

I followed her up the winding driveway, my eyes dancing over the house. Surrey had some pretty posh estates, especially in the countryside, but this place was ridiculous. Laurie guided us around the side to a wrought iron gate and we slipped inside. Music blared out of the speakers positioned in the corner under a wooden gazebo, and a boy I didn't recognise stood behind a laptop bobbing his head to the beat. The huge pool had been turned into a water polo match and half-naked boys jumped and lunged for the ball while girls huddled at the edge in little bikinis shrieking every time the water splashed up around them.

I suddenly felt very overdressed in my jean shorts and sparkly vest top, and very out of my depth.

"This is crazy," I murmured under my breath sticking close to Laurie. People waved and smiled at her, maybe at us. It was impossible to tell amidst the chaos.

"You came," Devon grinned sloppily when we reached him and Autumn.

"You're drunk," I said poking him in the chest. He stumbled back and chuckled.

"Busted." It came out slurred.

"Where's Liam?"

"Around." Devon answered Laurie, but his glassy gaze didn't leave my face.

"Do you want a drink, Lo?"

A drink sounded like a very good idea. Anything to tamp down the nerves vibrating through me. I nodded at Laurie and she disappeared.

"Come sit with me." Devon dropped onto a big chair. "Whoa, is everything spinning?"

Autumn rolled her eyes. "I can't believe you're already wasted. It's not even eight-thirty. Ignore him, Lo, he's a goofy drunk."

Devon caught my arm and pulled me down beside him. The close contact startled me. Sure, we'd hung out at school and chatted some, but this felt a little too close for comfort. "Devon," I scolded, my hand pressing against his chest as he tried to wrap his arm around me. "Not cool."

He immediately backed up giving me room. "My bad, maybe I drank more than I thought. Someone get me some water."

"Here." Laurie arrived with drinks. A cup of something for me and her and a bottle of water for Devon.

"You read my mind." He swayed as he reached for the bottle.

"Maybe you shouldn't have come if you were going to get like this." Laurie narrowed her gaze on him and I got the impression I was missing some piece of the drunk-Devon puzzle.

"I'm good." He waved the bottle. "This'll sort me out and I'll be fine. Don't sweat it."

"Whatever." Laurie turned away to face the pool and Devon squeezed his eyes shut. I threw Autumn a 'what the hell' look, but she pursed her lips with a quick shake of her head.

"Eloise is in the house," a voice boomed across the pool and Kyle sauntered over to us as if he owned the place. I groaned into my hands.

"I can still see you," he said with a hint of amusement.

"Seriously, Kyle, do you have to do that?" I peeked up at him. "I'm trying to blend."

"Why? You're like the new shiny toy everyone wants to play with." He arched his eyebrow toward the drunken boy who sat beside me.

"What do you want, Kyle?" Laurie sighed.

"I miss you, babe. Is it a crime to want to spend time with my girl?" He closed the distance between them, crowding her against the ornate brick wall.

"Kyle." She slammed her hands into his chest and he staggered back. "Don't do that, not in front of my friends. You're drunk. Go feel up some other girl or play beer pong with the guys or whatever it is you do for fun."

Kyle blinked as if she'd slapped him but his trademark smile slid back into place. "Oh, it's like that? We'll see." He winked at her and then pointed at me. "Don't be a stranger, Cous."

"Lo. It's Lo, arsehole," I murmured knowing he couldn't hear me. "Is he always so…"

"Hyper? Annoying?" Laurie said. "Take your pick."

"He misses you," Autumn stated. "It's his way of

forcing himself back in."

Laurie folded her arms over her chest, glancing over at where he stood with a group of girls. "Yeah, well, it will take more than that."

"Okay," I said jumping to my feet. "I thought we were here to party."

I could do this. It was crammed, sure, but we were outside. There was plenty of space and fresh air. Besides, the alcohol had already begun to calm my nerves.

Laurie and Autumn glanced at one another and back at me. "Well, yeah."

"So, let's go party. Devon, are you coming?"

He waved us off, looking a little green. "Go have your fun, I'll be here, puking into the plant pot most likely."

The girls followed me as I moved through the bodies. The pool was surrounded by a long lawn on one side and a patio area on the other. A huddle of girls had already carved out a dance floor, and I didn't give myself time to think about it as I moved my body to the beat. Laurie beamed, spinning seductively, dropping down, and gliding back up. Autumn joined us and the three of us danced. I felt the stares from around the pool. Girls green with envy. Guys hot with desire. But I shut them all out, letting myself get lost in the moment. I'd done this plenty of times in the last few months. Gotten drunk or high and partied until the break of dawn. This was different. I'd made a conscious choice to step up next to the other girls dancing. I wasn't motivated by the need to forget or drown out the pain. Sure, it was still there—it probably always would be—but this was a step toward healing.

To embracing my new life.

I hoped.

A couple of other girls joined us and the five of us danced until my skin had a fine sheen and my muscles ached.

"Water, I need water." I mouthed to Laurie.

"The kitchen's in there." She pointed to a door behind me. "Want me to come?"

"I'm good. I'll be right back."

Slipping past the crowd lingering near the doors, I headed inside and found the refrigerator.

"I don't think we've been introduced." A boy stepped into my view although he couldn't really be called a boy with so much muscle bulging out of the black tee hugging his body.

"Lo," I said trying to round him to get to the fridge. But he had other ideas.

"JB, I'm the captain—"

"Of the football team. I know who you are." I didn't, not really, but the glint in his eye told me he ate girls like me for breakfast—or liked to think he did.

"Nice," he smirked. "So, you're the new Stone kid?"

"If you mean, I'm the girl temporarily living with the Stone-Princes then yes, that would be me."

"JB, one of your jerk off friends is puking in Mom's violas." A petite blonde I vaguely recognised from school entered the kitchen and paused, her gaze landing on me. "Hello, I don't think we've met?" She gave me the once over, the way girls did when they were sizing up the competition.

I went to introduce myself but JB cut me off. "This is the new chick living with Prince." He gave her a pointed look and her expression slipped.

Interesting.

Something about finding out I lived with Maverick, or Macey, had her attention. I took one guess it wasn't Macey she was worried about.

Her face narrowed into a scowl. "You're Eloise Stone?" Despite the surprise in her voice, something told me she already knew exactly who I was.

It was my turn to narrow my gaze. "It's just Lo."

"Well, Lo, I'm Caitlin, though my close friends call me Cat." She dismissed me and addressed her brother. "Please go and do something about your friend, JB."

He pressed a thumb to his bottom lip, ignoring his sister and raking his eyes down my body. "On it. It was nice to meet you, Lo. See you around."

Why did it feel like a promise ... or a threat?

"One word of advice." The hostility in her voice caught me off guard and I blinked over at her. "Stay away from JB." She looked like she wanted to say more, but she smashed her lips together and sashayed out of the kitchen. I shook my head reaching for the fridge door. It really was like an episode of The OC around here. All I'd wanted was a bottle of water.

"Hey, there you are." I spun around to find Laurie smiling at me. "I was getting worried."

"Oh, I met JB ... and Caitlin."

She rolled her eyes. "How nice for you. JB is... well, he's a guy with a dick, but he's pretty harmless. Caitlin on the other hand, her claws are sharp."

"I suspected as much."

"She dated Maverick."

That had my attention. "You're kidding?"

"For almost a year. They broke up just before his junior prom. She's had a hard time letting go."

It explained the insta-hate radiating from her. I might have been 'family' but I still had tits and an arse. I knew the drill. To her I was a threat. She'd underestimated one thing though—Maverick's anger at my arrival. Then a sinking feeling washed over me and I quickly did the math. A year?

"They were dating last summer? Funny, Kyle never mentioned her," I tried to sound casual.

It wasn't funny. Not since he'd failed to mention anything about his stepbrother at all. The more I thought about it, the more I realised what a strange situation it was. I'd spent almost two weeks with the Stone-Princes last year. Hanging out at their house. Visiting the local sights. And not once had I seen a photo of Maverick or heard them talk about him. Other than to tell us he and Macey were away for the summer with their dad.

"They got together at the start of Maverick's junior year."

After we'd almost spent the night together.

Fuck.

"I feel like I'm in the middle of a bad soap opera," I groaned.

She laughed. "Welcome to my life. Come on, Devon finally revived. He's making a fool of himself on the dance floor."

I grabbed a bottle of water quickly and followed her back outside, pushing thoughts of Caitlin and Maverick and their drama far out of my head.

~

"I can't believe I almost missed my chance to get up close and personal with you," Devon whispered in my ear as he pulled my body back against his chest. We'd been dancing together for the last couple of songs. The boy had moves.

I looked back over my shoulder at him and smirked. "Keep your hands to yourself."

He grinned, running his hands up my waist. So, it was a little closer than I intended, but I was actually having fun. Devon felt safe—despite the vibes he was giving off. Maybe it was the fact he hung around with Laurie and Autumn or he didn't look at me as if I was his next meal, like some of the boys at school.

"I need to pee," Laurie announced and Autumn offered to go with her. I waved them off, sliding my fingers into Devon's and waving our hands in front of my body, rolling my hips to the beat.

The sun had set a while ago, but the amber glow of lamps hanging around the place illuminated the Holloway's garden. It was easy to get swept up in the moment. And when Devon turned me into his arms and his eyes dropped to my mouth, I almost let him kiss me.

Almost.

I turned my head and his lips grazed my cheek. "Burned," he murmured as his eyes shuttered with embarrassment.

"No hard feelings." I punched him in the chest. "I want to go slow." The words sounded like a promise I wasn't sure I was making, but I felt the prickle across the back of my neck. Of course, *he* had to pick this exact moment to arrive.

"Prince is throwing us daggers."

I let out a heavy sigh and bowed my head. "I don't know what his problem is."

"Well, I do." Devon dipped his head and slid his finger under my jaw, bringing us eye-to-eye. "You're his now."

"What?" I reared back.

"You're one of them. Like it or not, he owns your ass now. He closes rank, it's always been that way."

"Devon, I have no idea what you're talking about." I detangled myself from his grip. Aware we probably looked like a couple on the verge of a fight. Just what I needed. "I'm nobody's." I said, the defensive lilt in my voice obvious. "Definitely not a family that I just met."

And definitely not the boy who looked at me like I was nothing more than dirt on the bottom of his shoe.

He didn't look convinced as he raked a brisk hand over his hair. "Whatever. I need a drink. See you later, okay?"

I watched him leave. I'd been here a week and Maverick Prince was already screwing things up for me. My blood boiled, and I spun on my heels ready to march right up to him and give him a piece of my mind, but someone had beat me to it. JB was up in Maverick's face, speaking to him—and only him—as everyone else watched on. His face gave nothing away, a steel mask, but I saw the quiet storm brewing. His fists clenched at his sides and I knew he was one second away from losing his shit. I'd seen the same look in my brother's eyes more than once, usually right before he kicked someone's arse.

I don't know why I did it but I rushed over to them, acting as if I couldn't see the hulk of a football player glaring at my step cousin. "Maverick, can we go? I need to get out of here. Like now."

His eyes flashed to mine, and I saw confusion there. But then his cool exterior slammed back in place and he nodded tightly. "Go get in the car."

"But…" I glanced between the two guys.

"London."

It was a warning. Shit. Did I go and risk him getting into a fight or did I stay and risk making things worse?

I clutched my stomach and groaned dramatically, "I'm really not feeling well, can't we just go."

"If you need some help, I'd be more than willing to assist," JB's voice dripped innuendo and I felt Maverick tense beside me and felt sure the shit was about to hit the fan. But then his hand wrapped around my arm and he was all but dragging me out of the Holloway's yard.

Chapter Six

"You don't need to drag me, I'm coming." I ripped my arm free and ground to a halt.

"Just get in the damn car, Lon—"

"I swear, if you call me that again, I'll..."

Maverick's lips tugged up at the corners. "You'll do what?" His eyebrows rose in amusement and I glowered at him. "Fuck you, Prince. You should be thanking me, I just saved your arse."

He held my gaze for a second then shook his head and ducked inside his car. I did the same. When we were inside, he took a deep breath and raked a hand over his head. "Like he could take me."

"God, are you always this annoying?"

He didn't answer. The car purred to life, and he backed out of the driveway.

"Was it about his sister? Caitlin?"

"What do you know about Caitlin?"

"I know you went out with her last year and ended it before junior prom."

"Laurie Davison needs to learn to keep her mouth shut," he snapped, and I watched him through the corner of my eye.

"You don't need friends. You've got Summer and

Kyle and…" he stopped and I wondered if he'd been about to say his own name because that was a joke if I ever heard one. The only time he ever spoke to me was if he was bossing me around or dragging me to his car.

We were not friends.

Not even close.

Silence filled the car, and not the good kind. Ringing my hands in my lap, I took a deep breath and said, "So, what really happened back there?"

"Nothing you need to worry about."

"Fine." I folded my arms over my chest and turned away from him.

"Fine."

It was a football team party. Laurie said the basketball team wouldn't be there, and they weren't until Maverick showed up. Apparently, there was no love lost between the two teams, but now I wondered if it was because of the animosity between their captains, over a certain blonde-haired girl who had warned me off her brother, maybe? Or was it something else entirely?

These people I now called my family were exhausting, and I began to think Summer had the right idea keeping her head down. The car pulled into the Stone-Prince's driveway, but Maverick didn't cut the engine. "You're welcome," he said.

My head snapped over to his. "Please tell me it wasn't all some sham to get me to leave the party?" I said, eyes wide with disbelief.

He shrugged and held my glare, giving nothing away. I felt my anger levels shoot through the stratosphere.

"What the hell is wrong with you people? You ignore me most of the time, act like I'm no one, and then keep pulling this crap. It ends now." I sucked in a ragged breath. "I didn't ask to be dragged halfway around the world. I didn't ask to be moved into your pool house, and

I certainly didn't ask to end up on that beach with you last summer."

Maverick didn't speak, but I saw the muscle in his jaw tic.

He just sat there, his cold eyes boring into mine. That's how he wanted to play it? Fine. I could pretend it didn't happen either.

I threw my hands up in defeat. "You are quite possibly one of the most infuriating people I have ever met. Back off, Maverick. I'm a big girl, I can take care of myself. I don't need you riding in on your white horse trying to save me from imaginary bad guys. It might fly with Macey and Summer, but it won't fly with me. I. Don't. Need. You." I pushed the door open and slid out of the car, only pausing when his voice perforated the thick silence.

"Stay away from Holloway, London. I mean it."

I slammed the door and didn't look back.

~

The next day, I let Laurie talk me into spending the day at the Bay with her. Gentry was taking Dad to play golf and explore and I didn't want to be at the house alone. Not if there was a chance I would run into Maverick.

"A little birdie told me Devon tried to kiss you last night?" she said with excitement dancing in her eyes.

I pulled my knees up and shifted until I was comfortable on my towel. "He told you?"

"Jess saw it. She told Autumn who told me. You know how it goes. What's up with that, anyway? I thought I was sensing some serious lust-vibes between the two of you."

"Maybe. I don't know. He's cute and we have a laugh together, but I've been here a week, you know? I'm not looking to jump into anything with anyone."

It had absolutely nothing to do with a certain infuriating Prince.

Nothing.

"He likes you, a lot. Word of advice, don't lead him on if you're not interested."

"I'm not leading him on, Laurie." But I had danced with him. There had been some groping.

"He's a decent guy. Unlike some people."

I leaned up onto my elbows to see who she was talking about. Kyle and his friends were in the water playing football.

"You want him." I lay back down.

"Yeah, but he's a Stone-Prince. You guys aren't an easy bunch to fit in with."

"Hey, don't include me in with them. I'd met them once before moving here, hardly constitutes being family."

"Yeah, but you are," she sighed. "You're a Stone. I can't even imagine what that's like. I mean, no one really gets close to Maverick or Macey but we grew up with them. They've always been around. How are you finding it?"

"Honestly, I have no idea how to answer that. Kyle is… he's Kyle, and Summer seems like a nice girl. Macey is a total bitch and Maverick is…"

"I hear ya." Laurie laughed softly. "Kyle told me once Maverick is just like his father, Alec Prince. He's a hotshot businessman, owns half of Wicked Bay. Real piece of work. He married a model—she had a son from a previous marriage—and they had two kids together."

So, Macey and Maverick had a bad case of abandonment issues. Between Rebecca's new life with Gentry and Alec's new life with his model wife, they had gained two step-siblings and three half-siblings. It explained their hostility to some degree, but there had to be more to it.

"Wait," I said. "Alec is a Prince too? But that means Rebecca kept his name?"

Laurie's head nodded up and down slowly. "I know, right? Kyle told me she didn't want to have a different name to Macey and Maverick but I mean, come on, it's just—"

"Ladies, looking good." Kyle loomed over us, blocking the sun.

"Seriously, Kyle, Lo is your cousin, that's gross."

I sat up, tucking my legs to the side of me. "Are you stalking me?" He hadn't mentioned coming to the Bay over breakfast this morning.

He winked and chuckled. "So paranoid, Cous. No boyfriend in tow today?"

"Devon is not my boyfriend."

"The two of you looked cozy last night."

"Drop it, Kyle. If Lo wants to hook up with Devon that's her business. You don't see me jumping down your throat because you were all over Megan."

Kyle scrubbed a hand over his face and sighed. "I wasn't all over Megan. She was all over me. I can't help it if I'm this good looking. Besides, the girl I want all over me is playing hard to get."

Laurie blew out an exasperated breath and crossed her arms. "Go bother someone who cares. We're sunbathing and you're annoying."

He laughed again, but I sensed the strain. He really did want to fix things with Laurie—he just had a strange way of going about it.

"I'm out. If you need a ride home, text me. Or a few of us will be heading over to The Shack later if you want to come?"

I looked to Laurie to answer, I didn't want to force her into a situation she would rather avoid. "Maybe," she said earning her a goofy grin from Kyle.

"Enjoy the sun and don't burn." He gave her a pointed look before running back to his friends.

"He's so bossy."

Just like his stepbrother. I smiled to myself. Maybe the Stone-Prince boys weren't as different as I first thought.

Laurie and I sunbathed for another hour until my skin felt tight and Laurie told me a smatter of freckles had appeared across my nose. "I'm done," I announced, pulling the loose vest over my bikini top. Unlike Laurie who had stripped down to her bikini top and bottoms, I'd kept my shorts on.

"What do you want to do?" She pushed her glasses onto the top of her head and craned her neck as I stood up and dusted myself off.

"I'm easy. If you don't want to go to The Shack, we don't have to. I need food though."

"Ugh. Okay." Her smirk told me she was more than willing to go despite her attempt at being indifferent.

After rolling our towels and dumping our stuff in the boot of her car, we walked the short distance to The Shack which was exactly that—a wooden beach hut style diner with a wraparound deck housing tables and chairs. She held the door for me and I slipped inside. Kyle spotted me immediately. "Cous, get over here."

"Maybe this wasn't such a good idea," I muttered to Laurie, but she laughed me off, moving toward the group huddled into a booth with a circular table.

"Scoot up, Stone," she said to Kyle, and he shuffled along to let us in.

"Lo, you remember Matty and Trent?" He thumbed to the two guys on his other side. "Guys, meet Lo Stone, officially, and you already know the light of my life." Kyle tried to slip his arm around Laurie's shoulder but she elbowed him in the ribs.

"Don't be a dick, Kyle. We're here to eat. That's it."

"Yeah, yeah, keep telling yourself that."

"So, Lo, how is it living with this jerk?" one of the guys said.

I shrugged. "It's alright. Technically, I live in the pool house."

"Your accent is so cool. Say something British." He flashed me a smile that had me cocking my eyebrow.

"Like what?"

"I don't know, something posh or whatever."

"Dude, she's my cousin, not a freak show."

"Kyle," Laurie and I hissed at the same time, but his friend was watching me eagerly so I sat straighter and said, "How now, brown cow."

Four pairs of eyes stared back at me and then the booth erupted with laughter, but the mood changed when someone came up to the table. Kyle grumbled something under his breath.

"Stone," JB Holloway's eyes flickered to me but I knew he was addressing Kyle. "You said he wasn't going to be a problem. He came into my home, to my party—"

"Chill, JB, it was a misunderstanding. No harm, no foul, yeah?"

"You're on the team because I say it's okay for you to be on the team. Rein. Him. In. This shit is getting old."

"Everyone needs to chill the fuck out." Kyle laughed, but I heard the strain there. "You know how he gets."

"I don't need Prince fucking up the season for me. We clear?"

"Crystal."

JB turned his attention to me. "Feeling better?" He slid his thumb across his bottom lip, the way he had in the kitchen at the party and it made me shudder.

"Much, thanks." I flashed him an over-the-top smile.

"See you around, Stone." I heard the same promise in his voice I'd heard before. What was his problem?

"What just happened?" Laurie broke the silence.

"JB's just pissed Maverick turned up at the party looking for a fight."

58

"But they didn't fight, right?"

Kyle flashed me a knowing look. "No, because *someone* got in between them."

Laurie craned her head around to me. "Seriously, Lo, you didn't tell me it was you."

"I…" She was right. I hadn't. After my ride home with Maverick, I didn't know what to make of it all so I did what I did best, pushed it down and acted like nothing had changed.

And it hadn't, really.

When Maverick made a brief appearance in the kitchen this morning, he'd acted like the party never happened. So, I did the same.

"I can't believe you did that," her voice was low as the boys went back to talking about the giant stick up JB's arse.

"What was I supposed to do? Let them go at it? Maverick looked ready to kill him."

"It wouldn't be the first time." She glanced back at Kyle clearly uncomfortable discussing his stepbrother with him present.

"You've been holding out on me." I cocked my eyebrow but Kyle cleared his throat ending our conversation. "You girls okay?"

"Peachy," I said. "I'm starving. What's a girl have to do to get fed around here?"

The conversation turned to food, and all talk of JB and Maverick was pushed aside.

~

"Dad?" I stumbled over my slippers and reached out to steady myself. Light streamed in through the blinds even though it was the middle of the night. I didn't need to flip the switch to see his bed was still made, and for a brief second, I understood how it must have felt for him all those nights I stayed out, too drunk or angry to make it home. But my empathy quickly turned to irritation. It was two-thirty in the morning. Where the hell was he?

I stalked over to the windows and I peeled back the blinds. The main house was pitched in darkness, except for a light in the kitchen. Maybe he was in there, back from wherever it was he'd been. Slipping out of the pool house, I cut across the patio to the back door. It opened with ease, but the place was empty. I tiptoed through the house to the front door and peered out of the glass panel. Gentry's car was parked in its usual spot. So where was Dad? Hurrying back through the house to return to the pool house, I stopped to grab a drink. When I turned around, I almost jumped out of my skin.

"Maverick?" I squeaked. He was in the shadows, arms folded over his chest, watching. "Are you trying to give me a heart attack?" My voice wavered as I tried to catch my breath.

"It's late, London. What are you doing creeping around?"

Irritation etched into my face, I ignored the way his hooded gaze danced over my thin vest top, lingering on my chest for a little too long.

"Dad didn't come home yet." I raked my eyes down his body. It was impossible not to look. The way his t-shirt rippled over his muscles. Ugh. But that wasn't what caught my eye, it was the blood smeared across his knuckle. My gaze flickered back to his. "What are *you* doing up?"

He jammed his hands into the pockets of his sweat pants. The ones hanging far too low on his tapered waist. "You ask a lot of questions." Maverick stepped into the room taking the air with him and I gulped, suddenly feeling exposed in just my summer pyjamas.

"That's not an answer." I quipped back, searching his face for any clues, noticing an angry bruise forming around his eye. My hand moved to reach out for him, but

I stopped myself, tucking it behind my back.

"It's the only one you're getting." He leaned casually against the door frame. Maverick really was something else and I let out an exasperated breath.

"Do you have any idea where my dad is?"

"It's the middle of the night and he isn't home, where do you think he is?"

My jaw dropped at his insinuation.

No. Dad wouldn't—

"He wouldn't. We..." My throat closed, and I had to force out the words. "We just got here." And it was too soon after Mum. Dad wouldn't just move on like that. He wouldn't.

Something crossed Maverick's face, and he shrugged. "He might be your dad, but he's still a guy."

Why would he say that? A fresh burst of irritation coursed through me. "Is that where you were?" I arched my eyebrow.

"Is that what you want to hear? I was out fucking some girl?" Maverick moved closer, stopping right in front of me. His eyes were hard on mine, pinning me to the spot. Tension rippled around us. And then his hungry gaze dropped to my lips. I stepped back shocked by his effect on me. I wanted him to kiss me.

Shit.

My façade slid away, and I hated that he saw my surprise. That he kept doing this … baiting me. Blowing so hot and cold.

"Whatever, Prince. I'm going back to bed."

He didn't speak. He didn't move. With a soft shake of my head, I turned ready to leave, but I paused at the last second. "Oh," I said glancing back at him. "You might want to do something about your knuckles, I can still see the blood."

My heart galloped in my chest as I jogged back to the

pool house replaying the conversation with Maverick over in my head. He'd been fighting without a doubt. And the idea bothered me far more than it should have.

Wicked *Beginnings*

Chapter *Seven*

As if things couldn't get any worse, the next morning over breakfast, Rebecca and Gentry announced they wanted us to spend time together as a family. Macey kicked up a huge stink. But after Rebecca marched her out of earshot for a 'talk' she returned and gave Dad a half-hearted apology. In true Macey fashion, she ignored me. I hid out in the pool house until Kyle came and said Loretta was back with excessive amounts of barbecue.

"This should be fun," he chuckled under his breath as we joined the rest of the Stone-Princes on the patio. It was a beautiful area with a huge canopy housing a long wicker sofa, a matching table, and two chairs. Gentry was in the corner, standing in front of a built-in brick grill. He smiled over at us. "Go find the others."

Kyle nodded and disappeared off toward the house.

"I hope you're hungry, Lo, Loretta bought the whole store."

"I could eat a burger or two."

"Burgers? When I grill it's all about the steak," he laughed.

"Sounds good." Dad joined us dressed in board shorts and a Hawaiian print shirt looking every bit the surfer,

63

with his easy smile and a bottle of beer in his hand. I didn't know whether to be impressed or freaked out.

But I was still pissed how flippant he'd been about staying out for most of the night. When I'd confronted him this morning, he said he had been out with some of the team again. That it had turned into a late one at someone's house so he'd stopped over. But I couldn't help but wonder if Maverick was right … if there was something Dad wasn't telling me?

I left them talking and went to sit in one of the chairs. Summer was already curled up on the sofa, listening to her music. I gave her a small wave, and she slipped the buds out of her ears. "Hey."

"Listening to anything good?"

She shrugged, tucking her long hair behind her ear. "My friend is in a band. It's their demo tape."

"Oh wow, that's cool. Does he sing or play?"

Her eyebrows shot up in surprise and I flashed her a knowing smile. "A bit of both. It's his brother's band but they're letting him fill in until they find a new bass player."

"My ex played occasionally."

Something caught Summer's attention behind me, and I rolled my eyes. Maverick's timing was bordering on ridiculous. Choosing to ignore his presence, I continued, "Chris wasn't really in a band as such, but he liked to jam at open mic nights, that kind of thing."

Summer swung her legs over the edge of the seat and shifted forward. "Why'd you break up?"

It was my turn to shrug. "We weren't good for each other and then Dad announced we were moving here. Seemed pointless, you know?"

She nodded.

"Summer," Macey's voice rang out across the pool. "Come paddle with me?"

The youngest Stone-Prince child sighed, flashing me an apologetic smile.

"It's fine," I said waving my hand at her. "Go have fun." Although I wasn't sure fun ever went hand-in-hand with Macey.

"Why don't you get in, Lo?" Dad said. "It looks pretty inviting."

"I'm good." I slid my glasses down over my face. Maverick was close. I could feel him, but I didn't acknowledge him as he sat down on the other end of the sofa, furthest away from me. We clearly rubbed each other the wrong way, perhaps it was for the best we avoided one another. Especially around the rest of the family.

"Did you tell her?"

My ears perked up, and I strained to hear Dad and Gentry's hushed conversation. "Tell me what?"

Dad shook his head and gave his brother a stern look. "Hmm, Gentry and Rebecca invited your grandparents, they thought—"

"It's fine." What was another reunion?

"He's coming here?" Maverick's voice was strained, but Rebecca appeared and moved to him, laying a hand on her son's shoulder.

"Yes, and I'd like you to be polite, Maverick. It's one afternoon, it won't kill you." Her eyes bore into his as she looked down at her son. He wanted to bail, I saw it in his tight expression. But something held him back.

"Fine," he conceded.

"Excellent. Now, Lo, I have been dying to ask, did your father give permission for that beautiful tattoo or is there a story behind it?"

Dad cleared his throat and let out a strangled laugh. "Oh, there's a story, alright, Rebecca."

I groaned, tipping my head back. "It's not that big of a deal."

"I beg to differ, Eloise." Oh, I was in trouble now.

Dad only ever used my given name when he was pissed. Damn Rebecca and her questions.

"Dad," I pleaded, but he launched into the story. I got up and went to the pool, unwilling to relive it. So, I'd made a rash decision. It wasn't like I'd tattooed an angel on my left shoulder and a devil on the right, or the words love and hate across my knuckles. It was art.

Elliot's art.

He'd drawn the floral design as a present for me on my sixteenth birthday and until his death, it had hung proudly on my bedroom wall. So yeah, maybe it was an irresponsible decision to get it inked on my arm without parental permission, but it was my way of carrying a piece of him around with me. I wouldn't apologise for that.

"Hey, you okay?" Kyle dropped down beside me, dangling his feet into the water.

"I'll live."

He nudged me with his shoulder. "Is it true?"

"Is what true?"

"That you let your boyfriend tattoo you when you were drunk?"

"Ex-boyfriend, and yes. I was …" I hesitated, feeling the pain bubble under the surface. "In a bad place." Kyle knew the reason for the move—they all did—but no one had mentioned it. I didn't know if that was at Dad's request or because death wasn't something people liked to talk about.

"Because of the accident?"

I nodded, swirling my toes through the water.

"Well, I think it's badass. You're not like most girls, Lo."

My gaze slid to Kyle. He was grinning as usual. "I think there's a compliment in there somewhere," I said.

"There is." He shouldered me again. "You've been in Wicked Bay a little over a week, Cous, and you've already made friends and have a line of guys falling over their feet for your attention."

My eyes rolled skyward. Had it really only been a week? Kyle must have noticed my confused expression, and he barked a laugh. "You have no idea the stir you've caused, do you?"

"Stone," a voice boomed, and we both turned around to find Maverick standing by the table. "Get over here."

"The Prince calls." He waggled his eyebrows at me and I frowned. But Kyle ignored my confusion, tapping the end of my nose. He whispered, "so much to learn still, Cous. Catch you later."

Out of the corner of my eye, I watched him go to Maverick. They sat on the sofa, huddled together looking at Maverick's phone. Neither paid me any attention. The bruise around his eye looked sore but if it bothered him, he didn't let on. No one had mentioned it, and I wasn't going to be the one to bring it up.

"Let's eat," Gentry announced a few minutes later, and I reluctantly stood up and went to join them.

"This looks great, Dad." Kyle was first up helping himself to one of everything. Macey and Summer joined us and for the next twenty minutes we ate like a family. But I saw the cracks. Macey and Maverick hardly spoke. Summer was quiet, speaking only when someone directed a question at her. Kyle overcompensated, cracking inappropriate jokes about his dad's cooking. And the adults chatted on as if everything was normal.

"So sorry we're late."

I turned to take in the couple standing on the other side of the pool. Although we'd never met in person, I knew them to be my grandparents, August and Beatrice Stone. Yeah, this was completely normal. I pushed my plate away, suddenly not feeling hungry anymore.

"Eloise," my grandpa had a thick accent. "Get over here and give your grandpa a hug."

Oh, Jesus. I shot Dad a look that said 'help', but he pretended not to notice.

"Hmm, hi." I stood up and offered the approaching couple a small wave. The woman, my grandma, smiled wide. She had warm eyes, and I felt some of my anxiety ebb away.

"Oh, darling, it's so good to see you, at last. Come give me a hug." She extended her arms, and I went awkwardly, aware of the seven pairs of eyes watching us. Eight if you included my grandpa's.

"You look just like your mother." Her voice cracked as she enveloped me in her slender arms.

"Now, now, Bea, don't go getting upset. We don't want to scare the girl away."

Girl? My head whipped up, and I met my grandpa's eyes.

"Eloise, this is long overdue, sweetheart." He wrapped an arm around us both and squeezed. Maybe I should have felt something at meeting my grandparents for the first time in person. But they were acting strange. It wasn't like I didn't know who they were. They wrote, sent obligatory birthday cards, that kind of thing. It was just hard to feel excited about it given the circumstances.

"Where's my hug?" Kyle called over. "It's been at least three weeks since I saw you both."

I stepped away from my grandparents and flashed him a thankful smile. He always knew just what to say or do to cut through the tension.

"Robert, get over here and give your old man a hug."

Dad came over to us and enveloped his parents, smiling from ear to ear.

"We're sorry we weren't here for your arrival." Grandma whispered.

"It's fine, Mom. It gave us time to settle before you start worrying."

She smacked his arm. "It's a mother's prerogative to

worry. I'm just glad you're here finally."

Finally?

What did that mean?

"Is Ste—"

"Why don't we eat?" Dad interjected, guiding his mother to the table. "There's plenty of time to talk later."

I followed, feeling Maverick's heated glare lingering on me. As if he knew what was running through my mind. As if he knew what she'd been about to say. I didn't want to believe it because it wasn't possible. It couldn't be. Dad wouldn't do that to me. To Mum.

I switched off after that. Sure, I smiled at the right times, answered my grandparents' endless questions about the move and school, but I was checked out. Trying to figure out what was going on. What Dad wasn't telling me. I watched him discreetly as he joked and chatted with Gentry and their parents. My grandparents. He was like a different person. He looked like Dad and sounded like him, but something about him was different.

And I didn't like it.

Everything was changing. Coming here pushed *them* further and further away. But I didn't want to forget them or move on.

I didn't want to let them go.

"Lo?"

I blinked over at my grandma. "Excuse me?"

"I said are you free next weekend?"

"Oh, hmm, I guess."

"How would you, Summer, and Macey like to come out on the boat with me?"

Boat?

"I have practice," Macey spoke up and my grandma rolled her eyes.

"You say that every time I invite you to spend time

with me."

Rebecca gave her daughter a narrowed look, but she shrugged. "What? It's true. We have to be on point for the opening game. Sorry, Mrs. Stone." Her voice almost sounded sincere, but I knew it was a sham.

"Macey, I have known you since you were in diapers, please call me Beatrice." She glanced over at me. "I'd prefer grandma, but your cousins can be quite difficult."

Maverick's jaw clenched and things got even more tense.

Kyle's voice sing-songed. "I'm always free, Grandma, just say the word."

"Kyle Weston Stone, if I never take you out on the boat again it will be too soon."

"It was an accident, I swear I had no idea..." his voice trailed off when Gentry cleared his throat and stood. "I'd like to make a toast."

A low chorus of grumbles came from the other end of the table and I risked peeking over at Maverick. His eyes slid to mine, and I turned away quickly.

"I just want to take this opportunity to welcome Robert and Eloise into our family again. It feels right to have them here and I wish them well in their new life here in Wicked Bay. To Robert and Eloise. To family." He held his beer up in the air and the rest of the adults did the same.

"Excuse me," I rushed out suddenly overwhelmed by everything. "I'm... I'm not feeling so well."

I didn't look back as I ran for the pool house, not stopping until I was in the sanctuary of my room. The door closed behind me and my body slid down the wall like the tears that already ran down my cheeks.

Chapter *Eight*

"Lo?" Dad craned his head around my bedroom door. "Can I come in?"

I looked up at him and shrugged, too exhausted to answer.

Too devastated to care.

"What happened back there?" He removed the pile of clothes from the chair and sat down.

"Is there something you want to tell me?" I ground out, the words almost impossible to say. He couldn't be … he just couldn't.

Yet, in my heart I knew.

I fucking knew.

"What?" He choked, slamming a fist against his chest. "I..." His eyes gave him away.

"Who is she?"

I hated Maverick was right. Hated that this was happening. Back in Surrey, when things went to shit, I got drunk or high. My eyes darted around the pool house like a caged animal looking for a way out.

"Sweetheart, I... it isn't..."

"*Who is she?*"

Guilt flashed across his face and I balled my fists. "I wanted to tell you sooner," he said. "Before the move—

71

"

Eyes wide as saucers, I rushed out, "Before the move? There was someone before the move?"

"Lo, sweetheart..."

"Stop calling me that. I want to know who she is."

There was someone else.

Another woman.

Someone who wasn't Mum.

This.

Was.

Not.

Happening.

Tears burned the back of my eyes but I forced them down. "Who is she?" My voice was shrill as I clutched the pillow across my lap.

"Sweetheart, this is why I didn't tell you. I didn't want to upset you, not so soon after—"

"You didn't want to upset me? So, you thought you'd sneak around behind my back? Is that why we moved here? Is that why you dragged me halfway across the fucking world? For her? How long has this been going on, Dad?"

"Eloise, calm down."

"Calm down? Are you fucking kidding me? Mum died, Dad. She died, and you're shagging around like it's perfectly acceptable. It hasn't even been a year."

Eight months. He'd waited eight months until he moved on. I stared at the man who had been there to pick up the pieces when I finally got out of the hospital.

"I didn't mean for it to happen. We have a complicated history."

The pillow flew across the room and I was off the bed, pacing. They had history? What kind of history trumped a marriage?

A family?

My mother?

The woman Dad promised to love and cherish?
Forever.

"I have to get out of here." I rushed out of the room and slipped on my Converse. Dad followed after me muttering under his breath, but I was already out of the door.

Everyone watched me storm across the patio to the main house, I felt their stares, heard their whispers, but I kept going with no plan other getting the hell out of this place.

I grabbed a set of keys from the rack and started pointing and pressing the second I was out of the door, cursing under my breath when Maverick's Audi beeped. Of course, I chose his car because I was a pawn in the universe's cruel fucking game. But it was too late to retreat. I yanked the door open and slipped inside, realising my poorly thought out plan. I'd never driven a left-hand drive before, hell, I'd never actually driven properly before. A few laps around the local department store's car park didn't count. I managed to get the key in the ignition and fire it up. Pushing it into reverse, I eased my foot slowly off the clutch just the way Dad had showed me. But I missed the biting point, and the Audi lurched forward, stalling. My hands curled around the steering wheel as I inhaled a couple of deep breaths, but I was too far gone. I needed to get out of here.

Now.

As I was ready to try again, Maverick appeared out of nowhere, his wild eyes narrowed right on me.

Shit.

"Get out of the car, London," he mouthed, anger blazing in his inky depths.

I shook my head defiantly. It was the wrong answer. He stalked around to the driver's side and yanked the door open. "Move," he barked, and I flinched at the severity of his voice. "Either move over or get the fuck out of my car."

I climbed over the gearstick to get to the passenger seat, landing with a huff.

"Where to?" he said, and I shrugged. "Your plan kind of sucks."

"I didn't plan, I just ran."

The car roared to life and Maverick nodded. "I know that feeling."

What was happening? Again, I'd ended up with Maverick. Alone.

We didn't talk as he drove us to wherever it was he planned on taking me. So many questions lingered on the tip on my tongue. Why was he so closed off? Why did he hate Gentry? Why did he put on such a hard front?

What had happened that night last summer?

Maverick could be mean and cold and hurtful, but there were also moments like right now—like last year on the beach at the party—when he showed a softer side. It wasn't in the things he said or his demeanour. It was in his actions. He didn't have to get into the car and take me anywhere. If he hated me that much, he could have called the police. Or Dad. Or someone to try to get me to calm down.

But he didn't.

And I clung onto that one thought more than I should have.

"So, your dad is fucking someone new?" His voice punctuated the air, and I cringed at his words.

"So, it would seem."

"I'm sorry."

"Are you?" I shot back. He hadn't seemed sorry the other night when he'd suggested it.

Maverick dragged a hand down his face. "You're not what I expected," his voice was low and made my stomach dance.

"And what did you expect?" My eyebrow quirked up.

He glanced over at me, his eyes pinning me to the seat. "I don't know."

He wasn't going to tell me, fine. I crossed my arms over my chest and focused on the scenery. We drove through Wicked Bay and into a neighbourhood I didn't recognise. Gone were the mini-mansions and perfectly tended lawns replaced with smaller houses and graffitied walls.

"Hmm, Maverick, where are we?"

"Scared?" His lips curved in a smug smirk and a memory of him asking me the same question once before flashed into my mind.

I curled my fists into the soft leather. "No."

"We'll see." He cast me a sideways glance. "We're almost there."

He turned off the main road onto a dirt track leading to a warehouse. We were by the sea. I could see the moonlight glistening across the waves on the horizon, but this was a far cry from the Bay. It looked more like a derelict industrial area.

The car rolled to a stop and Maverick cut the engine. "You sure you want to come inside? You could always stay in the car." His eyes lit up in a challenge, and I narrowed my gaze at him in return as I reached for the handle.

"Stay close, okay?" he said with a hint of amusement.

I nodded, my heart pounding against my chest. Whatever was inside wasn't good. I climbed out of the car and ran my hands down my shorts, feeling the sea breeze nip at my bare legs.

"Here." Maverick appeared by my side and thrust a hoodie at me. "Put this on, the last thing we need is you being a distraction."

A distraction? I stared at him wide-eyed waiting for an

explanation. He didn't give me one. Slipping the hoodie over me, I pushed my arms through the sleeves. It hung low over my legs, and I rolled up the hem tucking it inside my waistband. Maverick watched. The intensity in his gaze made my stomach flutter. When I was done, he shook his head and started toward the warehouse.

I followed.

As we neared the warehouse, the low rumble of cheers filled the air. We slipped inside a half-open door and a wall of sweat and heat assaulted my senses. A sea of bodies took up every inch of space in the building, except for a space carved out in middle of the crowd. It was a ring, and the two men in the centre were beating the crap out of each other. My eyes widened and, for a second, I was completely paralysed. It was too much. The pulse of the crowd. The sticky heat. The deafening noise. But there was no time to freeze up as Maverick disappeared further into the crush.

"Maverick," I hissed, panic clawing its way up my throat. A couple of men leered in my direction, but soon forgot about me when the crowd erupted into a frenzy. I pushed onto my tiptoes to see through the heads, my eyes landing on the man sprawled on the hard floor, out for the count.

What the hell was this place? And what was Maverick thinking bringing me here?

I stuck close behind him, careful not to bump into anyone, grateful that he'd given me his hoodie to wear. Even if it did little to hide the fact I had tits and an arse.

"Rick, over here," a boy called over the chaos. Although, like Maverick, he couldn't really be classed as a boy with his broad shoulders and tall stature. But I recognised him from school. His gaze went straight to me as I peeked out from behind Maverick, and he shot his friend a questioning look. Whatever Maverick mouthed, I couldn't see from where I stood. The boy shook his head and moved closer. He leaned into Maverick and they talked in hushed voices, their eyes going to the middle of the crudely formed ring.

I stepped out from behind Maverick, my heart hammering in my chest, and folded my arms. "Is someone going to tell me what the hell is going on?"

It was obvious this was an underground fight, but I wanted to hear him say the words. Maverick scrubbed a hand over his face and grimaced. "No. Keep quiet, London, and stay out of trouble."

Trouble? Like I intended on being anywhere but glued to Maverick's side.

My brows drew together, waiting for an explanation, but all he said was, "You're not by my side, you're by Luke's, got it?"

Luke gave me a tight nod and went back to talking in hushed voices with Maverick. A voice echoed around the room and I peeked through the bodies in front of me, just glimpsing a man as they announced the next fight.

"He's up," Luke said and Maverick tensed beside me.

"Who's up?" I asked, earning me glares from both of them.

"London," he warned, and I rolled my eyes surprised how together I was given the size of the crowd.

"I'm not actually from London, you know?"

I was sure the corners of his mouth lifted, but then the crowd erupted again, and someone jostled into me, pushing me into Maverick. My heart lurched as the room started to close in around me. But then his hand was there, slipping around my hip steadying me. Calming me. I focused on his touch. The warmth of his fingers against my skin. When he realised what he'd done, he snatched it away as if the idea of touching me repulsed him. Ruining whatever had just passed between us.

Bastard.

Two men entered the ring: one wearing dark shorts, the other in shiny white shorts. My eyes couldn't help but drift over their sculptured stomachs and taut abs. They definitely didn't look like high school kids. The referee beckoned them forward, and the crowd settled, anticipation and blood lust crackling in the air. Both men stared at the other, fists clenched at their sides. It was then, I realised they intended on fighting fist to fist, no gloves. Jesus.

"Scared yet?" His voice was low in my ear and I shook my head, letting my hair cascade over my shoulder creating a barrier between us. Maverick was blowing so hot and cold, I didn't know which way was up. My stomach flipped with nervous energy and I didn't know whether to be excited or mortified … I went with both.

Luke chuckled, craning his head around Maverick's solid body and shooting me a wide grin. I gave him the middle finger and turned back to the ring, pretending not to notice him nudge Maverick and say, "She's feisty."

The referee yelled something and jumped out of the way. The two men danced around one another, testing the waters, throwing a bunch of mislaid jabs. Half the crowd cheered when White Shorts landed a painful upper cut. The other man's head snapped back, but he quickly righted himself, stretching his neck from side to side, shaking off what must have been a bolt of pain.

"Get him," someone close by me yelled. "Get him good, Sav."

Out of the corner of my eye, I watched Maverick watch the fight. He stood, arms folded over his chest, unmoving. He didn't flinch as the men in the ring landed punch after punch on one another. Blood trickled out of a cut on White Shorts' eye but it didn't deter him. He jabbed harder, quicker, catching the other man a couple of times to the ribs and once to the jaw. I winced with each hit. Imagining the crack of bone on bone. It was over quickly. White Shorts thrust his arms in the air, roaring with victory while the dazed man on the floor tried to stagger to his knees.

"He's quick, and did you see his right hook?" Luke said, launching into a dissection of the fighter's form while I watched the two opponents leave the ring.

The noise simmered while they got ready for the next fight, and I craned my head around Maverick's shoulder. "So, what happens now?"

He cocked his eyebrow at me. "You care?"

"Well since you kidnapped me, I might as well as pretend to give a shit. When will I get to see you in action?"

"I like her." Luke stifled a laugh and flashed me a grin. I smirked back but it melted away when Maverick expression turned thunderous. He leaned in close, out of his friend's earshot, and whispered, "Be careful what you wish for."

My body hummed at the warning in his voice but the moment passed when the announcer's voice boomed through the warehouse. "And now the one you've all been waiting for, the main event, Damien Lacroix versus Lyndon Ford."

If I thought the crowd was crazy before, this was something else. The roof seemed to blow off the place with the ferocity of the cheers and roars. I pressed closer to Maverick, trying to keep a sliver of space between us. And then I spotted the first contender. My heart lurched into my throat, my body rigid with shock. It wasn't him. It couldn't be. But God, it looked just like him—Elliot.

"London?" Maverick's voice barely perforated the looming panic attack as my mouth dropped open. But I couldn't breathe. I gasped, fighting for air, clutching my chest. I needed to breathe. Just one breath to kick-start my system. But I couldn't.

I couldn't move.

"I've… I've got to get out of here…" I stumbled back, pushing through the crowd. Angry yells and catcalls rolled off me as I ran out of the warehouse. Salty air hit me and I ground to a breathless halt. My hands dropped to my knees as I gasped for air.

"You okay?"

I hadn't realised he'd followed, but Maverick's form loomed over me and I shrank into myself further. Hating he could see how upset I was.

"London…" My name on his lips punctuated the air. Incomplete. Heavy with inclination.

"Just take me home, Maverick, please." My tear-stained eyes collided with his. He didn't speak, but I didn't really have him pegged as the kind of boy who knew how to deal with a girl mid-emotional breakdown. Not that I wanted to talk about it. Least of all with Maverick.

"Come on," he said, pulling out his phone and sending a text message. When he was done, he motioned for the Audi, turned and strode away.

In a way, I was glad he didn't ask questions. Questions led to answers, and answers led to memories. Memories I fought hard to bottle away.

We rode the whole way back to his house in silence.

Chapter *Nine*

"Hey," Devon dropped onto the bench beside me. "I'm sorry about the party. I guess I got jealous."

"It's fine." I gave Devon a weak smile, my gaze still settled on Maverick and his friends across the quad. He followed my line of sight and sighed, "I don't stand a chance, do I?"

My head whipped around to him and I said, "What?"

"It's the Prince effect. You think I'd be used to it by now."

I tilted my head. "What the hell does that mean?"

He dragged a hand over his face and blew out an exasperated breath. "Nothing, it means nothing. Forget it."

"Seriously? You think I..." I stuttered. "Me and Maverick?"

"Well, don't you?" He gave me a pointed look and I let out a strangled laugh.

"He hates me, Devon." After the way he'd practically kicked me out of his car and peeled out of the drive last night, and then ignored me at breakfast this morning, the feeling was mutual. And here was me thinking perhaps he wasn't a total dick. That maybe the boy I met last summer was still there underneath his hostile exterior.

"You mean you don't want him?"

I choked, slamming a hand to my chest. "You think I want him? You have met him, right? He's infuriatingly arrogant. He bosses me around like a child. No, I don't want him. Besides, it's weird, he's family." My eyes flickered back over to his group. If he felt me burning holes into the side of his face, he didn't show it. I was quickly learning Maverick Prince didn't show anything. He was a mask of calm and cool.

I turned back to Devon. "Hopefully my dad will hear from the agent soon and we'll be moving into our own place." That day couldn't come quick enough. Not that I relished the thought of being completely alone while Dad worked and did whatever else he did these days. Things I didn't even want to think about. Things I so far refused to let him tell me about. But I didn't constantly want to worry about bumping into Maverick or having Macey try to kill me in my sleep.

He leaned back casually against the table, but his eyes remained on me. I knew that look. I'd seen it before with my ex, Chris.

"What?" I lowered my eyes playfully.

Devon smirked. "Just thinking."

"About?"

His intimate gaze swept over my face and down my body. When his eyes landed on my face again his smirk tugged into a grin. "I have to get to class." He stood up. "I'll see you later though, Lo."

As he walked away, I realised it wasn't a question.

~

"So..." Kyle was waiting for me when I slid into my chair in History. "Where did you disappear to yesterday?"

He'd waited until now to ask me, probably because Summer rode to school with us, and I got the impression the elder Stone-Prince children liked to keep her in the dark about a lot of things.

"Nowhere." I kept my eyes upfront.

"Funny story. You ran out on us and ten seconds later, Maverick disappeared. Coincidence?"

I shrugged. "Must have been. I went for a run."

He leaned in closer, practically hanging off his chair. "A run? And how was that?"

"Good. It was good." My gaze slid to his, and his eyes danced with amusement.

"You two are almost as bad as each other. He's got his hands full with you, that's for sure."

"Kyle," I hissed low. "Nothing is going on with me and Maverick. Don't start spreading that shit, okay?"

He held up his hands. "Me? As if I would." After a second of silence he added, "So really, where'd the two of you go?"

With a shake of my head, I turned back to the front of class. Kyle was like a dog with a bone, and I knew he wouldn't let it drop until he knew something. But it wasn't my place to say anything. It was Maverick's business. I hadn't asked him to take me there.

And I wished he hadn't.

I'd hardly slept, unwanted images swirling in my head. Elliot in the middle of jeering spectators, getting the crap beaten out of him. Blood. Sweat. My tears. It all meshed together until the images became something else— something I never wanted to see again.

My eyes squeezed shut, forcing the memories out.

"You okay?"

Crap. I'd forgotten all about Kyle sitting beside me. I gripped the edge of the desk and nodded. I felt him staring, wondering.

"Cous…"

"Kyle…"

He smirked and relief swept through me. I didn't want to have the conversation here, in the middle of History.

"I'm good," I added, hoping he'd drop it but then his voice floated over to me.

"Maybe you should go on another run."

Bastard. He definitely wasn't going to let this drop.

The teacher kept us busy for most of the class, so I was able to avoid anymore of Kyle's questions. When the bell finally rang, I rushed out of the room with him yelling, "You can't avoid me forever."

I couldn't, but I intended on trying my hardest. Swallowed by the crowd, I hurried to my locker hoping his next class was in the other direction. Glancing back to make sure he wasn't following me, I didn't see the person coming toward me.

"Ow," I yelped as my body collided with Macey's. She glared at me, rubbing her shoulder.

"Oh look, it's Princess Lo."

I straightened and rolled my eyes. "Macey, it was a pleasure." Moving around her, she grabbed my arm and said, "Stay away from Maverick, Eloise. He doesn't need you. *We* don't need you."

I swung back to face her. "Are you kidding me? I don't know what your problem is, but I didn't ask to come here." *I didn't ask to be in the accident that took my mum and brother away from me.* "And I certainly didn't ask to move into your pool house. Stay out of my way, and I'll stay out of yours, deal? As for Maverick, I don't know what you think you know, but you're wrong."

My shoulder crashed against hers as I moved past her, anger seething through me. When I reached my locker, and looked back over at where Macey was, Maverick was there, leaning in close to her. He was pissed, his jaw clenched as he spoke. As if he felt me watching, his gaze snapped to mine, and he glowered. So, they were talking about me? I held his stare, lifting my chin, daring him to look away.

He didn't.

Rage seeped from his every pore. I could feel it from where I stood. But it only mirrored my own.

"Hey, how was yesterday?" Laurie's voice pulled me from my stare down with Maverick and I turned and blinked at her.

"Huh?"

"You know, with the fam-a-lam? Was it as bad as you expected?"

Worse.

Far worse.

I'd let myself believe maybe, just maybe, Maverick was a decent boy.

"It was pretty bad. I found out my dad is seeing someone new."

Laurie's face screwed up. "You're kidding, right?"

I pulled open my locker. "No joke. I didn't stick around to hear his excuses. Mum hasn't even been…" The words lodged in my throat and I swallowed hard. Laurie didn't know about Mum and Elliot. I hadn't gotten around to telling her my whole story. It wasn't exactly a great opener to make new friends.

"Your Mom what?"

"Long story. I'll tell you later. Are we doing something after school?" *Please say yes.* Anything to avoid the Stone-Prince house … and Dad.

Her face lit up with mischief. "You know it."

That sounded … ominous. But whatever it was, I was down. I needed to keep moving forward because if I stood still I knew the reality of my life would drag me down.

And I might never find a way back out.

~

"Devon?" I frowned as he approached me. "Where's Laurie?" Why did this feel like a set up?

He smiled but unlike his usual confident smirk,

nervous energy radiated from him. "Don't hate me, but I kind of asked her to do something for me."

I swung forward and pushed with my hands, leaping off the wall. "Okay, fess up."

Devon bowed his head, rubbing a hand through his hair. "I, hmm, I wanted to ask you out but wasn't sure you'd say yes so I—"

"She set me up." *Bitch.*

His eyes slid to mine. "She did me a favor. Now you can't back out."

"Who said I would back out, anyway? You didn't even ask me, Devon."

"You mean, you would have said yes?" Hope sparkled in his eyes and I shrugged. "Maybe. Guess we'll never know now, will we?"

Taking me by surprise, Devon dropped to one knee and grinned up at me. "Eloise Stone, would you do me the pleasure of going out with me, please?"

I reached down for his arm, yanking him. "Devon! Seriously!"

"Can't blame a guy for trying."

"Okay."

His eyes widened and his mouth dropped open. "Say what now?"

"Okay, I'll go out with you. But I don't want flowers or gifts or any of that crap." If we kept it simple—no pressure, no promises—maybe spending time with Devon would be exactly what I needed. If nothing else, it would keep Kyle and Macey off my back about Maverick.

"For real?" He glanced around the parking lot. "This isn't some kind of prank? Ashton Kutcher isn't going to jump out from behind the tree and Punk'd me?"

"Are you always so…" I searched for the right word but he beat me to it.

"Adorable? Eager? Persistent?"

I shook my head with laughter. "Okay, Devon Lions, show me what you've got."

He looped his arm around my neck and drew me into his side, guiding me toward his car. "Prepare to be wowed."

Conversation flowed easily between us while he drove us to 'the best damn diner in Wicked Bay'. He didn't ask any questions I didn't want to answer, but even if he had, Devon had a way of turning everything into a joke. He reminded me a lot of Kyle. But where my cousin was the epitome of the-boy-next-door with his all-American good looks and endless charm and wit, Devon was a lot more like my ex. He wore dark rinse jeans with a multitude of rips; and a white t-shirt underneath an unbuttoned dark shirt, sleeves rolled up at his elbows. It worked for him and, maybe in another life, before Dad decided to drag me halfway around the world, he would have been my type.

I didn't know whether that was a good thing or not.

I liked him, and there was something there, but he didn't make my skin tingle or my stomach flutter. He made me feel comfortable and at ease, and he made me laugh. And, unlike a certain brooding Prince I needed to erase from my mind, he didn't blow hot and cold.

Devon pulled into a small car lot and cut the engine.

"Pattie's," I said as I climbed out of his car. "Isn't that what you people call burgers?"

Devon barked a laugh as he held open the door and motioned for me to go inside. The smell of grease and meat wafted in the air and my stomach growled.

"Hungry?"

I waited for Devon and smiled. "I could eat a small cow."

"Then I brought you to the right place. Come on." He led us to a small booth. It was stereotypically American:

red leather seats, Formica table tops, with a jukebox in the corner, and checkerboard floor tiles.

"You have to get the Pattie's special with bacon and cheese fries."

"I thought I'd have a salad."

"Salad?" Devon rolled his eyes and slipped into the seat. "You can't come to a place like Pattie's and choose a salad."

"I'm joking, Devon. Pattie's special it is."

My eyes scanned the diner. It was busy, most of the booths filled with kids our age. Some I recognised from school, some I didn't.

The doorbell chimed drawing my attention to the group entering the diner. I let out a low groan and Devon craned his head around to see what the fuss was about. "Trouble in paradise?" He turned back to face me as Macey and her friends walked right past us as if I wasn't sitting there.

"She's a bitch."

He choked on his soda as he barked out a laugh. "Say it how it is, Lo."

I glanced back at their group. "I don't know what her problem is. It's not like I asked to be here."

"Macey is..." Devon leaned across the table and looked around conspiratorially. "Well, you're right, she's a total bitch. But it isn't just you, she's like it with anyone outside of her little group."

I wasn't so sure about that. She'd made it more than obvious she had a personal issue with me. But I didn't want to fuel any rumours.

The waitress arrived to take our order and Devon reeled off what we wanted. The more I looked at him, the more I realised just how cute he was.

"What?" He said, noticing I was staring at him.

"Nothing." I shook my head trying my best to look innocent. He was into me, I didn't need Laurie or

Autumn or Kyle to confirm that, but did I want to go there? So soon after arriving in Wicked Bay?

I didn't want to think about that. Not right now. It was early days and Devon had been nothing but nice to me. I needed friends. I needed people in my corner, and he seemed like a good choice.

"You sure you're okay?" Devon's eyes searched mine, and I nodded, flashing him a reassuring smile.

I was just a girl eating burgers with a boy. It was normal.

Comfortable.

It was *nice*.

Chapter Ten

"So, is it true?" Kyle shouldered me with a knowing grin.

"Is what true?"

"You and Lions? I heard Macey telling Rick she saw you guys."

Of course, he did.

I shrugged, slamming my locker a little harder than intended, and hitched my bag further up my shoulder. "I guess. We went to Pattie's and had burgers."

"And was this burger eating a date?"

"Does it matter?" I levelled him with a glare, and he held up his hands in defence, a hint of amusement shining in his eyes. "No. I'm just surprised is all."

"Do I even want to know?"

Slinging his arm over my shoulder he guided me toward class. "Nope. It's cool. As long as he treats you right, I'm good with it."

"I don't need your permission, Kyle." I snapped. He wasn't my brother. He didn't get to tell me who I could or couldn't date.

"True, but I'm giving it, anyway."

I glared at him. He was completely incorrigible. But then he flashed me his roguish grin and some of my irritation melted away. He made it almost impossible to stay mad with him.

"Well, thanks, I guess. It's not like it's anything serious. I like him. He's..." *Safe*, but the word, "Nice," rolled off my tongue.

"Nice, riiiight," he drawled in my ear.

"What's wrong with nice?" I shirked him off as we reached the classroom.

"Nothing, nothing at all." His eyes sparkled with mischief. "Nice is warm and cozy and safe. But it doesn't make your heart beat faster or get your blood pumping in other places." His eyebrows arched mischievously as I barged past him, muttering the word, "Pig" as I went.

But damn, he wasn't wrong.

~

Morning classes passed without any drama. Kyle didn't bring up Devon or Maverick again. But when I spotted Laurie waiting for me at lunch, I prepared myself for round two of the Devon-interrogation. She didn't even let me reach my locker before she said, "So..."

"So, what?" I played dumb.

"Oh, come on, Lo. Devon's been walking around like the cat who got the cream." She leaned into me. "Did you guys hook up?"

I reared back, my eyes wide. "Why, did he say that?" Because if he had...

"No, God no, he won't say anything, but I heard you guys went to Pattie's."

"For burgers, Laurie. *Burgers.* Did I miss the memo? Is Pattie's a front for some kind of dirty sex club?"

Laurie stifled a laugh. "My bad, I just thought..." she trailed off, giving me a sheepish smile.

"Well, you thought wrong. Is that what you hoped would happen when you set me up?" I gave her a pointed look, and she pouted.

"Oh, come on." She nudged me with her elbow. "You like him, I know you do."

"He's... nice." Ugh. There was that word again.

Every time I thought about it, all I could think of were Kyle's words earlier. But nice was safe. It was dependable.

Nice wouldn't leave me breathless and confused on a beach wondering what I did wrong.

"He's more than nice, Lo. He's got this whole indie sex god thing going on."

I choked on the breath I inhaled. "Indie sex god? That's one way of thinking about it."

"One way of thinking about what?" Devon appeared behind Laurie and she gave me her 'see what I mean' eyes.

"Lo was just telling me about your date."

His gaze caught mine, and I didn't miss the way his smile grew wider. "Oh, she was, was she?"

"Yes, she was."

I flashed Laurie an irritated look and said, "And now she's going to get lunch."

Their laughter followed me as I stomped my way toward the cafeteria.

~

I didn't catch a ride home with Kyle and Summer. I wanted to clear my head, and it was a nice day, the sun high in crystal blue skies. It was a world away from my life in England. I went through the main house. There was gated access to the garden, and Gentry had given us the code, but I wanted food, and our small kitchenette wasn't well-stocked. I suspected it was my Uncle and Rebecca's way of getting us into the house more.

"Ahh, Miss Lo, good day?" Loretta beamed at me as she went about wiping down the kitchen counters.

"It was okay." *Once Laurie and Kyle got off my back about Devon.* I helped myself to an apple and hopped onto one of the stools. Barely a minute passed before Kyle bounded into the room with his arms thrown wide.

"Ahhh Mama L, give me some sugar."

Loretta let out a hearty laugh as she hit him with the towel in her hand. "Kyle Stone, boy, keep your hands to yourself."

He dodged the towel and managed to wrap her into a bear hug before dropping a kiss to her head. "What's cooking? I'm starving."

She batted his hand again as he tried to intercept the spoon. "Out, it is no ready."

Kyle gave up and came over to the island, sliding onto the stool opposite me. "Where did you go? I waited."

"I texted you."

His eyes narrowed as if he didn't buy my excuse about wanting to get some fresh air. But he didn't press. "So, what are we doing tonight?"

"We?" I took a bite of apple.

"Yeah, I figure it's time we did a little family bonding. Stone to Stone."

"Don't you have football practice or a hot date or something?" Anything.

"Laurie is still freezing me out and JB is making us run plays tomorrow before school. So tonight, Cous, I am a free agent."

"Lucky for me," I grumbled under my breath as I faceplanted the counter.

"Ouch," Kyle protested. "That burns, Cous, burns."

"Okay." I peeked up through my lashes. "Fine, you win. I'm all yours. Just go easy on me."

Kyle fist-pumped the air with a grin. "Hells yeah. You ain't seen nothing yet, baby."

Oh, Jesus, what had I let myself in for?

Once we had eaten, Kyle told me to meet him at the Jeep in an hour. I went back to the pool house to make a start on my homework. When I was changed, I cut back across the patio. My phone rang, and I sighed when I saw *Dad* flash across the screen. My finger hovered. Did I really want to hear more of his lame excuses? Hear how he'd already moved on?

I hadn't spoken to him since running from the house on Sunday. When I finally dragged myself out of bed this morning and yesterday, he had already left for work.

"Hello."

"Lo, please," Dad's voice cracked, and I regretted answering. But he was my father—the only person I had in Wicked Bay. If I cut him out, I was alone.

"You should have told me." I sucked in a deep breath. "I deserved to know."

"I know, Lo. God, do I know. But you were hurting so much and I was losing you. I didn't want to push you away for good."

I doubled back and sat in one of the garden chairs, curling my legs underneath me. "Who is she?"

It hurt to even think the words, let alone say them.

He let out a heavy sigh. "I don't want to do this by phone, Lo. You deserve the truth, but I want to sit down and have this conversation. Like I should have all along."

"Fine," I clipped out unwilling to accept what was staring me in the face. There was another woman. Dad had someone in his life—someone who wasn't Mum.

"I love you, Eloise, more than anything. Losing your mother and Elliot, not knowing whether you were going to pull through or not, almost destroyed me."

Silent tears trickled from my eyes and I closed them tight, swallowing the rest down. I didn't want to remember—I couldn't. Remembering brought pain and hurt and regret. It left me hollow and empty.

Numb.

I'd spent the whole summer numb. And although I'd survived the accident, I wasn't really living.

"Eloise?"

"I'm here," I choked out, swiping away the tears with the back of my hand.

"Maybe I should leave work, come back home, and—"

"No, no..." I inhaled, opening my eyes. They landed on a blurry figure across the garden. I blinked until the water dissipated and Maverick's rigid profile filled my vision. "I'll be fine, Dad." I didn't take my eyes off him as he watched me fall apart.

"If you're sure? We can talk later? Maybe go for something to eat? Explore?"

"Sure thing."

"I love you, sweetheart."

"I love you too, Dad."

He hung up, but I clutched the phone in my hand as if it was my lifeline. Maverick didn't approach or speak. He did nothing. Just stood there, watching me. And although we were outside, the air felt heavy, thick, as it pressed down on me.

"Hey, Cous, I'm waiting." Kyle's voice filtered out from the kitchen, cutting the tension like a knife, and Maverick stalked off just as his stepbrother stuck his head out the back door. "Ready?"

"Yeah, I'm coming." I jumped up, rubbed my damp hands down my jeans, and started to move.

I just had to keep moving forward and everything would be okay.

It had to be.

~

"No way," Kyle tugged his hair, rolling his eyes dramatically. "No one beats me at pool, no one."

Unable to hide my smugness, I shrugged my shoulders. "First time for everything."

"Rematch. Rack 'em up, baby."

His friends—Matty and Trent—laughed, hurling

abuse at him for losing to a girl. I put the cue back in its holder and sipped on my coke. "I'm done for the night. Face it, Cous, you lost to a girl." I stuck out my tongue for good measure.

"Fucking awesome, wait until the rest of the guys hear about this," Trent said, earning him a smack around the head from Kyle.

"No one breathes a word. I have a reputation to uphold, you know."

It was my turn to roll my eyes as I hopped up onto the stool. A night out with Kyle had turned out to be pool at The Shack. It had been fun. No pressure, no questions.

No Maverick.

And I needed the distraction. Dad promised we would talk when he got home, but he'd already texted to call a raincheck. Yet again, I'd been put on hold for work, or worse, for *her*.

Kyle's phone vibrated, and I watched as he pulled it out and read the screen. Something was wrong. I saw it in the way his lips pulled into a flat line.

"Kyle?" I said, but he glanced at Matty and Trent and they shared a look.

"Time to get you home, Cous." He turned to me and I stared at him in disbelief.

"Are you kidding me? What's going on? Who was that?" My eyes dropped to the phone still in his hand. He noticed and slid it back into his pocket.

"Nothing you need to worry about." His voice was soft, but it only infuriated me more.

"You're cutting me out? Just like that? If something is wrong…"

He grinned. "Nothing is wrong. Are you always so paranoid? I have to be somewhere. Somewhere you," he pointed at me, "can't be. Guy stuff." Kyle winked, trying to ease the tension.

Well, screw that. I leapt down off the stool and

stepped up to him, my brows knitted together. "What aren't you telling me?"

I saw it. The brief flash of panic. He was hiding something. And I'd bet my arse it had to do with a certain stepbrother of his. But he didn't reply. We remained in a stare-down until someone cleared their throat behind us and I blew out a frustrated breath.

"Fine." I swung around and marched toward the door. The three of them talked in hushed voices behind me, but I didn't stick around to hear what they were saying.

When they finally exited the diner less than a minute later, Kyle's face was a stone mask I'd never seen before. He usually wore a smile. The one person you could count on to crack a joke or say something to break the ice.

This wasn't that Kyle.

And it worried me. Because if Kyle was worried… something was very wrong.

The Jeep bleeped and Matty and Trent piled in the back. I stood, hand gripping the handle. "Kyle…"

"Get in the car, Lo."

His words were like a punch to the stomach.

I was Lo now? He never called me Lo.

I climbed inside and buckled up, but I didn't meet his heavy stare, pressing my head against the glass instead. No one addressed the big fucking elephant in the room. But then, I suppose they didn't know Maverick had taken me to that warehouse. They had no idea I knew about his extra-curricular activities.

When we pulled up outside the house, I climbed out without so much as a goodbye, but Kyle followed me. His door slammed. I sped up, but he was right there, behind me, calling after me.

"Come on, Lo, don't be like this. If I could tell you, I would, but it's not my place."

I spun around and glared at him. "I thought we were family?"

"We are," he sighed, dragging a hand over his face. "But…"

"Don't worry, Kyle. I get it. And fuck you." My hand was on the door handle behind me. *Please be open*, I thought to myself as I twisted it. It clicked open, and I turned and ducked inside. He didn't call after me. But then I didn't expect him to.

The disappointment crushed my chest. I thought he was on my side. When I'd arrived here, I thought Kyle was the one person in this messed up family who would make things easier for me. But I was wrong.

The lines had been drawn tonight.

And he'd chosen Maverick.

~

I sat up for two hours watching the main house for any signs of life. Summer's bedroom light had turned off almost an hour ago. There was no sign of Macey. Rebecca was out with friends, and I figured—*hoped*—that Dad was with Gentry.

After running straight to the pool house, I realised I'd overreacted. Kyle didn't know about my brief history with Maverick. He didn't know I'd seen his bloody knuckles or gone to a fight with him.

At least, I didn't think he did.

To everyone else, Maverick treated me with the same contempt as Macey did. I was an unwanted stranger in his home. A home I was realising had its fair share of problems. It was almost midnight. On a school night. And three of the Stone-Prince children weren't home, and the adults of the family were all out, none the wiser.

Images of Maverick stepping into a crudely formed ring, plagued my thoughts. He harboured so much anger and bitterness. It radiated from him like a forcefield. Maverick was troubled. I didn't know why or what had changed since that night last summer. But something *had* happened. I knew because I had also changed.

When I'd woken up in hospital, barely able to speak or move, I knew. Knew something awful had happened. I had no memory, but it was a gut feeling. Intuition. Some higher power because I'd teetered the line between life and death.

Something was wrong.

Of course, I didn't realise what I felt was grief. I'd lost my mother and brother in an accident that should have also claimed my life.

But it hadn't.

I'd survived.

Physically at least, I was a survivor.

But I wasn't the same. Something was missing. Something I doubted would ever return. I was angry at the world. But unlike Maverick, I didn't beat the crap out of people to deal with my issues. Instead, I turned to drink and drugs. Anything to *not* feel.

Maybe that's why I felt drawn to Maverick? Even after last summer. Even after finding out who he really was. The damaged parts of him called to the broken parts in me. They recognised something inside of him and gravitated to him. I didn't want to. I wanted nothing more than to forget all about him.

But something happened that night—something that tethered us. Only we weren't the same people anymore. We were both hurting.

Both angry.

Both fighting our own demons.

Maverick's parting words when he left me cold and alone on that beach were *'You saved me'*. But we'd come full circle now. Because as I stared out of the window, willing for any sign of their return, I knew he had the power to ruin me.

l. a. cotton

Chapter *Eleven*

I'd fallen asleep.

Damn it.

I stretched my neck, rubbing the knotted muscles. The pool house was bathed in shadows and I strained my eyes to try to find my bearings. Dad's sofa bed was still neatly made, but I didn't have time to be angry with him. I was still furious at Kyle's stunt earlier.

And, for as much as it pained me to admit, I was worried about Maverick.

It was irrational—he didn't deserve my concern. But over and over, I'd imagined him in the middle of those blood-thirsty spectators, rivulets of red running from cuts and bruises on his annoyingly gorgeous face.

I slipped out of the pool house and walked over to the main house. Light streamed out of the kitchen window, and I paused at the low rumble of voices coming from inside. Pressing my back to the wall, I stayed in the shadows like a thief in the night. It was wrong. So wrong. But Kyle had cut me out, treating me like I was no one. Pushing me out, like I didn't need to know. Like I didn't matter.

It stung.

"The fuck were you thinking?" Kyle spoke. His voice

cracked with frustration, a stark contrast to his usual light-hearted banter.

"Back off, Stone. I'm okay."

"Okay?" My cousin laughed bitterly. "You look like you went ten rounds with Mayweather. Your mom will shit a brick when she sees you. I don't even want to know what my dad will do. Remember last time?"

Last time? How long had this been going on?

"I don't need you getting in the way, okay?" Maverick's voice was low. More of a growl, really.

Kyle scoffed, and I imagined him shaking his head, his messy blond hair falling over his eyes. I inched closer to the door, my back plastered to the wall, and craned my head around the glass. Kyle's form disappeared leaving Maverick alone. Hands pressed hard against the counter, he leaned forward, the muscles in his back straining against his t-shirt. His head was bowed, hiding his face, but I saw the tape around his spread hands, the red smears across the dirty material. My hand lingered on the handle. I didn't want to go in there, but my actions were no longer my own. I wasn't in control anymore.

When it came to Maverick Prince, I never was.

I hesitated, and he twisted, two dark pools stared back at me. Had he heard me? Or did he sense me there, lurking?

The spot lighting illuminated his face. His lip was split and swollen and a new bruise was forming over his old injury. I didn't make a move to go inside and he didn't approach.

We just stood there.

Watching.

Waiting.

I cracked first, overwhelmed by the intensity in his eyes. Yanking my hand away, I staggered backward and jogged back to the pool house. The door slammed shut behind me and I fumbled to lock it. My eyes fluttered shut as I tried to catch my breath—tried to tell my heart to calm.

"London." There was a soft knock at the door. It was jarring. Maverick wasn't gentle. I froze. I hadn't expected he would follow me.

"Go away, Maverick," I called back, unable to disguise the quiver in my voice.

"Not until you open the door… please."

My resolve cracked—like I had a choice when it came to him—and I turned around, twisting the lock. It swung open, and he slipped inside, pressing it shut behind him. "Didn't anyone ever tell you it's rude to spy?"

"I wasn't spying." My voice caught in my throat, and he gave me a look that said he didn't believe me. I lowered my eyes, looking anywhere but him. "I was worried." It came out barely a whisper.

Why had I admitted that?

He closed the distance between us and then he was there, warm fingers gliding underneath my jaw, tilting my face. I met his gaze. Some of the darkness was gone, replaced with something else. Something that made my stomach flip wildly. "You shouldn't waste your time worrying about someone like me."

I could see his face now. The bruises forming under the surface. The cuts and grazes. My heart ached, imagining every time a fist connected with his skin, and before I could stop myself, I reached out for him. He caught my wrist. Holding it in mid-air.

"Why do you do this to yourself?" I asked, searching his eyes for an answer.

"You wouldn't understand." His voice was quiet, and I saw a glimpse of the vulnerable boy from that night. His eyes shuttered, and he leaned closer, inhaling a shaky breath, until his face almost touched mine. At the last second, he pulled up and his lips connected with my forehead.

"Maverick?" I swallowed hard. I didn't understand what was happening, but I didn't want it to end either. I felt it. The flow of energy between us—the same thing I'd felt last summer.

"Are we just going to pretend it never happened?" My voice was quiet, and I hated how insecure he made me feel. I wasn't that girl anymore.

I wasn't.

He didn't get to hold power over me. No one did.

So why couldn't I tell him to go?

"What happened that night, Maverick?" I whispered. I had to know—deserved to know—but he tensed and I didn't need to see his face to know his mask had slammed back down.

"I should go." He was already pulling away, but it was my turn to catch his arm. "Wait, talk to me." I pleaded, my stomach twisting with pain, knowing if I let him walk away that would be it.

His gaze slid to mine again, but my Maverick was gone. "It was a mistake. I was never supposed to be there that night. You need to let it go, London. Forget about it. It. Was. A. Mistake." His words were measured, but I didn't miss the way his jaw clenched as if he was in pain. "*This* is a mistake."

I reared back at his words and narrowed my eyes, calling his bluff. But he didn't flinch. He'd already pulled away. I felt it in the air shift around us. For a brief moment, it had been warm and electrified with anticipation, but now it was cold and empty. Maverick moved for the door, pausing to look back at me. "It's better this way, Lo." His expression was torn, but I was too angry to care.

When he was gone, I sank to the floor and hugged myself tight. I didn't cry—I wouldn't. Not over Maverick Prince and his mind fuck games. He wanted me, I could

104

sense it. Had sensed it that night last summer. But something held him back then, and it was holding him back now.

As I fought back the tears, I realised for the first time since arriving, he'd called me Lo.

~

"You look like shit." Devon offered me a tight smile. "But not as bad as Prince."

"Oh my God, did you see his face? Principal Delauder hauled him into her office this morning." Autumn's eyes flickered to where he was sat with his friends, hunched over. "Maybe he finished what he started at JB's?"

"JB doesn't have a scratch on him," Laurie added.

"Maybe that's because Prince got his ass handed to him, it's been a long time coming." Devon's voice was bitter, and he glanced over at me. I don't know what he expected to find, but I schooled my features, feigning indifference.

When I realised the three of them were watching me intently, I said, "What?"

"Well," Laurie spoke for the group. "You do live with him. Didn't you see anything? Hear anything?"

"Seriously?" I stared at her incredulously. Even if I did know anything did she really expect me to go running my mouth off?

About my family.

Ugh. I hated that word.

Laurie's eyes dropped away, but Devon finished what she'd started. "Come on, Lo, you can't expect us to believe you live there and know nothing? I bet his mom lost it, your uncle too?"

I felt the irritation growing into something darker and clenched my fists at my side. "If you're only friends with me to get the latest Stone-Prince gossip, you've got the wrong girl."

Devon rubbed his temples, guilt flashing across his face, while Laurie and Autumn's mouths dropped open. I didn't stick around to hear their apologies. I shoved off the bench and cut across the lawn toward the main building. It meant walking right past Maverick and his friends, but what other choice did I have? Besides, he'd made it perfectly clear where we stood last night.

They were talking and joking but as I neared them one of them noticed and nudged the boy beside him. Then Luke spotted me. He gave me a small nod, so small I doubt anyone saw. But then another couple of the boys looked up and before I knew it they were all looking. All except Maverick. Then he twisted around and our eyes collided. I forced myself forward. Forced myself to break the connection.

And I didn't look back.

When I reached my locker, my body hummed involuntarily. What was that? The way they'd looked at me—the way *he'd* looked at me. My pocket vibrated, and I pulled out my phone and read the text from Kyle.

Kyle: What was that about?

Lo: Nothing. Leave me alone.

His reply came straight back.

Kyle: Don't be like that. I'm sorry, okay?

Lo: Not good enough.

I turned off vibrate and stuffed it back in my pocket just as something caught my eye at the end of the hall. Summer ducked out of a room and into the girl's bathroom. From the way her head hung low and her body folded in on itself, it didn't look good. I took off after her.

"Summer?" I called as I burst through the bathroom door. She was in there, I could hear her uncontrollable sobs echoing off the wall tiles. But she didn't reply.

"Summer, I know you're in there," my voice softened, and I crouched down looking for her feet. Bingo. I pushed the right door, and it swung open. Tears streamed down her face as she met my concerned gaze.

"What happened?"

"N-nothing, I'm fine." She swiped at the tears with her sleeve but a fresh wave poured out.

"Bullshit." I closed the stall door behind me, slipped my bag over the peg, and crouched down in front of her.

"If something happened, you can tell me. I won't tell anyone, I promise."

Her lips quivered as she considered my words. We had spent little time together since I arrived, but other than talk about her friend, the musician, I hadn't seen her with a group of friends. And knowing how her elder siblings behaved, I doubted she had many people to confide in.

"Summer, talk to me…"

"It's Nick."

"Nick, your friend in the band?"

She nodded, choking back an ugly sob.

"What happened?"

"Isleptwithhimandthecondombroke." It came out a garbled mess of words and sniffles.

Fuck.

"Okay, did you see someone? Family planning? The doctor?"

She shook her head violently unable to form words.

"Summer, is there someone I should call. Macey? Your mom?"

"No, no." She clutched my hand, and I stumbled back almost falling flat on my arse. I shimmied onto my knees and wrapped my arms around her trying to ignore the fact I was on the bathroom floor.

"Ssh, it's going to be fine. Everything will be fine. Let's get out of here and figure out what to do, okay?" I held her at arm's length, searching her eyes. She looked broken and my heart ached for her. "Come on," I said. "It's still lunch break, maybe we can sneak out without being noticed."

I highly doubted that with the way Kyle seemed to know my every move. But I had to try. There was no way she could stay in school in this state.

Scrambling to my feet, I pulled Summer with me, and unlocked the door but not before shoving a handful of tissue paper at her. As I stepped out, she grabbed my hand again. "Wait." Panic flooded her voice. "I'm not sure I can. What if someone sees, what if…"

"Hey, I'm not going to tell, okay? And if we run into someone we'll say you got your period or something. People don't want to know about that kind of stuff."

Summer nodded again, sniffling back the tears.

"Dry your eyes and then I'll check the coast is clear."

We slipped out of the main building through the back door without being spotted. I still wasn't over familiar with the school campus, but Summer pulled herself together enough to lead the way. We slipped out unnoticed through one of the side gates. I didn't know how long it would be before someone realised we were missing, but I couldn't throw her to the wolves, I wouldn't.

"What now?" she asked, huddled close to me, her arms holding herself together.

"We go back to the pool house to regroup. Everyone's at work. And if we use the back entrance, Loretta doesn't have to know we're there." I hoped.

"Thank you."

"You don't have to thank me, Summer," I said with a

strained smile. "We're family."

There was that word again.

By the time we reached the house, my phone was blowing up with notifications. I cursed under my breath as I punched in the code on the gate and we slipped inside. The grounds were quiet, and I silently prayed Loretta had left for the day. Inside the pool house, Summer sat in the chair, waiting for me to come up with a plan.

"Can we call your doctor?" I didn't know the first thing about healthcare in the States but I knew enough to know it wasn't like our free health service in England. Summer's face fell flat, and I had my answer.

We needed another plan.

"Okay." I retrieved my phone.

Kyle: What the hell Lo? You skipped class?

A minute later.

Kyle: Where are you?

A minute later.

Kyle: Seriously, Lo, cut the shit and text me back.

Ten minutes later.

Unknown: Kyle said you skipped school. What the fuck are you doing?

There was one more sent only minutes ago. And I didn't want to think about how Maverick how gotten my number.

Unknown: London...

Now he cared? I deleted them all—but not before storing his number—and opened Google, searching for the nearest family planning clinic. I read the list off to Summer who confirmed it was a fifteen-minute walk to the clinic Dr. Google recommended.

"Lo, I'm scared. What if—"

Rushing to her, I sat down and hugged her close. "Ssh, everything will be fine. We'll get you checked out and I'm sure they can give you something, you know, as a precaution."

"Okay."

I grabbed some money from Dad's 'emergency fund' and hid our bags in my room. At least if Loretta was around, she wouldn't spot anything.

"Come on, let's go. Hopefully we can get back before anyone else gets home."

Because if we didn't, I wasn't sure I could protect her from her family.

Chapter Twelve

"Sum, open up, I know you're in there. Loretta said she saw you."

Damn Loretta and her Spanish spidey-sense. Summer's eyes went wide as the banging continued.

"We will have to tell them something," I urged, squeezing her hand in reassurance.

We'd made it home before school ended, but Kyle knew Summer was missing. He'd texted me at least six times. Which meant, Maverick and Macey probably knew.

"We can't tell them, Maverick would..."

"Ssh." I smoothed the stray hairs from her face. "I'll think of something, okay? Just go along with me." I went to move but Summer clutched my hand. "They can't know," her voice cracked.

I nodded, but it was more of a grimace. Neither of the Stone-Prince boys would be easy to convince, but I had to try. And if I had to choose one to battle with, it would be Kyle every time.

"Sum—" Kyle's eyes narrowed with suspicion as the door swung open. "Where is she?" He glared at me.

I pushed the door open further but didn't move. "She's here, and she's fine. See." I flicked my head to the

111

bed where Summer was curled up.

"Summer?" his voice softened as he craned his head over my shoulder. "What happened?"

"Girls stuff," I said.

"Girls stuff? You both ditch afternoon classes and all I'm getting is 'girls stuff'? Not good enough, Cous. You need to starting talking, now."

I folded my arms over my chest and stepped forward, forcing him back into the hallway. "Well it's all you're getting, *Cous*." I smiled wryly, arching my eyebrow for good measure.

"Lo." He dragged a hand over his face and part of me felt bad for him. Kyle cared, I didn't doubt that, but the last thing Summer needed was an interrogation from him. He leaned in, lowering his voice. "Did something happen with Nick because if it did—"

"Kyle." I pressed a firm hand against his chest. "You need to back off. She's here, and she's fine. She doesn't need this right now."

He cupped his jaw again. "You'd tell me, right, if something bad happened?"

I nodded. "Everything is fine. I promise."

"Can I talk to her?"

"I don't think that's a good idea, not yet. Give her time."

I saw the pain in his eyes. His unwillingness to walk away, and couldn't blame him. Elliot would never have left me if he knew I was hurting. He was my big brother. My protector. But Summer didn't want him to know, not yet. And I vowed to keep my promise.

Kyle released a strained breath and finally relented. "Fine. I'm out of here. But I will find out one way or another." He stalked away without his usual bounce, and I closed the door and returned to Summer.

"Should I get Macey? Maybe she would—"

"No, I don't want her to know. Not yet," Summer

rushed out. "I'll tell her, I will. Just let me deal with this first, okay?"

I sat on the edge of the bed and stroked her hair. "Of course. Whatever you need."

"Thank you, Lo, for everything. I thought Nick would be there for me, you know? But when I told him I should go the family planning clinic, he stared at me like I was talking another language."

"He probably panicked." I hesitated. I'd wanted to ask earlier but didn't want to upset Summer any more than she already was. "Can I ask you something?"

She nodded.

"He didn't force—"

"What? No! We've been friends forever. I don't have many girlfriends, being a Stone-Prince is intense, you know? If it's not Maverick, it's Kyle. Even Macey is always warning me to watch my back. It's made life at school hard. Nick didn't care who I was. Over the summer, we got closer. One night we were hanging out, and he kissed me. It felt right, I guess. We've been dating for a month. But I wasn't ready. It changed things. As soon as it was over, we both felt it."

"You're only fifteen, Summer. There's plenty of time for all that."

"I know. I want to put this whole thing behind me."

My phone vibrated, and I dug it out of my pocket.

Kyle: Tell Summer I'm sorry. If she needs anything, I'm here

I showed her the screen, and she smiled. "He's a big, soft, teddy bear really."

"Nothing like Maverick," the words slipped out before I could stop them. But Summer didn't notice the slight inflection in my words.

"He's just overprotective. He doesn't let people in easily. It's like he has this wall around him. He wasn't always like this," she paused, letting out a soft sigh. "Actually, he was, but it wasn't always this bad. Something changed last year. Obviously, no one has asked him about it and if they had, they wouldn't get an answer. Maverick is a closed book."

And didn't I know it.

"You don't have to stay." Summer sat upright. "I'm okay, I promise. The nurse said the chances of … anything happening is virtually nothing. I'll be fine."

"You're sure? I can stay a while longer."

"Um, I think I'm going to call Nick. I don't want him to worry."

I hadn't noticed it before—I'd been only concerned for her wellbeing—but I saw it now. The youngest Stone-Prince didn't just have a crush, she was in love.

"Okay, but if you need anything, you know where I am."

I left Summer dialling her *friend*. If Maverick and Kyle found out I didn't want to think about what would happen to him. But it was her decision to make.

"What do you think you're doing?"

My heart lurched at the sight of Macey at the end of the hallway, arms folded firmly over her chest.

"Nothing."

"Seriously? You're going to shut me out? I'm her sister."

I held her stare. "That's between the two of you. Summer needed me, I was there." It was a low blow, but Macey had made no effort to make me feel welcome. Her usual scowl deepened, and I readied myself for her reply, but it never came. Her glare burned into my back as I made my way downstairs.

There was no sign of Maverick or Kyle. I helped myself to a drink and some cookies and headed for the pool house unable to shut off my thoughts. Here was Summer, the youngest Stone-Prince, surrounded by elder siblings, but still lonely. Alienated. And I got it. Maverick and Macey were intense. And Kyle, even though he was different, was overbearing.

I knew all about over-protective brothers. Elliot had been the same, but he hadn't pushed me away. He'd been my best friend, and before he went off to uni, we'd done everything together. Being only one year apart, we shared a lot of the same friends, and he was always around.

Until one day he wasn't.

I hadn't only lost my brother in the accident, I'd lost my best friend. And sometimes, when I let myself stop and remember, the pain was too much to bear.

Inside the sanctuary of the pool house, I kicked off my Converse and yanked my hair out of the ponytail, letting the waves cascade down my back. I hadn't even been here two weeks yet, and it felt like I was caught up in a whirlwind. My phone vibrated again and I let out a groan. Kyle was incessant. But when my eyes fell on the screen a whole other feeling took hold.

Maverick: Thank you

Thank you? What did he mean? I couldn't imagine Summer had told Maverick what happened in the time it took me to get to the pool house. Or had he found out some other way? Or was I misreading the situation entirely? Maverick was angry—a loaded gun waiting for an excuse to fire. But somewhere underneath all the brooding and hostility was the boy I'd met last summer.

~

The ride to school the next day was uncomfortable. Kyle muttered the odd word while Summer sat silent in the back, refusing to make eye contact with anyone. But by the weekend, the tension slowly evaporated. I'd checked in with her a couple of times and she reassured me everything was okay. She and Nick were working through things, but after their scare both of them had decided to take it slow. Macey watched me like a hawk, and Maverick didn't look twice at me.

After his text message, it stung.

"So, you'll come after, right?" Laurie said. After apologising all week, I finally relented and agreed to go to the opening game pep rally with her, after dinner with Dad.

"Yes, I'll come. Dinner should be done by nine, at the latest."

She shrieked down the line and I held the phone away from my ear. "Sorry, I'm just excited. I love football."

"I bet you do." I laughed accusatorially.

"Hey, I do. It has absolutely nothing to do with Kyle."

"Keep telling yourself that." I swung my legs over the bed and stood. "I need to go get ready. Dad will be here soon."

"Okay, have fun. I'll see you later. Text me when you're done."

We hung up, and I searched through the small closet for something to wear. It was just dinner with Dad, but I didn't know what to expect after. Laurie had told me how big of a deal football was at Wicked Bay High. And these people didn't do things by half.

A knock at the pool house door startled me. I called out, "Come in."

"Lo? It's me," Uncle Gentry's voice floated through the house. "Are you decent?"

I went into the living area. He stood poised in the doorway with a strained smile on his face. "How was school today?"

"Okay, thanks."

"Good. I feel like we haven't spent enough time

together but things at work are..." he paused something clouding his eyes. "Busy."

"It's fine, I'm a big girl." I hadn't meant for it to sound so bitter.

"Everything is okay, though? The kids are making you feel welcome? I know Kyle is happy you're here." He ran a hand through his hair and it occurred to me he was nervous. Uncle Gentry was nervous. That couldn't be a good sign.

"Is everything okay?"

"You're different, Lo." His voice was sad. "What you went through. I can't ever imagine. But know you're loved and your Dad just wants the best for you, sweetheart."

"Okay." I frowned, caught off guard by his little speech.

"Just go easy on him, okay? It hasn't been easy for him, none of this has."

I wanted to ask what he meant, but my phone blared and he was already out of the door.

~

"Looks fancy." I eyed the restaurant. It was on the main street, downtown. And it looked worlds apart from the places I was used to eating at. With its deep red curtains and gold furnishings, I suddenly felt very out of place.

"It'll be fine." Dad squeezed my hand reassuringly, and I smiled. The ride over had been nice. We'd chatted about our first couple of weeks in Wicked Bay. Dad told me about Stone and Associates, and his new role there. It was pleasant. It almost felt like old times. Which made the fancy restaurant seem over the top.

"Seriously, we couldn't have just gone to The Cali Grill?" It had been my favourite place to eat last summer.

He laughed softly as he held the door open and I

slipped inside. If the outside looked upmarket, the inside was something else, and I sucked in a sharp breath. But Dad didn't seem fazed as he guided me to the hostess, talking in hushed voices. The maître d smiled and picked up two leather bound menus, leading us to the back of the room.

My eyes scanned the tables, a sinking feeling washing over me as I realised there were no empty ones.

"Dad?" My voice cracked as he slowed in front of a table occupied by a beautiful woman. Feet rooted to the spot, my body lurched forward to catch up to the jarred movement.

"Tell me this isn't what I think it is?" My voice was low, cracked with betrayal.

"Eloise, I'd like you to meet Stella."

Stella.

Was it possible to hate a name? To take offence to the word that gave someone their verbal identity?

Because all I felt was hatred.

Blood curdling, heart wrenching hatred.

"I can't..." the words started to form, and I saw the maître d's confusion at my reluctance to sit down.

Dad moved in front of me, shielding me from her view. Or maybe it was the other way around. Maybe she was the one he was protecting... from me.

"You ambushed me." I stared up at him, blinking away the tears.

"I knew if I told you, you wouldn't come. Please, Eloise," his voice was quiet. "I'd really like you to meet her. She's important to me."

More important than me?

The words were right there, on the tip of my tongue. But I couldn't speak. I couldn't do anything but let him guide me into a chair as he moved around to the blonde-haired woman watching our exchange with caution in her eyes.

"You look lovely, darling." He leaned in and kissed her cheek and it was like a knife to my heart.

"Lo, I'd like you to meet Stella Drake. Stella, my daughter, Lo."

"Hello, Lo, it's lovely to finally meet you."

Finally.

There was that word again. The word my grandparents had used.

Dad sat down across from me and next to Stella. I didn't miss the way his hand patted hers, or the longing in his eyes as he gazed at her.

Fuck.

He loved her.

My father wasn't just seeing a new woman, he'd fallen in love with one.

"Lo?" The hard edge to his voice had my eyes widening.

"Sorry, what?"

"I said this is Stella." He gave me a pointed look.

"Hello," I croaked.

"I love your shirt, Lo. It really complements your hair and skin. Robert didn't tell me how beautiful you were."

What was I supposed to say? That I had my mum's eyes and complexion? Did she want to hear that? To hear all about my dead mother?

Thankfully, I didn't have to answer. The waitress arrived to take our drink order and Dad made light conversation. It was like a dream—an out of body experience. They talked like two old friends and I realised Stella Drake was someone who knew my father before he moved to England. Before he met Mum and got married and had a family. This woman sitting in front of me with her perfect hair and warm smile was privy to a man I'd never met.

The knife twisted.

"How are you finding school?" She attempted to pull me back into the conversation. "It can't have been easy?"

I shrugged, picking the hem of the black tablecloth. "It's been okay, I guess. My cousins have been very welcoming." I swallowed down the lump.

Something flashed over her face and she smiled again. "Good, that's good. At least you have... people."

What the hell did that mean?

Once again, we were interrupted by the waitress. She delivered our drinks and took our order. I didn't miss the way Dad ordered for Stella, and I couldn't help but wonder who this man before me was. He certainly wasn't the man I knew.

My dad.

Our food arrived, providing a buffer between Stella's questions and Dad's attempt at building bridges. As far as I was concerned he was trying to salvage something that was ruined before it ever got started.

He'd set me up.

Instead of asking me to meet her, he'd forced her on me. I wasn't ready. It was too much, too soon.

I pushed the chicken parmigiana around my plate, unable to stomach it.

"Stella is an editor for the local paper," Dad said.

"That's nice."

"It pays the bills and means I can work from home sometimes so I'm around for Beth."

"Who's Beth?"

The colour drained from Dad's face and he placed down his cutlery and Stella let out a garbled sound. "Oh, I'm sorry, I thought Robert had told you. Beth is my daughter, she's six."

The knife hit an artery, and I felt myself plummet. The blood drained from my face.

"She's great, Lo. You'll love her."

I stared at my father as I calmly placed down my own

cutlery and met Stella's uncertain gaze. "Actually, he didn't tell me. Until last weekend, I didn't even know anything about you. Now, if you'll both excuse me I have somewhere to be."

Stella let out a shaky breath as I rose from the table and walked away. Dad didn't follow. I didn't expect him to. After all, he had Stella to comfort.

Chapter Thirteen

"Wow, Lo, I had no idea. I'm so sorry, I just thought that perhaps they'd separated and you didn't want to talk about it."

"Yeah, well." My gaze lowered, matching my voice. "It's not exactly a conversation starter."

"I'm so sorry. I can't even imagine…" Laurie's voice trailed off. "I'm here, if you need anything, okay?"

"Thanks, I appreciate it." I smiled at her but felt the sadness in it.

I'd left the restaurant and called Laurie to come get me. Now we were at school for the opening game pep rally. Girls had painted their faces red and white, the team colours; and the crackle of anticipation and the sound of blow horns filled the air. It was like nothing I'd ever experienced. Back home, school sports teams were lucky to pull a crowd of twenty, but from the sea of kids in their war paint it looked like everyone had turned up to show their support for the football team. I was just relieved it was outside and that we weren't all crammed into the gym.

"Come on, let's find the others." Laurie grabbed my hand and pulled me through the crowd. A couple of people smiled and said hello, their faces vaguely familiar from classes.

We reached Autumn and the others just as the band burst into chorus.

"Wow, its loud," I yelled, earning me an eye roll from them.

"No band in England?"

I shook my head, jamming my hands into my lightweight jacket. "Not like this, no."

From our position in the bleachers, we had a good view of the football field where the band marched in neat rows while the cheerleaders did their thing. I spotted Macey then Caitlin Holloway. Her blonde hair whipped around her face as she twisted and twirled revelling in the attention. Macey looked less enthused but still moved gracefully. Organised sports were never really my thing, and my eyes moved on to the sidelines where the team were gathered in full kit.

"There's Kyle." Autumn nudged Laurie, with a giggle, and even I could appreciate their infatuation. The boy looked good, the whole team did. Until my gaze landed on JB and a shudder worked its way up my spine. Laurie had told me he was harmless, but there was something about him. Something that made my skin crawl.

The band finished and a man in a red and white baseball cap, emblazoned with a W, stepped up onto the podium, silencing the crowd. Laurie elbowed me and winked and went back to watching. He talked about team spirit and hard work and kicking ass and by the end of it, the crowd was in a frenzy again. Even Autumn and Laurie were bouncing on their feet, cheering and chanting.

I didn't understand a lot of what Coach Munford said, but it was hard not to be swept away with the atmosphere. I felt it, the thirst for the win. It oozed from the team, reflected back at them from the crowd. Dad and Stella Drake became a distant memory as I watched Kyle jump on his teammates, enacting some kind of male bonding ritual. A hand slipped through my arm and Laurie nestled closer. "And now," she said, "we party."

~

This party was different to the previous two I'd attended. Girls were dressed down in team colours, some in football jerseys. But even though the dress code was lower key, it was just as crazy. It was at a boy called Brendon Palmer's house, right next to the ocean. I'd thought it couldn't get much more extravagant than the Holloway's, I was wrong. His house backed onto a private part of the beach and there was a big bonfire. Laurie informed me his family were huge football fans and it was customary for the Palmer's to host the opening game party. The youngest of four brothers, Brendon lived, breathed, and slept football, and his parents were all too willing to host.

"Aren't you even a little bit curious?"

"Huh?" My head snapped over to Laurie's. We'd found a few lawn chairs and dragged them to the edge of the beach.

"Where Devon is." Her brow lifted a little.

"Hmm, where is Devon?" It hadn't even crossed my mind he wasn't here, but then since walking away from him at school the other day, he'd been avoiding me.

"Giving you space." She smirked. "After your little outburst the other day."

"Oh, come on." I kicked my legs out in front of me and leaned back. "You deserved it and you know it."

Laurie held up her bottle. "True, but you underestimate your cousins' position in Wicked Bay High. Look around you, Lo." She swept her hand through the air. "It's always about money in Wicked Bay. Who's got it, who hasn't. But it's more with your cousins. Because of Alec Prince. Because of who he is. Our parents want to be in his circle and their kids want to be in Maverick's."

"I don't want to talk about them. Or my dad. Or anything that reminds me this really is my life now. I just want to drink and dance." *And forget.*

Her eyes flashed with mischief. "That, we can do. But not too much, Kyle will—"

"Laurie!"

"Fine, fine. No more talk of them tonight. Just don't let me get drunk and go with him, okay?"

"Promise."

I still hadn't cleared the air with Kyle. But I had bigger problems to deal with—like Stella Drake. Ugh. Annoyed at myself for letting my mind go there, I tipped back my beer and finished it off, wiping my mouth with the back of my hand. "I need another."

I stood up and Laurie's eyes bugged. "Lo," she warned. But I was already moving. Maybe it was foolish breaking the one promise I'd made Dad before moving here. But he'd broken promises too. Besides, Kyle wouldn't be far away, lurking in the shadows, spying on my every move.

The path up to the Palmer's house was littered with empty cups and I wondered who would clean up tomorrow. Although they probably had a cleaner too. From the size of their house, they probably had a whole team of them.

"Stone," a deep voice said as I reached the back door. I swung around with a sigh, my eyes landing on JB as he sat on a low wall, clutching a bottle in his hand. "Didn't expect to see you here."

I don't know if it was the adrenaline from the pep rally or the couple of beers in my system, but I closed the distance and tilted my head to one side. "Well, here I am."

A wicked grin tugged at his lips as he stood up, his biceps straining underneath his jersey. "Here you are indeed."

"Well, thanks for the chat," I said. "But I need a refill." I waved my empty at him and turned on my heels.

"Stone, wait up." He was behind me, huge and imposing. I went rigid. Shit. Why had I engaged? His fingers swept my hair off my shoulder, lingering. His touch felt violating. I couldn't explain it but it felt wrong. About to shirk him off and get the hell out of there, a saccharine sweet voice called, "JB, come swim with us. We need warming up."

I rolled my eyes, stifling a groan. He didn't move straight away and, for a second, I thought he might turn them down in favour of me. To my relief, he didn't. "I'll be right in," he said in a husky voice.

It was my signal to get out of there. My body lurched back into action, and I slipped into the house. The kitchen was full of bodies, and every surface was covered with drinks or snacks. Dragging air into my lungs, I pushed forward, helping myself to a handful of crisps as I scanned the room for beer, but someone stepped in front of me. "We need to talk." Kyle grimaced.

"No, we don't. I'm here to party, not talk."

His eyes narrowed. "Are you drunk?"

"No," I snapped, barging him out of the way and helping myself to a beer.

"Lo, come on. This is me."

"If she wants you to know, she'll tell you. Give her time."

"Seriously? She's fifteen. If he did something—"

"Kyle." I swung around almost colliding with his solid frame. "You're only a year older. Did you forget that in the middle of your knight in shining armour quest?"

"Yeah but she's a girl."

"I'll pretend I didn't hear that." I moved around him and headed for the door, but he was quicker and cut me off at the end of the island.

"She's really okay?"

"She'll be fine. And maybe if you tried talking to her instead of treating her like a child, she'd come to you with stuff."

He raked a hand through his hair and nodded. "Okay, okay." His gaze slid to my drink. "Now, how many of those have you had?"

"Bye, Kyle." I ducked my head and hurried out of there. He was worse than... well, worse than a dad who actually cared. I hadn't heard from my own father since I fled the restaurant.

I swallowed a mouthful of beer, letting the sharp taste wash away my own feelings of bitterness. It wasn't that I didn't want Dad to be happy, of course I did. But he'd lied, and for all I knew, this whole move was a sham. It wasn't a fresh start for us—it was a chance for him to move closer to his new whatever she was.

Something pricked at the back of my mind.

What if—

No.

He wouldn't.

He loved Mum.

They were happily married.

But this was all so sudden. Much too sudden for a man grieving.

Oh, God.

I ground to a halt and downed the rest of the bottle. Beer wasn't going to cut it, I needed something much, much stronger.

~

"Kyle help me..." the girl sounded annoyed but I couldn't figure out why. My head lolled backwards, smacking against something hard, and a groan of pain gurgled in my throat.

"She weighs a ton, what the fuck did she drink? And

127

why weren't you watching her?"

"Seriously, Kyle, I'm not her keeper. She wanted to cut loose, and I don't blame her after what her dad did."

"What her dad did?"

My body felt like it was being dragged in two.

"Oh crap, maybe I shouldn't have said anything."

"Laurie..." Now the boy sounded annoyed. Did I know him? Was that Kyle?

"Kyle."

"Ssh, Lo, we've got you. Just sleep it off, okay."

"Sleep, I like sleep." The words came out slurred and someone chuckled.

"Okay, get the door."

I landed with a thud against soft leather and alcohol sloshed around in my insides. "Ugh," I groaned, clutching my stomach. "I don't feel so good."

"If she pukes back there, you can clean it up."

"Me? It's not my fault."

"Did you try to stop her?"

"You have met her, right? She's not one to fall in line, Kyle. And she was hurting, so back the hell off!"

There was a distant grumble. It reverberated into my body. Another door slammed and everything went black.

"What the fuck happened..."

I teetered on the edge of darkness. Something had pulled me out of its claws. Strong hands cushioned my head and slid underneath my legs.

I was floating.

Up.

Up.

Up.

"Drank too much."

"You don't say."

"Maybe I should—"

Growl.

Did someone growl?

A door slammed. And another. The noise trying to drag me back from the darkness. But it was no use. I gave over to it once more.

"Do you want me to—"

"I got it."

"Whatever you say, Prince."

Prince? There was a Prince here? I hope I looked okay.

"What am I going to do with you?"

Who?

Me?

Darkness.

The hands disappeared and my body began to fall.

Down.

Down.

Down.

Until my back hit something soft. I sighed and then hiccupped.

Gross.

"Jesus," a voice said. Was that the Prince? I really should have made more effort to speak. Say something, anything. But my lips wouldn't work. They felt detached from my face.

"Lo? Do you need something? Water?"

I tried. Imagined opening my mouth, saying the words... but nothing happened. I no longer had control over my body.

Someone smoothed my hair out of my face. There were fingers. Long, deft fingers. I blinked my eyes open trying to fight my way through the haze. Two inky black pools shone back at me. Then I was moving, being dragged onto my side.

"I'll be right here, okay?" Warmth connected with my forehead. Soft and lingering.

Then the Prince was gone.

~

I woke with hair matted across my face, dribble crusted on the corner of my mouth.

Ugh.

My head splintered into a thousand pieces as I opened my eyes and tried to get my bearings. What the hell had happened last night? I expected it to all come flooding back but it didn't. The memories were there, I felt them, but they remained tightly locked behind the haze of an epic hangover.

Slipping my hand under the covers, I made a tent and peeked down. Still fully clothed, I breathed a sigh of relief. Clothes were a good thing. Or were they? Had I gotten so drunk that someone had to put me to bed?

Shame washed over me, and I flopped onto my back and listened for any signs of life, but was met with eerie silence. Sunshine poured into the room through the blinds and I rubbed a hand across my eyes vaguely able to recall the night before.

There had been dinner with my dad and a woman? St... Stella Drake.

My stomach rumbled and then churned violently. I threw off the covers and staggered into the small bathroom, dropping to my knees.

Oh God. I remembered.

Dad had taken me to a fancy restaurant and ambushed me.

I retched into the bowl, dry heaving until my throat burned. But nothing came up as I remembered clearly the way he'd looked at her.

Stella Drake.

The woman my father was in love with.

I slipped off the bowl and laid face down on the cool tiles, pressing my cheek to the marble.

Dad was in love.

How had this happened?

More importantly, how had I not known?

My phone blared from somewhere inside my bedroom but I didn't move. I couldn't, as I tried to piece together the rest of the night. I'd fled dinner. Laurie picked me up. There was a pep rally at the high school. A party.

Lots of beers at the party.

It all came back like a bad home movie. I'd been on a mission to forget. Laurie watched on as I drowned myself in beer after beer until hitting the strong stuff.

But the memories fluttered away into oblivion like a piece of string in the wind.

How had I gotten home?

Another thought crossed my mind… did I want to know?

After another few minutes, I finally dragged myself off the bathroom floor. I splashed some water on my face and brushed my teeth, swilling my mouth twice for good measure. What I really wanted was a shower, but my legs were like jelly, barely able to support my body as I shuffled around the bedroom. So, instead, I opted for a change of clothes, swapping my jeans, sheer blouse, and vest top for sweats and a clean t-shirt. Running a brush through my matted hair, I swept it up in a ponytail and sat on the edge of my bed, scrolling through my phone.

Kyle: How's the head?

I swallowed my pride and texted Kyle back asking if he knew how I got home. His reply came straight through.

Kyle: That's for me to know and you to find out

Ugh. I was too broken to play games so I moved onto Laurie's text message.

Laurie: Hey, just wanted to check you're okay? Sorry I let you get so wasted.

I texted back.

Lo: You didn't let me do anything, I'm a big girl. Guess I just needed a blowout. No more though. I think I burned away my stomach lining.

Laurie: Ouch. We'll see you at the game, right?

Lo: Maybe. I'm not sure I'll make it out of the house today.

There was a good chance, I'd need a whole day to recover. Possibly two.

Laurie: You have to come. Call me later xo

I ignored the two text messages and one missed call from Dad, and went in search of fried food and water.

Chapter *Fourteen*

"**O**h look, it's awake."

I shot Macey a severe glare. The throb in my head didn't have time for her crap. All I wanted was grease and liquid, and to sleep off my hangover ... preferably, in that order.

"I heard you made quite the spectacle of yourself last night." Her accusation hung in the air between us and I slammed my hand down on the island. "I heard you're a complete bitch, but life goes on, right?" My saccharine sweet voice had the desired effect, and she blanched.

"You should—" her words died on her lips as Kyle bounded into the room looking as fresh as a daisy.

"You look like shit." He came around the island, leaned in close and sniffed. "And you smell like it too. Jesus, Lo, did you drink enough to sink a ship?"

"Don't," I groaned. "Please, don't remind me." I moved to the refrigerator to get some water.

"Where's Dad?" he asked Macey.

"Golf. They left an hour ago."

"And Momma P?"

"Seriously, Kyle? You know she hates that." She snorted. "Mom's here. She's taking me and Summer to the mall later." I didn't miss the inflection in her voice. It was a family thing, and I wasn't invited.

My inner bitch refused to stay quiet. I met Macey's smug smirk and said, "How is Summer today?"

Her face paled again, only this time she pushed her plate away and stormed out of the kitchen.

"Must you poke the beast?" Kyle dropped onto the stool opposite me.

"She's a bitch."

"I don't disagree, but she's family."

"Whatever, Kyle. My head feels like it's going to explode." I sipped the water, testing my stomach. When it didn't rush back up my throat, I drank the rest in small doses.

"What happened last night?" He looked concerned. "Laurie said something happened with your dad?"

"Did you know?" I met his eyes.

"I feel like you're setting me up to fail here, Cous."

"About Stella, did you know about Stella?"

"Ah, that." His smile slipped, and I had my answer.

"You knew?" I felt sick again.

"Whoa, it's not like that. It's not some huge conspiracy against you. Uncle Robert wanted to tell you himself and he wanted to wait until—"

I slid off the stool and hurried out of the kitchen and toward the pool house. If Kyle knew, what's betting they all knew. Which meant when Maverick taunted me about it... he knew!

I burst through the door, slamming it behind me.

They knew.

They all fucking knew.

"Lo, Cous, come on, don't be like that." I glanced back at the door. Kyle was pressed up against the glass pouting like a child. "He asked us not to say anything," he said as he slipped inside, holding out his peace offering of more water and a pastry.

My body trembled with anger, and something else I

134

didn't want to succumb to. But I couldn't fight back the tears.

"Oh shit." Kyle dropped the peace offering on the counter. "Don't cry. I have to leave soon for the game, but I can't leave you like this, and Coach will kick my ass all the way into next week if I'm late."

I stifled back a laugh and dried my eyes. "You can't be late, you have a game to win."

He puffed out his chest. "Damn right, I do. But seriously, Lo, are you okay? Rick would—"

My eyes widened at the mention of his name. "Maverick would what?"

"Nothing." His eyes darted around me.

"Kyle, how did I get home last night?"

"I drove you." He continued, avoiding my eyes.

"Thank you. I can't imagine it was a pretty sight."

This got his attention, and he smirked. "I've seen worse."

"So, it was you who tucked me in? That's kind of weird."

"Hmm." He ran a hand down his face. "Are we good here? I really need to shoot."

I narrowed my eyes, the pieces I was far too hungover to assemble slowly falling into place. "Yeah, we're done. I'll see you later if I can shake this awful hangover."

"You'll live. Besides, you have to be there for my first game, you're family."

~

Five hours later, I found myself back at the high school, in the bleachers watching Kyle do his thing. Laurie insisted I go. Even after I found out Dad planned to go with Gentry and Summer. And after a ten-minute lecture on all the reasons I should go, I realised she was right. Just because we were both going to be there didn't mean I had to talk to him.

"How are you?" I leaned in close to Summer.

She nodded, but didn't take her eyes off the field. "Okay, thanks."

"Things are okay? With Nick?"

She nodded again, but I didn't miss the way her lips pulled tight.

One of our players broke through the defense and the crowd went wild. Even Summer, the quiet, shy, Stone-Prince, cheered. But the noise was nothing compared to the roar when we scored. The place erupted, and I covered my ears to stop my head from exploding.

Laurie was talking, her mouth moving rapidly with excitement, but I couldn't hear a word she was saying. I smiled along until she went back to watching. Then my eyes roved over the crowd, landing on Gentry. He and Dad were nearer the front, in seats reserved for family members, both sporting red and white Wreckers caps. A bolt of envy flared through me. Dad was so comfortable here, so settled. It was almost as if he hadn't spent the last twenty-five years living in England, he'd slipped so easily back into his old life.

His life before Mum and Elliot and me.

When the final whistle blew, our team had won by seven points. Laurie informed me it was the perfect opening game. Knowing nothing about American football, I could only agree.

"You're coming to JB's, right?" She asked as me and Summer trailed after her and Autumn.

"I don't think so. I need sleep."

"You have to come. We won, we need to celebrate. Kyle will—"

"Live without my presence for one night. Go," I waved them off. "Have fun and remember alcohol is the devil. Trust me, I know."

They disappeared into the sea of people and I turned to Summer. "Are you heading back with your dad?"

"I, hmm, I was going to meet Nick. But I can come with you."

"No, go. It's early. I'll be fine. I promise."

She smiled and tucked her long hair behind her ear. "I'll see you tomorrow."

"Bye." I waved and scanned the crowd. There was no way I was riding back with Dad. I wasn't ready to deal with him yet. Which left me no choice but to walk.

Hands jammed deep into my pockets, I wound through the bodies until the crush cleared and I could see the parking lot.

"Lo, wait up." Devon jogged toward me. "You're leaving already?"

"Yeah," I said. "I don't know if you heard but things kind of got messy last night. I feel like death."

He laughed. "I thought getting wasted at parties was my trick? Want to talk about it?"

"Not really." I spied his car behind him. "But I could eat. Peace offering?"

Devon's whole face lit up. "Yeah?"

I nodded. "I owe you an apology," I said as we walked to his car.

"No, you don't. I pushed and I shouldn't have. My beef is with Prince, not you. I'm sorry. Forgive me?" He grinned over the roof and I smiled.

"Forgiven."

We climbed inside. I was glad we'd cleared the air, but something still bothered me.

"What is it with you two, anyway?"

Devon's hand gripped the wheel a little tighter. "Long story. Maybe one day I'll tell you all about it. I know he's your cousin, Lo, but you can't trust him. He only looks out for one person. Himself."

Well, okay then. I had no comeback for that so I kept quiet, waiting as Devon turned the key and the car roared to life. He peeled out of the parking lot, and I couldn't help but wonder exactly what had happened between the two of them.

Devon didn't drive to Pattie's this time. He chose a little place on the outskirts of town, claiming that it would be quieter after the game. I was relieved I wouldn't have to see anyone from school. It had been a crazy few days, between Dad, Summer, and Maverick. It was hard to believe I'd only been here two weeks.

"Shall we?" Devon held open the door to the diner, and I ducked inside. It was nice. Quiet. We sat in a window booth that overlooked the sea.

"Cool view," I said playing with the menu.

"Yeah, it's nice. What do you feel like?"

My stomach rumbled, and we both laughed. "Apparently, I'm finally ready to eat." I'd barely managed a piece of toast earlier.

"That bad, huh?"

I shot him a look. "Like you didn't hear all about it?"

Devon smirked in response. "Laurie may have said something."

"Of course, she did," I mumbled under my breath, focusing on the menu and not the heated gaze he was throwing me.

The waitress came and took our orders and we settled into easy conversation. I liked Devon, I did, but it was like he was holding back. Keeping secrets. And I'd had enough of that lately. So, I brought up the elephant in the room.

"You weren't at the party yesterday? Or the game today?"

"The party, no, but I was at the game. You just didn't see me."

"You're avoiding me," I said, and he shrugged.

"I was giving you space. It's no secret I like you, Lo, but you seem, I don't know, unavailable. I didn't want to crowd you and after the other day, I figured space was the best course of action."

"Well, thank you, I appreciate it. It's been a crazy two weeks."

"That's all you have to say?" His eyebrow quirked up.

"Look, Devon." I met his gaze head on. "I like you, I do, but I just got here. There's a lot of stuff I'm still dealing with, and I'm not sure jumping into anything with anyone is what I need right now."

The blood drained from his face and I quickly added, "But I could really use a friend."

"A friend?" He threw my words back at me and I nodded. He wanted more. I knew that. But I wasn't ready and besides, girls and boys could be just friends, couldn't they? I wasn't leading him on if I was being upfront with him.

"What kind of friends are we talking? The kind who hold hands and have sleepovers and share all their deepest, darkest secrets?" The corners of his mouth lifted in amusement and I wafted my menu at him.

"Devon! I'm being serious. I want to be friends, I don't want things to be awkward between us."

He threw his hands up. "I'm only joking with you. Friends, got it. I've been told I make an excellent friend." It didn't come out sarcastically, but there was an undertone to his words I couldn't quite place.

Our food arrived, and we ate and chatted like two friends would. Maybe it was a mistake thinking we could just be friends, but back home in England, I'd had plenty of male friends. And Devon hung around with Laurie and Autumn and I didn't get any lusty vibes between them. It would be fine. Totally fine.

My phone vibrated, and I debated ignoring it but Devon said, "Aren't you checking that?" so I retrieved it from my pocket and swiped the screen.

Dad: I'll be at Stella's tonight, but I'd really like for us to talk tomorrow. I'm sorry.

"Everything okay?" Devon motioned to the phone still in my hand.

"Yeah," I replied. "Everything is fine." I slipped it away and pushed my plate away. Suddenly, I wasn't very hungry anymore.

~

Devon dropped me back at the house after we argued about splitting the bill. He wanted to pay, but I'd insisted friends didn't do that. I won, much to his disappointment. But I didn't want the lines to blur into dangerous territory.

Gentry's car wasn't in the driveway and when I entered the house the place was empty. I sent Summer a quick text checking she was okay. As I cut across the garden to the pool house, my eyes swept over the pool. It looked so tempting. I hadn't dared swim in it yet, not wanting to strip off in front of my new family. But if they were all out...

I hurried to change into my bikini, grabbed a towel, and went back outside. Curling my toes over the edge, I closed my eyes and took a deep breath, lifted my arms into a point and pushed off. My body sliced through the cool water and I gasped when my head surfaced. It wasn't ice cold, but it was still a shock to the system. I moved in slick lines, front stroke on the way up, twisting to back stroke on the return. I wasn't competition worthy or anything, but before the accident, I'd loved the water, and it was something I hadn't done in a long time.

Breathless, I finally hoisted my arms onto the side, my feet treading lazy circles beneath me. The Stone-Prince's garden was something I'd only ever dreamed of. And for the meantime, it was home. But despite its beauty, its perfection, it was all an allusion. Gentry and Rebecca put on a united front for Dad and me, but I saw the cracks. They were barely ever home. If Gentry wasn't at work, he was out playing golf or meeting friends for drinks, and his wife was the same. Rebecca worked as an events planner which meant lots of late nights and weekends scouting venues and putting the final touches to banquets and galas. Which left their children to come and go as they pleased.

Lost in my daydreams, I didn't notice Maverick and his friends enter the garden before it was too late. Their laughter and chatter died at the sight of me but I only had eyes for Maverick as I silently pleaded with him to do something. I didn't want to have to climb out in front of five boys.

When no one moved to help me, I snapped, "Are you all just going to stand there and leer, or is one of you going to get my towel so I can get the hell out of here?"

A fair-haired boy jerked into action and moved toward the sun chair where my towel was, but an arm flew out and stopped him. Maverick turned to his friends and said something in a hushed voice. His friends nodded, craning over his frame to have one last glance at me as if they hadn't ever seen a bikini-clad girl in a pool before. Which given how many parties they had, I highly doubted.

They disappeared inside and Maverick turned to me. Anger blazed in his eyes, or was it frustration... or something else entirely? He didn't utter a word as he fetched my towel and brought it to the edge of the pool, dangling it in front of me. I snatched it from him and placed it by the steps.

"Okay, you can go now," I said.

"Why are you acting like this?"

"Like what?"

"Like you're embarrassed?"

"You just turned up with four of your friends while I'm half-naked in your pool. I am embarrassed." I wasn't, but he didn't need to know that.

Maverick regarded me for a second before raking a hand down his face and saying, "We were going to hang out here for a bit. We can go somewhere else, if you want?"

I gaped at him. He was asking my permission about things now? His mood swings gave me a serious case of whiplash.

"It's fine. I was just getting out anyway. I have homework. Don't worry, I wouldn't want to cramp your style."

He looked ready to say something, but someone yelled his name from the kitchen. Maverick didn't say another word as he stalked off, and I hopped out of the pool as quickly as I could, wrapping the towel around my body and making a run for the pool house.

Chapter *Fifteen*

I spent the rest of the night holed up in the pool house. The laughter from Maverick and his friends drifted through to my room, but I did my best to ignore it, jamming my iPod buds into my ears and turning up the volume.

The next morning when I woke up, Dad was already waiting. His shirt was pressed, matching the undisturbed bed sheets on the sofa bed. Since I hadn't heard him return, I figured he'd never made it home. But there he was, sitting at the small breakfast bar as if everything was fine.

"Morning," he said, a guarded smile playing on his lips. "I'd wondered when you were going to show."

"What time is it?" I yawned, ignoring the bright pink elephant in the room he had failed to address yet.

"Nine-thirty. You must have needed it. Did you enjoy the game?"

I shrugged, going for the coffee pot. "It was okay, I guess."

"I thought you'd stick around for the party, but Kyle said—"

"You saw Kyle?"

"Yes, he's in the house. Rebecca is insisting they have breakfast as a family. I made our excuses though." He blew out a long sigh. "I'd like to clear the air … and apologise."

Propped against the counter, cup in hand, I clipped out, "I'm listening."

"Eloise, please, be reasonable."

"Reasonable?" I clenched my jaw. "Are you kidding me? You ambushed me, Dad. And as if it isn't bad enough, I had to find out from Kyle that the others all knew about her. Talk about a knife to the stomach. How long?"

His eyes widened a fraction. "How long what?"

"Don't play dumb, Dad. How long have you been seeing her?" I couldn't bring myself to say her name.

He blanched, but I wasn't going to give him an easy ride.

"It has to be before the move, right? I mean, that's why we're here. For her. So, I figure it's got to have been going on a while. Maybe even before Mum—"

"Eloise, please," he snapped, but quickly regained his composure. "It's complicated."

"That's your reply? It's complicated? Seems pretty simple to me," my voice was shrill as I glared at him.

"Eloise, this isn't how I wanted to do things."

"Oh, please, Dad, tell me how you wanted to do things? Enlighten me. Because from where I'm standing, you walked me into that fancy restaurant knowing exactly what you were doing. Did it ever occur to you to talk to me first, instead of dropping her on me and expecting me to be okay with it? Mum just died, she just…" Tears rushed from my eyes and I doubled over, reaching behind me to place the cup down, overcome by emotion.

Dad hurried from his stool and tried to comfort me, but I pushed him away. "No," I yelled. "You don't get to do that. You don't get to pretend everything is okay.

Everything is not okay!"

The ounce of colour left in his face drained away. "I messed up, didn't I?"

"You think?" I stared at him incredulously. "I don't even know how we come back from this, Dad. You lied. That's all on you. You can't just expect me to accept it. Accept her." Swiping at the tears with my hand, I sucked in a ragged breath. "You brought me here, left me in this bloody house, and what? Just expected me to be okay with it all? I don't even know who you are anymore."

"Lo," his voice cracked and a small part of me felt guilty, but I was too angry to be reasonable. Too hurt to care.

"I need time, Dad. You need to give me time."

He nodded, defeat shining in his eyes as I walked away and back into my room. I wanted him to follow me, to make me listen, to make me understand his reasons. But he didn't.

And it spoke volumes.

I picked up my phone, sent a text, and headed into the bathroom. Maybe if I stood under the water for long enough, it would wash away all the pain.

Maybe.

~

"That sucks," Devon said as he slathered sun lotion over my shoulders.

"Yeah, I feel like a fool for not realising, but I haven't exactly been checked into life for the last few months."

He dropped the bottle into my bag and leaned back onto his elbows. I'd texted him to see if he wanted to hang at the beach with me and Laurie, but she hadn't shown up yet.

"Want to talk about it?"

"Not really." I was thankful for my sunglasses. They hid the pain I knew would be reflected in my eyes.

"I get it, but if you ever need to talk, I'm here. No strings, okay?"

I nodded, my head laid on my folded arms. "It's so beautiful here."

"What's England like?"

"It's okay, I guess. I lived in the country so it was very green. Lots of fields and farms. It's worlds away from here." My eyes wandered over to the sea where a group of kids ran in and out of the white-capped waves lapping at the shore. "I could get used to this."

"It's home now, Lo. You don't have to get used to it, you just have to embrace it."

Home.

The word sounded strange. Was this really my home now?

When Dad announced we were moving, I hadn't been lucid enough to fully understand the implications. My relationship with Chris had reached toxic levels, and I was drunk or high more than I was sober. I just wanted a way out.

An escape.

So, I went along with it because I couldn't stand the look of desperation in Dad's eyes every time he found me barely conscious, strung out on my choice of poison at the time. But now, I wondered if he was desperate to save me or to escape himself. To leave behind the memories, the suffocating reminders of Mum and Elliot. They were in everything: our house, the walls, the furniture.

Could I really blame him for wanting to leave?

"Lo?"

"Huh." I twisted my head back to Devon and smiled. "Sorry, I zoned out."

"It's cool. Listen, I was wondering—"

"I'm here, I made it. Sorry, Mom wanted to bond." Laurie made air quotes and sighed. "What'd I miss?"

"Not much. Devon was just telling me he wanted ice

cream." I stifled a laugh as he protested, but Laurie cut him off, "Ooh, yeah, get me one? Thanks." She flashed him an eager smile, and he rolled his eyes, wiping his hands down his board shorts as he stood up.

"Guess I'm going to get ice cream."

"Thanks," we both said in unison. When he took off toward The Shack, Laurie laid out her towel beside mine and slipped the thin summer dress off her body. "So, this looks cosy."

"Laurie," I warned, and she laughed.

"I'm only joking around. I get it. Friends only, right?"

"It's all I'm capable of right now," I said.

"So, the chat with your dad was that bad, huh?"

I let out a groan and shifted onto my side, propping my head up with a fist. "I love him, but he's so clueless sometimes."

"Tell me about it, families are the worst. But I'm glad you texted. We can hang out and then if you don't want to go back to the house later, you can stay over at mine. My parents are out of town for the night."

"That'd be okay?"

She nodded enthusiastically. "Of course. Autumn's brother is back from the military so she's busy doing family stuff and I don't like being home alone. We can watch a movie and get pizza, then I'll drive us to school in the morning."

"You don't know how good that sounds." I needed space. Away from Kyle, away from the house. Away from a certain brooding Prince who refused to stay off my mind.

"Two ice creams, at your pleasure." Devon appeared over us. "You both owe me three dollars."

"Devon," Laurie gasped and I let out an amused chuckle. She glanced between us. "What?"

"Ask Lo, here. She seems to take issue when people

147

try to do nice things for their *friends*. Isn't that right?" He gave me a pointed stare as he held out my ice cream. I sat up and took it from him.

"Look, I like to pay my way, okay?" I shrugged, running my tongue around the dripping cream and then licking the top clean off.

Devon grumbled something under his breath, thrust Laurie her ice cream, and stalked off.

"What was all that about?" I craned my neck to watch him backtrack to the diner.

"For real? He's totally got it bad for you."

"I told him I'm not interested."

"You know that, and I know that, but he's a guy, Lo. They have a one-track mind. He might say he's cool with it now, but one day he's going to want more, and then what?"

I grabbed my cover-up, balling up the chiffon, and threw it at her. "Stop, okay? We're just friends. He said he's cool with it." But the look in her eye told me she was anything but convinced.

~

We spent the rest of the day hanging out at the Bay. Some of Devon's friends joined us and by the time we were ready to leave, they were trying to persuade Laurie to have a party. I'd shook my head discreetly and mouthed, *"No more parties."* I just wanted to hang out with her and give myself time out to catch a breath.

"Laurie, you're killing us here. You have a free house, you have to let us come hang," a boy called Jared said with a suggestive grin.

"Bite me, Jared. You know I'm dating… was dating Kyle," she corrected herself. Jared closed the distance between them, caging her against her car.

"Come on, Stone's out of the picture. We could have some fun together."

I watched them out the corner of my eye, hoping Kyle

didn't appear out of nowhere. Because although they weren't official, something told me it was only a matter of time.

"Like you'd know what to do with me," she shot back, shoving him backward. He barked out a laugh and shook his head as she rounded her car to the driver's side.

"You don't know what you're missing, babe."

"Give it up, J, she's Stone's." Devon stepped up beside me. "Sorry about Jared, he gets…"

"Don't sweat it." I nudged his side with my elbow. "Thanks for hanging out with me today. I'll see you tomorrow at school?"

There was a spark of some unknown emotion in his eyes as he looked down at me, and I braced myself, but all he said was, "Yeah, of course. But if you girls get lonely later and want company, you know where to find me." Devon winked and jogged off to catch up with his friends and I climbed inside Laurie's car. She looked flustered.

"Something you want to tell me?" I said with a smirk.

"He's just so… ugh!"

"You will have to be a little clearer than that. Are we talking about Kyle or Jared?

"Jared?" Her eyes bugged. "Puh-lease. He's a dog. I'm talking about Kyle, that infuriating cousin of yours."

"Why don't you just smooth it over with him?"

"If only it were that simple." She turned the key, and the car whirred to life. "We can stop by yours and grab your stuff and then go straight to mine, okay?"

"Sounds good."

Ten minutes later, we pulled up outside the house. It was the first time I'd seen the driveway full of cars. The only one missing was Maverick's.

"Front or back?" Laurie asked, and I remembered she'd been here before, when her and Kyle were officially dating.

"I guess we should go through the house."

She looked as excited by that prospect as I did. I dug out my key and opened the door. "Hello," I called. "It's me."

"Lo? We're in here." Rebecca's voice floated out from the kitchen. I nodded to Laurie to stick close by. Her face scrunched up, but she followed.

"Hey." I lifted my hand in a small wave as I entered the kitchen. Rebecca was busy fussing over a pan on the stove while Summer and Gentry were seated around the island. Macey was in one of the chairs outside, catching the last rays of the afternoon. Kyle and Maverick were nowhere to be seen.

"Did you have a nice day, honey?" Rebecca's eyes widened when she spotted my friend. "Laurie, is that you hiding behind Lo?"

"Hi, Mrs. Stone-Prince." She stepped out from behind me and raised a stiff hand.

"Enough with the formalities. Please, call me Rebecca. It's so good to see you again."

"Lo, Laurie," Uncle Gentry flashed us a smile and went back to his papers.

"Hey, Summer," I said, silently asking her if everything was still okay. She gave me a tight smile.

"What have you two girls got planned for this evening? I'm making lasagna, if you'd like to join us?"

"Actually, I'm going to stop at Laurie's for the night. Her parents are out of town and she doesn't want to be home alone."

Rebecca paused from her stirring and turned to me. "Does your father know?"

Like he cares. "I'll text him."

"Sounds good. Oh, how exciting." She clapped her hands together. "Your first slumber party."

"Mom, I think they're a little old for slumber parties," Summer added, surprising all of us. When she realised we were staring in her direction, she ducked her head and continued doing her homework.

"Well, I'm going to pack a bag and then we'll head out. If you need me I have my phone. I guess I'll see you tomorrow."

"Don't stay up too late, and Laurie, I'm sure Kyle will be disappointed he didn't get to see you."

Laurie stifled a snort as we hurried out of the kitchen and cut across the garden to the pool house, ignoring Macey.

"That was… weird." Laurie said once we were inside. "I get a total *Stepford Wives* vibe from her."

"She's not so bad. It's like she tries too hard, you know?" I went into my room and started packing a bag. "I bet she's on the phone to Kyle right now telling him to hurry home so she can play matchmaker."

"Bitch," she shot back. "Come on, let's get out of here quick, in case you're right."

Five minutes and one overnight bag later, we were back in her car and reversing out of the driveway.

Chapter Sixteen

A night away from the Stone-Prince house was exactly what I needed. For a few hours, I'd been able to shut it all off.

Dad.

The past…

Summer.

The present…

Maverick.

The tensions, secrets and lies that were slowly eating away at me like poison. And for those few precious hours, I'd been a normal teenage girl hanging out with her friend. We'd rented a movie off Netflix and ordered pizza. Laurie even broke out a bottle of her mum's wine and we sipped Chianti while giggling every time Channing Tatum's perfect arse filled the screen. It was nice. Fun, even. But the next day at school, when my eyes landed on Maverick across the hallway, I knew something was wrong. His friends laughed and joked around him but his attention was elsewhere. His jaw clenched as his hardened gaze, the one I'd come to recognise, searched for something.

Or someone.

It happened so fast.

One minute he was standing there, the next he was gone, storming through the huddles of kids, while his friends stared after him, confusion shining in their eyes. I slammed my locker shut and went after him. I knew I shouldn't care about whatever he was doing—whoever he had his sights set on—but the same girl who stumbled across him on the beach last summer, refused to let me walk the other way.

When I turned the corner, my feet skidded to a halt as I watched him wrap his hand around a shaggy-haired boy's throat and slam him against the wall with such force it echoed down the hall.

"Maverick!" Summer yelled, panic flooding her voice. I rushed to her side and slipped an arm around her shoulder, hugging her into me.

"Touch my sister again and you're dead, got it? Dead!" His free hand collided with the wall and we both winced.

"Maverick, stop, stop, you're hurting him." Summer tried to get to him, but I pulled her back. He looked possessed, anger pulsating from him.

"Maverick," I said calmly but loud enough for it to be clear. "Think this through."

The poor boy trapped between the wall and Maverick's arm looked ready to crap himself, his eyes wide with terror.

"Maverick," I repeated and this time his head moved a fraction. He didn't meet my eyes, but I knew I had his attention. "You need to let him go."

It was the wrong thing to say. Maverick's arm pushed against Nick's throat, and the boy clawed at his human restraint, gasping for breath. Maverick was unaffected. He didn't budge, didn't flinch a muscle as Nick thrashed against him. He was completely lost to his rage.

"I should beat the shit out of you right here. What the fuck were you thinking?" His voice was raw with anger as

Nick spluttered and choked out a string of garbled words that had Summer sobbing into my shoulder as her body shook with fear.

"What the ... Fuck." Kyle appeared out of nowhere and rushed straight over to Maverick and Nick. He was too calm. As if he was used to dealing with this version of Maverick all the time.

And it occurred to me, maybe he was.

He laid a hand on Maverick's shoulder and squeezed. "Rick, come on, man. You can't afford to get benched which is exactly what coach will do if he finds out about this. Let him go."

Maverick let his arm fall away but fisted his hands into Nick's hoodie still holding him in place. "Stay away from her."

The blood drained from Nick's face as his frantic gaze searched for Summer. Maverick shoved him hard before releasing him fully, and Nick hesitated. I didn't blame him. Maverick still looked ready to kill, his eyes icy and unresponsive.

"Get out of here," Kyle urged. "And the rest of you, show's over." The crowd dispersed in a frenzy of hushed whispers.

"I hate you," Summer choked out as she stepped toward her brothers.

"Sum—" It was Kyle who spoke, but she silenced him with a narrowed glare, turning her head to Maverick. She laughed bitterly. "And you wonder why I never tell you anything. You need help Maverick. Before you hurt someone. *Really* hurt someone." Summer spun around, barged past me, and ran off down the hallway.

"Shit," Kyle murmured under his breath just as Maverick said, "Lond—"

"Don't." I clenched my fists at my side. "Did you tell him?" I looked to Kyle and his expression grew serious.

"Don't put this on me. I'm only just finding out

exactly what that fucker did because you wouldn't tell me."

"You knew she knew?" Maverick's voice was scathing, but we both ignored him.

"Macey told you," I sighed. "Didn't she?"

"Answer the question, Kyle."

Kyle's eyes widened, but I kept going. "Fuck you, Maverick. I'm going to find Summer because someone needs to try to fix your mess."

When I turned around Macey was standing there, guilt written all over her face. "What did you do, Rick?"

"Oh, this just gets better and better," I exhaled a shaky breath. "What did you think telling him would achieve?"

Macey looked to her brother, but he remained silent. When her eyes flickered back to me she stuttered, "I... I don't know."

"And you wonder why she kept it from you." I shouldered past her and went in search of Summer.

~

I found her sobbing into Nick's chest, in an empty classroom at the end of the hallway. "Hey, can I come in?" I whispered.

Nick nodded, and I stepped into the room, closing the door behind me. "Are you okay?"

He let out a shaky breath. "I'll be fine. I'm more concerned about her." He motioned to the girl breaking in his arms.

"Can I?" I inched forward.

"Sure, I think I should lie low anyway. Give Prince chance to cool off. I'll call you later." He dropped a kiss to Summer's head and turned her into my arms.

"Hey, Summer, it's me, Lo." Brushing damp strands of hair out of her face, I tried to soothe her.

When the tears subsided, she lifted her head and smiled weakly. "This is becoming a regular occurrence.

I'm embarrassed." She swiped her eyes with her sleeves.

"Don't be. Maverick was out of order."

"Nick left?" Her eyes darted around the room and I nodded. "He said he'll call you."

"I think I checked out for a minute. I'm so embarrassed. Now everyone will know and they'll look at me and..."

"Hey, hey, none of that. Maverick probably did you a favour," I said. "At least now boys will know you're off limits." It was supposed to be a joke but Summer burst into tears again.

"Crap, I'm sorry." I hugged her tight, rubbing soothing circles over her back.

"I hate him."

"No, you don't. He's an impulsive prick, but he's just looking out for you."

"Nick will never want to—"

"Nick's not going anywhere, okay?" I'd seen the resolve in his eyes. The way he held her like she was the most precious thing in the world. "This will all blow over, you'll see."

Because someone needed to put Maverick straight— even if that person was me.

"I told Macey. She wouldn't let it drop so I told her. She promised not to tell him, she promised ... I should have known, they tell each other everything."

Not everything, my mind whispered. Something told me if Macey knew about me and Maverick, she'd be making my life a lot harder than she already was.

"Ssh, it doesn't matter. All that matters is Maverick didn't hurt Nick." His ego had taken a hit but physically, he was nothing more than a little shaken. Knowing Maverick, the way I'd begun to, it could have ended a lot worse.

"But what if he—"

"Maverick won't touch him again. I promise." Even if

it meant going head to head with him, I'd do it. Someone had to. I brushed more loose wisps of hair out of her face. "Do you think you can get through the rest of the day?"

Summer sniffled and dried her face with her sleeves. "Yeah, I think so."

"Good, because I don't think we can cut class again."

She managed a strained laugh. "Yeah, you're probably right. Thank you, Lo, again. I don't know what I would have done without you."

I hugged her into my side and guided us toward the door. "Like I said before, that's what family is for."

~

I met Summer outside her last class and Kyle gave us a ride home. He tried to apologise to her, but I shook my head warning him not to push. She needed time. And the elder Stone-Prince siblings needed to let Summer come to them, on her terms, when she was ready.

When we arrived at the house Summer fled the Jeep and ran straight inside, and me and Kyle sat there, staring at the house.

"That shit was messed up," he said, his voice laced with regret.

"Are you really surprised?"

He ran a brisk hand down his face. "Rick is..." he searched for the right word but I said, "A loose cannon. Summer is heartbroken, and what about Nick? He didn't deserve that. And you want to know why I didn't tell you? This is precisely why, Kyle. Because you would have run off to Maverick and who knows how it would have ended."

Kyle shifted, so he was facing me. "I know, I know. Is she... okay? She wouldn't even look at me on the ride home."

"What do you think?" I bit out. But I could see the regret in his eyes. He wasn't happy about how things had gone down either. So I added, "She'll be fine."

"Good. That's good." Respect shone in his eyes. "She's lucky to have you, Cous."

"She should have the three of you, too."

"I know." He swallowed and then cleared his throat. "It's just different with her. We've tried to protect her from…" Kyle's voice trailed off and I knew he was shutting me out again. "Listen, I need to get to back for practice. You'll be okay?"

"Go, I'll be fine, and I'll check in on Summer later."

He nodded, and I took that as my sign to leave. I climbed out of the Jeep and headed inside, going straight to the kitchen. Loretta had left some pie on the counter. Loading a plate with a healthy slice, I sat at the island. The front door rattled, and I smiled to myself. "What did you forget?"

But Kyle didn't reply because it wasn't him.

"Oh." My eyes settled on the person standing in the doorway. "It's you."

I went back to my plate of sugar, ignoring Maverick as he stood rigid. "Is she ups—"

"Don't even think about it. You've done enough today."

"I want to apologise. I saw red and lost it."

I slammed my fork down. The clink of metal against marble pierced the tension rippling in the air. "It's a bit late for that, don't you think?" I met his conflicted gaze. "Not only did you embarrass her in the middle of school, you hurt the one person she cares about."

He flinched.

"Summer isn't a child, Maverick." My voice was shrill, and I lowered my tone. I didn't want to risk her hearing this. "They know they jumped into things too quick. They know it was a mistake. But it was her mistake to make and deal with. Not Kyle's, not Macey's, and certainly not yours." I rose from the stool and moved toward him but didn't let myself get too close. He was my Kryptonite and I couldn't risk getting distracted.

"You treat her differently. You all do. Everyone keeps her at arm's length, wraps her up in cotton wool. It's not fair on her."

"I just want to protect her. You don't think I know what guys that age are thinking? Macey told me you had to take her to the clinic for fuck's sake. She's fifteen."

"I was only sixteen last summer."

His face turned ashen but Maverick was an expert at schooling his features, and his impenetrable mask slid back into place. "That was different."

"Different, right."

"We didn't do anything."

We'd done enough, but obviously it didn't matter to him.

"Whatever you tell yourself so you can sleep at night," I murmured.

Maverick's eyes darkened suddenly as he inched forward. I stepped back, maintaining my distance. I couldn't let him get too close.

"London…"

"You need to give her time. Nick isn't going away, Maverick. They're in love. She loves him. They might be young but they care about each other. Don't get in the way of that or you'll lose her forever. And you might want to think about apologising to Nick. Something tells me you need to make a grand gesture if you want to get back into her good graces in the next ten years."

Maverick blew out an exasperated breath and scrubbed a hand over his face. I could see his temper rising. He didn't like being told what to do. But he didn't intimidate me, not like he did others.

"You know I'm right," I said.

He didn't reply.

He continued staring at me—his darkened gaze cutting right through me. I wanted to get inside his head, to hear his thoughts, and experience the world through his eyes. To find out what made Maverick Prince tick. But something told me I might not like what I found, so I left him standing there hoping that if he cared for his sister— if he cared for me, at all—he'd do the right thing and fix it.

Chapter *Seventeen*

After the shit hit the fan with Summer and Maverick, life in Wicked Bay settled down. The morning after Maverick had almost pummelled Nick into a bloody mess, he walked into school and apologised. I didn't witness it with my own eyes, but news circulated the school hallways like wildfire and everyone was talking about it. Summer was a different story. She refused to forgive so easily and two weeks on, things were still frosty between her and Maverick.

Had I only been in Wicked Bay a month? In some ways, it felt longer. But in the ways that mattered, I still wasn't sure I'd ever feel truly at home here.

For starters, I was still living in the pool house. Dad came and went. We were like ships passing in the night. Strangers in a strange place. It was okay, though. I wasn't ready to forgive him, and it seemed that spending time with Stella was more important than spending time with me and trying to fix our relationship. Besides, I'd asked for time and space, and for as much as it stung, he'd given it to me.

A hat landed on my head and I turned to find Kyle propped against the counter grinning at me. "Much better."

I whipped it off and brought it in front of my face. "I'm not wearing this."

"Sure, you are." His head shook with silent laughter. "Team spirit, Cous."

My eyes dropped to my white t-shirt. "I am the epitome of team spirit." I pointed to the red heart emblazoned on the front. "And it comes with love."

"Just wear the damn hat, Stone," he barked, but I heard the amusement in his voice.

"You're extra bossy today. What happened?"

"Nothing." He raked a hand over his face. I learned it was Kyle's way of showing everything was not fine.

"Trouble in paradise?"

"I asked Laurie to Homecoming, and she said no."

Ah yes. The dance next weekend. Any excuse and it seemed high schools in the States threw a dance. In England, we were lucky to get a tacky leavers ball held in some dated musty-smelling hotel. Not that I'd attended any.

"Ah, so it's girl trouble." I stifled a laugh into my hand.

"Fuck you." He walked away grumbling to himself.

"Kyle, wait. I'm sorry." He liked Laurie—*really* liked her—and I was fed up of seeing them mope over each other when it was obvious they both still cared.

He paused and turned, looking at me like a lost little puppy dog. "I thought she would have forgiven me by now. But it's not working. Every time I think I'm forcing my way in, she pushes me back out." Shoulders slumped, he looked defeated, and I wanted to give him a big hug. It was so unlike my cousin to bare his soul. He usually laughed his way through his problems.

"Have you tried asking her what she wants?" I gave him a pointed look.

"What's that supposed to mean?"

"You said it yourself, you've tried forcing your way back in... has it ever occurred to you that's the reason she broke it off? You Stone-Prince boys are intense, Kyle. And newsflash, not all girls want to feel like they're dating a stalker."

"You're calling me a stalker now?" His eyes widened with disbelief.

"That's not what I meant, and you know it, but have you actually listened to anything she's been telling you? Have you ever given her space to figure out what she wants?"

Realisation flashed over his face. "Fuck."

"Yeah, fuck." I laughed softly. "Laurie wants you, Kyle. Anyone can see that. You need to give her what she wants."

His gaze darkened, and he blew out a frustrated breath. "You girls are as confusing as shit. So, what do I do? Back off? Give her space?"

I shrugged. "You'll figure it out. I have every faith in you. Now go do whatever it is you do before a game because I expect to see you kick some arse tonight."

"Damn right, I'll kick some *arse*." He smirked, and I flipped him off.

"I do not sound like that," I protested.

"You bet your *arse* you do." He slammed his fists against his chest and roared with laughter. "I'll see you later." He left but glanced back at the last second. "And Cous, wear the hat."

Smiling to myself, I finished my cereal. Macey wandered in and helped herself to juice and left without a word. The girl knew how to hold a grudge of epic proportions, and since the mess with Summer and Maverick, she'd been extra moody. But I figured if she hadn't accepted Gentry after all these years, there was no use holding my breath that she'd accept me anytime soon.

"Good morning." Dad breezed into the room, grinding to a halt when his eyes landed on me. "Lo, what are you doing here?"

"I live here, remember?" Anger sizzled in my veins. 'Kind of like you were supposed to.'

"That's not what I meant, sweetheart." His face was ashen. "I was just surprised. I thought you'd be—"

"Staying at Laurie's?"

I'd stayed over the last couple of weekends. Her parents were out of town a lot and she liked the company which worked out well for me since I'd rather be anywhere but at the Stone-Prince house.

Something changed after the incident with Summer and Nick, and, if possible, Maverick had become even more guarded around me. If our paths crossed around the house, he always nodded curtly or said a flat hello, but he never looked at me. And at school he completely ignored me.

The Lo from last summer would have felt hurt. She probably would have curled up on her bed and cried at the universe's sick game her life had become. But I wasn't that girl anymore. So, although I felt the electricity between us—the pull—if he wanted to be a twat, that was fine by me.

Two could play at that game.

I had friends now. Kids no longer looked at me like I was the British freak—even if Kyle's friends liked to crack jokes about my accent in almost every class we shared—and my grades weren't completely sucking.

Elliot would be proud.

So would Mum.

Except for that one blowout at the pep rally party, I only ever drank a couple of beers, and I hadn't touched a joint since arriving in Wicked Bay. Inhaling people's second-hand smoke didn't count. Not really.

"I've missed you." Dad changed tact but I ignored his

half-hearted apology and took my bowl to the sink. He followed, leaning back against the counter beside me. "You'll be at dinner tomorrow?"

"Do I have a choice?" I met his eyes.

"Eloise, please. You can't shut me out forever. The house is almost ready. It shouldn't be much longer and then we can move and start afresh."

"Afresh. Really Dad? Are you that fucking clueless?" The bowl slid from my hands and splashed into the soapy water. "A new house isn't going to fix us."

"Lo…" his words trailed off. He knew as much as I did, no words could fix us.

Maybe we were past the point of salvage.

"Are you bringing her tomorrow?"

His gaze dropped to the floor. "I'd like to bring her, yes." His eyes snapped back to mine. "But I won't. Not if you don't want me to, I won't."

This was a turning point. I felt it pressing against us, filling the silence. I could say no, like a petulant child, and we could pretend for one dinner that everything was okay. But everything was not okay. Dad would not end things with Stella—he loved her. She was part of his life now. And to keep him in mine, I would have to accept her eventually.

I didn't have to like her though.

"Do whatever you want, Dad. She's important to you, right? You love her, she should be there. She's your family now." I dried my hands and shoved past him and didn't look back.

She was his family.

But she wasn't mine.

~

"Holy crap, my heart is beating so hard," Laurie screamed as she clutched my hand. I was pretty sure she'd done damage. I broke free, stretching out my fingers to test their strength. Relieved to find no broken digits, I slipped my arm into hers again, and leaned in close. "Your boy did good."

"My boy?" Her face craned around to mine and I grinned. Soon she was grinning too. "He did, didn't he?"

Laurie played a good game, acting unaffected by Kyle's advances, but she still loved him, plain and simple. And part of me envied her. I'd never had that kind of connection with anyone, not since... who was I kidding? What Maverick and I had was toxic. Confusing. Like an annoying scratch I couldn't quite reach.

When the final whistle blew, the benched players rushed out to their teammates and celebrated their fourth win of the season. I still didn't entirely understand the rules, but the buzz was addictive and although I liked to give Kyle a hard time about attending games, I'd developed quite the addiction. More than that, I was proud of my cousin. He was only a junior, but he'd already proved himself to be a worthy player, scoring touchdowns in the last three games.

"He's so getting laid tonight," Laurie whispered.

"What happened to making him work for it?" I arched my eyebrows accusingly.

"Oh." She winked. "I will."

As if he heard her words, Kyle tore off his helmet and searched the crowd. When his eyes landed on our section, he covered his heart with his hand and pointed right at her.

"Oh my God," she breathed out, and I smiled to myself. He was so getting lucky tonight.

"Come on, lover girl. I need to get my party on."

And we did.

Brendon Palmer's house looked different through sober eyes. We met Autumn, Devon, and Liam, carving out a spot next to the pool. Devon and I shared a lounger, while Laurie bounced nervously on her feet, waiting for the rest of the team to arrive.

A roar of cheers told us they had, and I watched in awe as Kyle and his teammates strolled through the house and into the garden like they owned the place. And I guess, right now, in this moment, they did. High school was funny like that. People placed the athletes and jocks on a pedestal. I'd quickly learned it didn't matter if your grades were good or if you were going to get a full academic scholarship to a top college, what mattered was your place on the social ladder.

I'd never been bothered about those things back in Surrey. Our school was small, much smaller than Wicked Bay High. Everyone knew everyone, and you were either friends, or not. It was different here. Kyle was popular. People gravitated to his fun-loving nature, and he played on the varsity football team which gave him his top rung status. It was the same for Maverick. Although the basketball season hadn't started yet, his team were untouchable. And they were mostly seniors. They ruled the school. Macey was on the cheer squad, and despite her surly attitude, most girls wanted to be her. For her access to the football team... and Maverick.

They were the Stone-Princes. They had it all. Popular because of their name and popular because of their status on the teams.

Summer was different. She didn't crave the attention or the recognition. And then there was me. The latest addition to the Stone-Prince family. My name gave me some weight—I saw it in the way my classmates treated me. They were polite and interested, but never *too* interested. Kyle saw to that on my first few days of classes. In a way, he'd drawn a line. I was his.

Theirs.

Aside from Laurie, and in turn Autumn, Devon, and Liam, no one tried to become my friend or really get to know me. It hadn't occurred to me before that maybe Kyle had orchestrated that. I looked over at Laurie and smiled, but it felt forced. I didn't want to doubt her motives—we'd become good friends. But now the seed was there, I couldn't help but wonder.

"Another drink, Lo?"

I blinked up at Devon. He was standing over me. I hadn't even felt him move. I really needed to pay more attention.

"Hmm, okay, just beer." Even though my body already craved something stronger, I didn't want to lose control again. Not after last time. But I hated feeling like this—that I'd let my mind go there.

Kyle broke away from his group and came over to us, rubbing the back of his neck. "Hey, Cous." His eyes flickered from me to Laurie. "Laurie."

My mouth tipped up watching their exchange. He was out of his comfort zone. But Laurie made it easy for him, launching herself into his arms and kissing him hard. They staggered back and Autumn smirked at me. *"About time,"* she mouthed.

"Yeah," I replied through a tight smile.

"We'll, hmm, I'll be…" Laurie's voice turned into murmurs and giggles of delight as Kyle grabbed her hand and yanked her away from us.

"What'd I miss?" Devon handed me a beer.

"Kyle and Laurie made up," I said.

"Jared will be pissed. He really likes her."

"For real?"

He nodded, taking a drink. "Serious. He thinks she's the one to tame his wild ways."

"Don't ever let Kyle hear you say that."

"Don't worry, I don't have a death wish."

We sat in comfortable silence, watching the party unfold around us. Autumn and Liam cuddled up opposite us, unable to keep their hands off one another. After watching them make out for five minutes, Devon snapped, "Go get a room, I am sick of seeing your tongue, Liam."

"Chill," he laughed at his friend. "We're just messing around."

Devon huffed. "Well mess around somewhere else."

Autumn shot me an apologetic smile, but I shook my head. It didn't bother me. Couples were doing the same thing all over the place. But Liam stood up taking her with him and they disappeared down the path toward the beach. I nudged Devon with my shoulder. "What's gotten into you?"

"Nothing," he sighed, refusing to look me in the eyes.

"Devon?"

"I'm fine, Lo, I promise. I'm going to take a piss and get another drink. You want anything?"

"I'm good," I said watching as he disappeared back into the house leaving me alone.

Just brilliant.

We hadn't even been here an hour, and I'd already been abandoned by all my friends. Refusing to sit and wallow, I got up and wandered down to the beach. Groups of kids huddled near the bonfire, and some boys were playing volleyball. I kept going until it was quieter. Slipping off my sandals, I sat down and slid my feet into the sand, feeling the tiny grains rub against my skin. Wrapping my arms around my knees, I watched the sea lap gently at the shore. The sound was hypnotic. It really was like being in another world out here. So far away from my life back in England.

It was so peaceful, and I felt a calm settle inside my chest I hadn't felt in a long time.

My eyes danced along the ocean. Far off in the distance was the Bay. In the other direction was a long stretch of rocks acting as a breakwater separating the beach from the small port in town, the tips of the sails just visible. Then my eyes landed on something not so beautiful.

Maverick with Caitlin Holloway.

They stood close, closer than you would expect friends to stand, but not so close they looked 'together'. My blood warmed with jealousy, a million thoughts running through my head. He was here. At a football party.

For her?

I'd asked him once about Caitlin and he'd made it sound like there was no love lost between them. So why was she touching his arm? And why wasn't he brushing her away?

Warmth turned to scolding heat as I twisted my body to get a better look. It was wrong, I knew that. Watching their private moment like some obsessed stalker. But it reminded me of a different time—a time when I'd been the girl in a quiet corner of the beach with him. I hadn't known then who he was.

Who he was to me.

But it didn't stop the sting of dejection rippling through me.

Maverick ran a hand over his head. I couldn't see the lines of his face, the finer details, but I saw enough to know he was frustrated. Annoyed, even. Caitlin's hand slid up his arm and over his shoulder, and she inched closer until her body was almost pressed up against his.

Stop her, my mind urged. Silently screaming as I balled my fists.

But he didn't stop her.

He didn't move a muscle as she leaned up on her tiptoes and pressed her lips to his.

I scrambled up and ran. I couldn't watch him kiss her back. My heart couldn't take it. Because although I knew Maverick Prince wasn't mine, I couldn't bear the thought of him being hers.

Chapter Eighteen

"Someone grab me the plate, this steak is about done."

Beatrice answered her eldest son's request and got up from the table.

"I love your house, Rebecca. The pool is amazing. Isn't the pool amazing, Bethany?" Stella hugged her daughter close into her side and the little girl flashed my aunt a sickly-sweet smile, while I continued picking at the piece of bread on my plate trying to look anywhere but at her or Dad. Unlucky for me, I was surrounded by people I wanted to avoid. Them on one side. Maverick on the other. There was no bloody escape.

"Eloise," my grandma sang. "We still need to arrange that boat trip. Are you free next weekend?"

"I guess," I grumbled catching Summer's eye across the table. She stifled a snigger, sitting a little straighter when Beatrice reached us and placed the plate of meat down.

"You too, Summer Ellen. It's been too long since we spent any quality time together. Now dig in, everyone," she declared and, unsurprisingly, Kyle was first to jump in, helping himself to the biggest steak.

"So, how's business, son?" August cut into his meat

with precise, firm movements unlike his grandson who was tearing into the slab of meat like a boy starved.

"It's good, Dad. Having Robert join us came at the right time, it'll be good for business." Gentry glanced at my father and they shared a look. I felt like I was missing something but no one else seemed to notice, tucking into their meals. Smiling.

Even if it was all fake.

"This steak is simply divine, Gentry. Thank you for inviting us."

"You're more than welcome, Stella. You're part of the fam—"

I slammed my cutlery down a little harder than intended. The crystal glasses shook, and all heads whipped up in my direction. Shit. I reached for my glass of water and chugged down a mouthful, flashing everyone a strained smile. "Meat got stuck."

Kyle thumped his chest to disguise the rumble of laughter in his throat. When my eyes slid over him to Dad, I caught Maverick watching me. I was relieved my glasses hid my eyes because I didn't want him to see into my soul. The one crushed when I saw Caitlin kiss him.

August quizzed Kyle on yesterday's game and soon the men, minus Maverick, were in a heated discussion about the upcoming 49ers game against the Oakland Raiders. I only knew about it because Laurie hadn't stopped talking about it, and I realised maybe she really did love football. Not just the blond-haired, blue-eyed running back who I got to call cousin.

I played with my food, smiled when spoken to and forced the odd answer here and there. The whole thing was a sham. Maverick and Macey barely spoke to Gentry or my grandparents but no one acknowledged the frosty atmosphere. The adults made Stella and her daughter welcome, but failed to recognise how much it was killing me inside to sit there and watch them treat her as one of the family. And I was there in body, but in mind I was planning my escape, preferably via Uncle Gentry's liquor cabinet.

The urge to run was deep. It flowed through my veins like an addict twitching for their next hit. But where would I go? Aside from Laurie and Devon, everyone I knew in Wicked Bay was here. Seated around this table.

And I couldn't trust most of them.

My hidden gaze flickered to Maverick again. After stumbling across him and Caitlin at the party, I'd fled the Palmer's house and returned to the pool house. I don't know what I expected to happen with us—Maverick had made it clear I was a mistake—but I was sure he felt the pull between us. It was there, blazing in his eyes, every time he looked at me.

He really was a wolf in sheep's clothing.

"Lo?"

My head snapped over to my grandparents. "Excuse me?"

"I asked if you wanted more salad, dear?"

"No, no thank you," I said pushing my plate away. I couldn't eat. It wouldn't quench the thirst I felt. I needed something else. Needed the superficial high to numb the pain. I wouldn't get high—it was a promise I'd made not only to Dad, but also to myself—but it didn't make the craving any easier to bear.

Excusing myself from the table, I went into the kitchen under the guise of getting myself another drink. I needed to breathe before I suffocated out there.

"How are you holding up?" Kyle followed me, closing the door behind him.

"I either want to get shit-faced or high, so you tell me."

His eyes narrowed on me, no doubt trying to figure out if I was speaking the truth.

"Don't worry," I said. "I'm not a junkie, but I made some less than stellar choices over the summer."

"You were hurting."

"I still am." I turned my back on him, gripping the counter and closing my eyes.

"Hey, Cous." He was closer now. Right behind me, his hand hovering over my shoulder. "If you need to talk, I'm here. I know it's a mess. I know your dad fucked up, but you're not alone."

I swallowed, the tears building and turned slowly. Kyle dropped his hand and stepped back, giving me space. I smiled weakly. "Thank you, but I'm a big girl, Kyle. I'll be fine."

It wasn't like I had a choice. I couldn't run off to Chris's when shit got too much and spend my days and nights high or wasted.

Kyle sighed behind me and then he was gone. The door opened again, and I spun around ready to tell him I needed space and I couldn't do that with him breathing down my neck. But the words dried on my lips as Maverick filled my vision.

He filled everything.

The cracks in my chest…

Stole the air from the room…

Made my stomach swim with desire.

"What?" I snapped, throwing my arms around my waist. Holding myself together.

He held up two empty glasses and glanced at the refrigerator. I stepped aside letting him do his thing. My eyes fluttered shut as he passed me. So close. And yet so far away. We were strangers, but in some weird way, I felt like I knew the pieces of him no one else got to see.

And it was screwing with my mind.

Maverick disappeared behind the door, but his voice penetrated my walls. "Just say the word and we'll get out of here." He reappeared, settling his gaze on my face. His eyes dropped to my mouth, and I sucked in a sharp breath. He wanted to kiss me. Then, like a bucket of ice cold water, I remembered Caitlin kissing him.

"I called Devon. He's coming to pick me up."

The muscles in his jaw clenched, and I knew if he had an internal anger-o-meter, it had just exploded. Whatever was between those two, wasn't just some high school beef. Maverick looked ready to commit cold-blooded murder.

Shaking my head with a sigh, I turned to leave, but his voice pinned me to the spot. "You're playing a dangerous game, London. Stay away from Lions."

I walked away from him with only one thought on my mind.

Maverick Prince could go to hell.

~

I did text Devon. Not because I wanted him to bail me out, but because once the words were out of my mouth, I couldn't give Maverick the satisfaction of finding out I'd lied. But I also texted Laurie and the three of us went to The Shack for milkshakes. Autumn and Liam met us there. When the conversation turned to Homecoming, I regretted fleeing the house. Laurie and Kyle were back on, and naturally going together, so were Autumn and Liam. Which left me and Devon.

He'd stayed true to his word over the last couple of weeks, acting nothing but friendly. But Laurie was right. I didn't miss the way he watched me when he thought I wasn't looking. Like right now, I could feel the heat of his stare as I pretended to check my phone underneath the table.

"So, we'll all go together, right?" Laurie declared and my head snapped up in her direction.

"All go where?"

"To Homecoming."

"I, hmm, I hadn't planned on going." Weren't these things quite formal? All corsages and expensive limos.

Her face dropped. So did Devon's.

"You have to come. It's the first dance of the year."

"Laurie." I silently pleaded for her to drop it but she was like a dog with a bone. They all were.

"Yeah, Lo, you have to come. Besides, we hmm..." she glanced to Devon who flushed crimson.

"You already bought the tickets," my voice was flat as I rolled my eyes unable to hide the irritation flashing behind them.

The fact they thought to include me should have made me feel happy—and, in a way, it did—but I was worried it was an attempt to push me and Devon from friend zone to more. And I wasn't ready for that. Besides, hadn't Laurie warned me about not leading him on?

"If it makes you feel any better," Devon said, smiling apologetically, rubbing a brisk hand over his head. "I told them it was a bad idea."

He had?

It comforted me a little. Maybe he really did know it would never happen between us. Because I was still healing. Because I couldn't be emotionally available in the way that was fair to someone. It had absolutely nothing to do with the wicked smile I couldn't forget no matter how I tried.

"Fine. I'll go. On one condition." I met each of their gazes, landing on Laurie last. "I don't have to wear a dress."

The table exploded with laughter. And even I found a rumble of amusement spilling out of me. It felt good. Screw my so-called family with their bullshit secrets and fake smiles. As long as I had good friends, I could get through the days.

"It kind of comes with the territory," Liam said and I

groaned, faceplanting the table imagining trawling round the mall being forced into excessive dresses and skyscraper heels.

Laurie and Autumn must have heard my thoughts because their eyes danced with excitement as they both said in unison, "Shopping trip."

And just like that, it was decided.

We would all attend Homecoming. Two couples with two friends accompanying them. Maybe it wouldn't be awful—maybe it would even be fun. I'd never been to a dance before, not the way they did it here. Loud chatter pulled my head up. It was a voice I recognised.

Caitlin Holloway's gaze landed on me and her eyebrows pulled together as if she was confused to see me here. I quickly scanned the group, relief sinking into my chest when I realised Maverick wasn't with her. That would have been… I shook the thoughts out of my head. I had no claim on him, despite my irrational attachment.

She followed her friends to a booth, but didn't break eye contact. I'd seen her around at school. We shared a couple of classes. But since the party at her house—when she'd warned me to stay away from her brother—she hadn't paid me much attention. This was different.

I felt the contempt flowing from her. She didn't like me. And the feeling was mutual.

"Lo, psst." Laurie stamped on my foot under the table. "What are you doing?"

I finally dragged my eyes away and faced my friend. "What?"

"The serious death stare you're sending in Cat's direction."

"She's a bitch."

"Whoa," she gasped and our table fell silent. Shit. Had I said that out loud? "Did something happen? You never said—"

"Nothing happened." I shrugged, taking a long slurp

of milkshake. "I just don't like her."

My answer seemed to pacify the others, and they went back to making plans for Homecoming. Laurie, however, narrowed her eyes. She didn't buy my excuse, but it didn't matter. I couldn't tell her the real reason I didn't like Caitlin.

She leaned over the table slightly, lowering her voice. "Seriously, did something happen?"

I mushed my lips together and shook my head. This was not good. Not good at all.

"Lo," she warned. "She's still staring at you."

Unable to stand her inquisitive glare, I slammed my hands down a little too harshly and said, "Who wants to do something a little more adventurous?"

Everyone stared blankly at me, no doubt wondering what the hell had gotten into me. But that was for me to know.

And them to never find out.

~

The house was cloaked in darkness when Devon dropped me off. After Caitlin's appearance at The Shack, I'd persuaded them to go down to the Bay to skinny dip. But the boys chickened out, so we hung out for a while instead. I made him pull over at the bottom of the winding drive. Just in case. I said goodbye and melted into the shadows of the tree-lined path. But something stopped me, and I took shelter behind a giant trunk, craning my head around to get a better view.

Maverick was at his car, hand poised on the handle. Kyle and Macey stood together, the sight of them united threw me for a loop, until realisation punched me in the stomach. It was dark. Late. He was leaving to fight, and they were trying to stop him.

Their hushed voices carried on the gentle breeze but not enough for me to make out more than the odd word.

Part of me wanted to run up to them. With three-on-one, maybe he would listen? But the irrational betrayal I felt seeing him with Caitlin rooted me to the spot. And I didn't want to reveal I knew about his little secret. I suspected that, aside from Luke, no one knew where Maverick had taken me the day I fled from the house. And some sick glutton-for-punishment part of me, wanted it to stay that way.

It was ours.

Another brief moment in time where he had cared.

I didn't want to taint that. Even if clinging onto it made me pitiful. It reminded me that the boy I'd fallen for on the beach last summer, was still in there somewhere. That my younger, naiver self hadn't dreamed him up.

Kyle got in his face. He didn't look happy. Macey neither, but she hung back, her arms folded firmly over her chest, eyes narrowed and cold. My heart skipped a beat when Maverick shoved Kyle hard, yanked the door open and slid inside, leaving my cousin looking defeated—and worried—in a heap on the ground.

The Audi peeled out of the drive, tyres screeching and a plume of smoke billowed into the air. Kyle scrambled to his feet, hands balled into fists. He said something to Macey and her face blanched. The ice queen had a heart after all, the fear evident in her features.

Whatever Maverick was about to do, wasn't good.

Macey disappeared back inside the house but Kyle stared after the empty driveway. I could have stayed hidden. Could have waited until he went inside too. But I didn't. I slipped out of my hiding place and strolled up toward him like I was none the wiser. "Hey, what are you doing out here?"

He ran a hand down his face. It was creased with worry. "Waiting for you." Kyle slung an arm around my shoulder and guided me inside. "You have some explaining to do, Cous."

It was the last thing I expected to fall from his lips. And I glanced back over my shoulder unable to shake the feeling I was still missing some piece of the Stone-Prince puzzle.

Chapter Nineteen

"Lions wants you," Kyle said around his trademark lazy smirk. "But you need to be careful, Cous."

"What does that mean?" I glanced back to the door, wanting to ask about Maverick. But I didn't want to out myself so I swallowed down the words.

"It means things could turn ugly if you two hook up."

I balled my fists and ground to a halt. "Kyle, stop with the cryptic riddles. Is there something I should know?"

He spun on his heels and shrugged, his features illuminated by the soft glow from the kitchen. "Just be careful, okay?"

Ugh. I barged past him and went inside.

"Hey, come on. I'm just looking out for you."

"Whatever. It's not like I plan on dating him, anyway. We're just friends."

He shot me a pointed look. "Friends, right. That's why you called him to save you earlier?"

"I called Laurie too, not that it's any of your business."

"You did? Huh." Something clouded in his eyes. "Rick didn't mention—"

"He didn't know."

He cupped his jaw, rubbing gently. "That explains it then."

"Explains what?"

"Nothing."

"Screw you, Kyle. It's late, I'm tired, and we have school tomorrow." I moved to the back door, my hand curling around the handle.

"Your dad did a shitty thing today. We all did. I'm sorry."

I craned my head around to him. "It's not your fault he's an insensitive arsehole."

Kyle stifled a laugh. "No, but it is my fault you were blindsided. We all knew. I should've given you a heads up when you arrived. For what it's worth, I'm sorry."

It was my turn to shrug. "What's done is done. Night." I pushed the door open and slipped outside but not before I heard Kyle say, "He might be an asshole, Lo, but he's your dad and he loves you."

He sure had a funny way of showing it.

Inside the pool house, I kicked off my Converse and peeled the baggy t-shirt off my body. It wasn't as if I needed to worry about someone seeing me prance around half-naked since Dad hadn't slept here for days, the covers on his bed still smooth and untouched.

Kyle's cryptic warning played on my mind. I got the impression he wasn't only trying to protect me, but Maverick too. Which made no sense. Maverick was with Caitlin again. What did it matter who I was interested in? Even if they did have a bad history, Devon had been nothing but a good friend to me.

When I thought things couldn't get any more confusing my phone bleeped and I read the incoming message.

Maverick: Are you okay?

I texted back.

Lo: Fine. Back at the pool house now.

No reply came, but then, I didn't really expect one. Maverick was in full-on protective mode. Not because there was something between us, but because I was family. I hit the light switch, slipped between the sheets, and closed my eyes.

~

Maverick didn't have any fresh cuts or bruises the following morning, and things went back to the normal I'd come to accept living with the Stone-Princes. Macey and Maverick ignored me, Summer kept to herself, and Kyle drove me crazy, especially since he was around more now he was dating Laurie again.

By the time Homecoming rolled around, I wanted to drop out—or gouge my eyes out—just so I wouldn't have to survive their explicit PDA's. But the whole night was planned. The girls were getting ready at Laurie's and meeting the boys there. Laurie informed me they saved the limos and corsages for Winter Formal which was in six weeks.

The thigh length rockabilly black and teal dress cinched at my waist and scooped low on my chest. It was as near to a dance-worthy dress the girls could persuade me into. I refused to give up my Converse but did let Autumn curl and pin my hair into a loose style framing my face.

Autumn clapped her hands with a little shriek of approval when she saw Laurie's completed look. "Kyle will die when he sees you in that."

"He'd better. It cost Daddy a small fortune. And Lo, you were so right to go with that dress. It looks like perfection on you."

I smoothed down the skirt, layered with net to make it flare out from my hips. It did look good. From the fitted bodice and halter strap to the teal floral embellishment down one side matching the detail of my tattoo.

"I can't believe you're wearing sneakers though," Autumn sighed, sinking back into the seat.

"Oh, I've never been a heel girl." I flashed her a smirk, kicking out my sparkly new glitter Converse in front of me. "Give me flats any day of the week."

Laurie pulled into the school parking lot. There were already streams of kids milling about, heading toward the gymnasium. A ball of nerves drilled through my stomach. It wasn't a date. I'd reminded Devon enough over the last week and he'd agreed. But it sure felt like more—something I wasn't entirely sure I was ready for. At least, not with him.

"Come on, Kyle, just text. They're waiting at the door."

"How chivalrous of them," Autumn huffed and Laurie batted her arm. "Dude, it's the twenty-first century. Besides, we can make them suffer at Winter Formal."

Sure enough, Kyle, Devon and Liam were waiting by the entrance. My eyes swept over the three of them, lingering on Devon for a second longer. He looked good in the dark pants and shirt. He'd rolled the sleeves up to his elbows giving him a casual look but his hair was styled more than usual. Laurie was right, he totally had an indie sex god vibe. But I felt nothing. No flutter of wings against my stomach. No heart skipping a beat or doing a leap of excitement.

Nothing.

It would have been easier if I felt something—if I could reciprocate the longing in his eyes as he raked his gaze over my body. "Wow, Lo, you look…" he swallowed hard clutching at the skinny tie hanging loosely around his neck. "Wow."

"Okay, dipshit." Kyle smacked him around the back of the head. "That's my cousin you're checking out. No funny business."

"Kyle," I hissed, my eyes boring into his. "I can handle myself, thank you very much."

He mumbled something as Laurie slipped her arm through his and dragged him inside. Kyle wasn't outwardly rude to Devon—he wasn't outwardly rude to anyone—but I felt the tension between them at school. Laurie seemed immune, no doubt used to it.

"Come on, I need a drink," I lowered my voice, keeping my hands to myself as I walked beside Devon.

The gym was brimming with people, excitement dancing in the air, and it was impossible to avoid brushing my arm against Devon's as he leaned down, whispering in my ear, "You do realize the only drink you'll be getting is a soda." He laughed, but the joke was lost on me.

I scowled up at him only to be interrupted by Kyle thrusting a red cup in my hand. "Here," he said glancing between the closeness of me and Devon. His eyebrows quirked up. "It's soda."

"So I've heard," I shot back.

"Kyle, come dance with me."

It was my turn to raise my eyebrows glancing between my cousin and Laurie. "Have fun *dancing*," I called after him as she dragged him out to the dance floor. He flipped me off with a shake of his head. Autumn and Liam trailed after them and when I turned back to Devon, he was looking at me with those eyes again.

"Don't get any ideas." I gave him a pointed look, and he held up his hands.

"I need to hit the bathroom," he said. "Be right back. You'll be okay?"

"I think I can manage."

Devon disappeared into the sea of bodies and I

located an empty table and made my way toward it. The whole place looked like Hobby Craft had thrown up on it. Red and white balloons, streamers, and foil confetti adorned the tables. A huge hand-painted banner hung above the stage where the DJ was stationed welcoming the class of twenty-seventeen.

"Looking good, Stone." Warm breath glided over my bare shoulder and I jolted with a shudder, turning slowly.

"JB, always a pleasure."

His eyes swept down my body, lingering on the low-cut neckline of my dress. I snapped my fingers under his nose and arched my eyebrow in annoyance. A slow smirk broke over his face and he laughed. "You're feisty, I like that." He stepped closer.

I stepped back. "Did you need something?"

"Maybe." His eyes sparkled with mischief as he dragged a thumb over his bottom lip.

"Don't you have a crown to collect, or something?" I flicked my eyes to the stage.

"The crowning isn't until later."

My gaze darted toward the dance floor, hoping to catch Laurie's eye but she was too busy cuddled up against Kyle, enjoying every second of letting the entire school know he was hers again.

"Looking for someone?" JB stepped closer again, and I stepped back but the edge of the table hit the backs of my legs jolting me forward. My hands flew to his chest to steady myself.

We both looked down to where I was touching him. He smirked, and I sneered, snatching them away with a frustrated sigh. "What do you want, JB?" I was growing tired of his bullshit. But he remained unaffected, leaning down to my ear.

"I've always wondered what it'd be like to kiss a British chick. Do you do it differently?"

I pulled back and stared him dead in the eye, anger searing through my veins. "Never going to happen."

"We'll see. Never say never, little Stone." He patted my head as if he was petting his dog. "Enjoy the dance."

"What did he want?" Devon appeared at my side, confusion clouding his eyes.

"Nothing. Come on, let's dance."

Turned out high school dances were kind of fun. After my run in with JB, we joined the others on the crowded dance floor. Laurie and Autumn managed to tear themselves away from their boys and we danced, the six of us, for what felt like hours. Naturally, Kyle drew a crowd and before long our six was half the junior class. Halfway through the night, they crowned the Homecoming Court. JB made a big scene with the queen, a senior girl I recognised as class president. I felt sorry for her as he wrapped his thick arms around her and tried to kiss her. Caitlin, Macey, and another cheerleader were crowned princesses, and Kyle, and two other footballers were crowned princes. I caught the flash of jealousy in Laurie's eyes as my cousin received his honour, but when he snatched the mic of a speechless Principal DeLauder and declared his love for her, she melted. Like literally. Autumn and I had to hold her up as she gushed at his grand gesture.

Devon had disappeared and when he returned, the smell of vodka lingered on his breath. "You're drunk," I accused him as he stood a little too close for comfort. He shrugged, a lazy grin plastered on his face.

"Want some?"

"No, I don't want some," I lowered my voice. "You could get into trouble, Devon."

His brows knitted together. "I thought you were fun, *London.*" There was no disguising the bitterness in his voice and I narrowed my eyes right at him, choosing to ignore his dig.

"Are you done?"

"Sorry, I'm sorry." He threw up his hands almost taking out a girl behind him. I mouthed an apology to her, grabbed his arm, and dragged him away, not stopping until we were out in the hallway.

"What is your problem?" I snapped, unable to hide my irritation.

"Ease off, I'm just drunk. These things are a drag."

"So, why'd you come? No one made you, Devon."

He'd pushed it. Not me. I would have been happy staying at the pool house.

"Like you have to ask."

I dropped his arm and stepped back. He looked physically pained, his eyes dropping to the space between us. "Devon, you knew how I felt. I didn't lead you on."

"I know, I know, it's just..." He closed the distance between us, staring down at me with such longing. It was a different feeling to the way JB cornered me. It didn't scare or intimidate me—but it wasn't comforting either. Because I knew it meant something different for Devon. Something I couldn't reciprocate. But I had no time to explain. His mouth crashed to mine, and I stumbled backward into the wall. He came with me, mistaking my shock with an invitation to continue.

"Devon, stop," I gasped, pressing my hands against his chest.

"Come on, Lo, I know you feel something for me," he murmured through the kiss. I pushed harder.

"No."

His body jerked away from me, his eyes searching mine. "Fuck," he ground out, dragging a hand down his face. "I thought... I mean... Fuck."

"Goodbye, Devon," I said calmly, smoothing down my dress. I didn't look back as I made my way out of the building and into the cool, inky night. "You've got to be fucking kidding me," I muttered as my eyes landed on the couple arguing in the corner of the parking lot. Maverick looked tense as Caitlin got in his face, mouthing words I couldn't quite decipher, and didn't want to hear.

But they heard me, their heads snapping over in my direction. I kept walking. It was too much. First Devon. Now this. Throw in Dad and his new girlfriend and I was pretty sure the universe was sending me a giant fuck you.

"London, wait up." Maverick jogged up beside me and I glanced back to find Caitlin sending me daggers.

"Your girlfriend doesn't look too happy you left her hanging. You should probably go fix that."

"Shut up," he said falling into step next to me. "What happened?"

"What makes you think something happened?"

"Because I know you."

I shot him an incredulous look. He held out his keys and bleeped open the Audi. "Get in, I'll drive you home."

"I don't think that's a good idea."

"Just get in the damn car, London."

"Fine." It wasn't like I had any other options except to walk home. But it was late and a two-and-a-half-mile walk. Even in flats it didn't sound appealing.

We rode in silence. I began to think it was the way we communicated. Silent looks and unspoken messages. When Maverick turned onto the winding road up to the house, he finally spoke. "Ready to talk about it?"

I twisted to look at him. His eyes were still fixed ahead. "No. I told you everything is fine."

"You're a shit liar."

A heavy sigh escaped my lips. "What do you want from me, Maverick?" I rested my head back against the seat and closed my eyes. I was so tired of these games.

The car came to an abrupt stop outside the house, making my head hit back against the seat. My eyes flew open. Then he turned slowly, his narrowed expression giving nothing away. He wore an impenetrable mask, only letting you see underneath on his terms. My question hung in the air between us. Pulling us closer like two magnets.

I couldn't think.

Frozen in time, I couldn't see past his dark intense gaze pinning me to the spot as I stared back at him. My heart thudded in my chest, while the silence seemed to amplify the tension.

One...

Two...

His mouth crashed down on mine, and the world fell away.

Maverick was everywhere.

Hands buried in my hair, breath tickling my skin, tongue exploring my mouth. I was transported to that night—when he'd given me my first proper kiss. Only I wasn't that girl anymore. I wasn't some shy, innocent teenager now. My hands slid down his chest, tugging the hem of his t-shirt. I wanted to feel him again. Feel the contours of his stomach, run my fingers over every smooth ridge, but one of his hands slid down to mine and captured my wrist.

"We can't." Maverick's mouth hovered over my lips as he touched his forehead to mine, our chests heaving between us. "We can't." His voice was thick and unsteady as if he was saying one thing but meaning another.

Because of Caitlin... I wanted to scream. What had I done? I'd known getting into his car wasn't a good idea but I'd done it, anyway. Anything to be close to him, to pretend.

I heard the torment in his voice. Felt it in his kiss. But it didn't change anything. He wasn't mine to kiss. He wasn't my anything.

He was hers.

And I'd let him kiss me. Worse, I'd kissed him back. I eased out of his hold, unable to look him in the eye.

"London, look at me."

"I should go," I said schooling my features. Locking down the emotion in my voice.

I twisted away from Maverick and pushed open the door.

"Lo, wait, please."

Glancing back, I gave him a weak smile, said goodbye, and didn't look back.

Chapter Twenty

I shuffled along the pier, sunglasses blocking out the midday sun and curious stares.

"Oh, to be young again," my grandma chuckled, taking a right onto a floating dock where the larger boats were moored. She glanced back at us. "The two of you look like death. Nothing some sea air won't fix."

Macey grumbled something under her breath and Summer sniggered.

"Don't," the elder sister warned, but Summer was unaffected, looking as fresh as a daisy. Unlike Macey, my mood wasn't the result of a late night and too many drinks.

I'd been surprised to see her waiting outside the house this morning. She'd made it clear at the last family dinner she didn't want to spend time with Beatrice, and I was certain she and her friends went to the after party last night at Brendon Palmer's.

"Here we are." The old woman stopped at a pristine white cabin cruiser. My eyes widened behind my glasses as I took in the beauty of the vessel. In the sanctuary of the pool house it was easy to forget just how rich Dad's family were. But out here, in Wicked Bay marina, it was impossible. The whole place reeked of money.

"How wonderful." Beatrice clapped her hands together as she started up the catwalk. "You made it."

I paused, my head snapping toward my grandma's saccharine sweet voice. Stella and Bethany were already on board, standing there in all their father-stealing glory. She offered us a weak smile while her daughter scowled. It was a good job my sunglasses covered most of my face because I was sure my own sullen expression rivalled the little girl's.

"Come now, everyone on board." Beatrice looked the part in her cut-off navy chinos, pin-striped blouse, and loafers. She'd even tied a white sweater around her shoulders. It was all very nautical, and I'd stifled a laugh when she picked us up from the house. No one else batted an eye. Because it was normal. Their kind of normal.

Macey and Summer followed her across the narrow walkway, but I couldn't move, rooted to the spot by the anxiety washing in my stomach. They were all so eager to force this woman on me.

A woman I wanted to nothing to do with.

"Eloise, dear, are you coming?" Her eyes offered reassurance, but I found little comfort there.

"I'm not feel—"

"Eloise," her voice was firmer this time and with a heavy sigh I traipsed on board. Macey looked as excited as I felt, and maybe for one day, we could unite in our aversion to the Stone-Prince women bonding trip.

"You look lovely, Eloise," Stella said as I took a padded seat furthest away from the rest of them. "You too, Summer, Macey."

Macey scoffed, leaving Summer to answer for us. "Thank you, Stella," she said. "It's nice to see you again."

Traitor.

She flashed me an apologetic smile, but I lifted my feet onto the bench and leaned onto my knees, tucking my chin into my folded arms. Beatrice was busy barking orders to the man who helped us on board. My guess was he was the captain. He didn't look a day over twenty, dressed in crisp white shorts that hugged his arse a little too closely, and I smiled to myself when I caught Macey checking him out too. It seemed she wasn't completely immune to people, especially ones with a cute smile and fit body.

As the boat cut through the water and the marina shrunk in the distance, I tilted my face to the side, letting the rush of sea air lick my skin. Beatrice was right, it was refreshing, and maybe by the end of the trip, all thoughts of a certain Prince would be blown far, far away.

Who was I kidding?

After that kiss, I didn't expect to forget about him anytime soon. It had seared itself into my memory—my heart—and although I knew better, I couldn't undo it. I just had to push it to the recesses of my mind and pretend it never happened. Just like Maverick would, no doubt.

Beatrice was content talking to Stella and the captain—I heard her call him Daniel—until the boat slowed to a stop. I pushed my glasses up onto my head. The marina was barely visible, but the coastline was beautiful and I drank in the picture-perfect view.

"It's pretty, isn't it?" My grandma appeared at my side and I nodded.

"Very much so."

She sat down beside me and I slid my feet off the bench. "I know what you're probably thinking, dear. That, like your father, I blindsided you today. But sometimes people need a gentle push in the right direction, Eloise." I followed her gaze as she glanced to Stella who was helping her daughter peel an orange.

"All a parent wants, is to see their child happy. Stella is a good woman. I hope, in time, you'll find it in your heart to give her a chance." She patted my leg and left me.

"What did she want?" Macey plopped down beside me.

"Just giving me the 'get over it' speech."

"She's a real piece of work." She sneered. "Where'd you go last night, anyway?"

I frowned. When I thought me and Macey could bond over our displeasure of being here, I hadn't expected this. "Just home."

"Home, right. Funny, because I noticed Lions was missing too." Macey shot me a sideways glance that said she didn't believe a word I'd just said.

"What do you want, Macey?" I sighed.

She stood up and wiped her hands down her shorts. "Nothing. Nothing at all. My bad for thinking we might be able to have a civilized conversation."

She stomped inside the cabin while I sat there wondering what the hell had just happened. But I was too exhausted to dwell on it. Beatrice asked Summer to help her prepare lunch, and they both disappeared inside too, leaving me with Stella and Bethany. I curled up on the bench again, slid my glasses back down and looked out at the ocean. If I ignored her, maybe she'd get the message.

It lasted all of two minutes.

"Eloise, do you mind if I join you?"

I craned my head around to Stella. Bethany was nowhere in sight. She didn't wait for my answer, perching on the end of the bench. "Isn't it beautiful out here?"

"Yeah." That one word almost choked me. I didn't want to do this—be here, talking to this woman. It wasn't her. She could have been the Queen for all I cared. It was what she represented.

"Robert said it was Homecoming last night. Did you have fun?"

I shrugged, hating the way she said his name with

obvious affection. "It was okay, I guess."

"We didn't mean to hurt you, Lo. I want you to know that. Your father loves you very much. I don't want to come between the two of you. I know how hard it is raising a daughter on your own." Her gaze moved to the cabin door and I couldn't deny the sadness in her voice. It irritated me. I didn't want to feel sympathy for this woman.

I didn't.

"Bethany's dad, well, he's been out of the picture since she was just a baby. Life hasn't always been easy but you just get on with it, you know. I can't imagine what you went through and I'm not looking to replace your mom. But I love your father very much and one day, I'd like the chance to get to know you."

Stella left to go inside while I sat there, numb.

I had nothing.

No words.

No arguments.

Just an ache in my heart and the silent tears flowing down my face.

~

It was Summer who eventually came to see if I was okay. I was relieved they'd given me space. But I knew I had to pull it together. For no one else but myself. I couldn't keep letting the actions of others define me.

Nine months had passed since I woke up in hospital a 'survivor'. When my ashen-faced father burst into tears when I asked to see Mum and Elliot, I didn't want to be a survivor. I wanted the crippling pain—the physical heartache—to stop.

I wanted to end it.

To be dead.

People say time is a healer. But it's a lie. Time doesn't heal, it just masks. Sure, there are days when the pain is less, when it seems that things aren't so bad, but scratch underneath the surface and the grief is still there. Raw and real. It isn't a wound to fix. A hole to fill.

When I finally left hospital, I couldn't return to life before. I couldn't stand the constant looks of pity and words of sympathy. Life stopped the day I woke up in that sterile bed. Dad understood that; he understood I needed that little old medicine 'time'. But he was wrong. I didn't need time.

I needed a freaking miracle.

And I found it inside a vodka bottle or the bitter smoke of a joint. But even that wasn't enough and before long, I was inhaling or swallowing anything that took me away. That transported me to a euphoric plane. I didn't become addicted to any particular drug or the high. I became addicted to the escape.

The weightlessness.

Moving to Wicked Bay saved my life, I didn't doubt that. And I only had Dad to thank for making that choice for me. But now I was here, trying to live, trying to 'get over it', and people were pushing me too quickly. Just because it seemed like I was coping on the outside, didn't mean that on the inside everything was okay. That the gaping hole Mum and Elliot left was slowly being filled.

It wasn't.

I tried so hard to think 'what would Elliot do?', but I wasn't Elliot. Not even close. Growing up, he was the strong one. The fearless one. If he wanted something, he chased it down until it was his. And I was only too happy to live in his shadow. To share the light that permanently shined down on him. Because Elliot was going somewhere in life.

And now he was gone.

And I was still learning how to live without him. My brother. My best friend. The person who had always been there to pick me up when I fell, to give me a voice when

I couldn't speak. In a way, my older, wiser, over-achieving brother, Elliot had always been my crutch, and I was learning to walk unaided now he was no longer here.

I shifted on my knees, leaned over the side of the boat and inhaled a deep breath, letting the salty air fill my lungs.

"Hey, are you okay?" Panic laced Summer's voice and I couldn't blame her. She probably thought I was ready to throw myself overboard. But I just needed to feel.

Something.

Anything.

Feel the rush of salt air lick my skin, the sticky sea breeze in my hair, the sharp sting in my lungs just to know I was alive. And that no matter how hard, empty and painful the days were, I would get through this.

"Lo?"

The blood had drained from my knuckles where I gripped the rail, but as I turned to Summer, I smiled. It wasn't strained or forced or fake.

It was real.

"I'm good," I said. "Come on, let's go eat. I'm sure everyone is fed up of waiting." I climbed down and motioned for her to lead the way. Because I could do this. My way, on my terms.

For Mum.

For Elliot.

For myself.

~

"Thank you for a wonderful day, Beatrice," Stella said. And she meant it. She wasn't being fake or conceited. My grandma was right—as much as it pained me to say it— Stella was a good woman. I'd spent the rest of the afternoon watching her interact with her daughter and Summer. She radiated warmth and compassion, and whilst I was in no rush to let her into my life anytime soon, part of me—the part that didn't want to vomit every time I saw them together—was happy Dad had found someone like her.

"It was really lovely spending the day with you all." Her eyes lingered on me and I mustered a weak smile.

Beatrice and Stella hugged and did that rich-people air-kiss thing while the rest of us stood around waiting. Then my grandma leaned down and whispered something in Bethany's ear. She giggled, nodding eagerly, and took her mummy's hand, and they disappeared down the dock.

"What'd I miss?" Kyle's voice boomed across the pier and I was surprised to see him, arms folded across his chest, leaning against his Jeep.

"What are you doing here?" I said as we reached him.

"Your chariot awaits."

"You're such a weirdo, Kyle." Summer kissed Beatrice and hopped into the back. Macey managed some half-hearted thanks before rounding the Jeep and getting in beside Summer.

"Grandma B, always a pleasure." Kyle pulled her in for a hug, peppering her wrinkled face with kisses.

"Kyle Weston Stone, put me down, this instant," she insisted and he released her, his eyes dancing with laughter.

"Eloise, please don't be a stranger. You are always welcome at the house. In fact, I'll arrange a dinner. It's about time I got to cook for my whole family."

I let her hug me. "Thank you, for trying." Her parting words sank into my bones. Had she known all along how hard it was for me today?

She waved us off, and Kyle launched into twenty questions about our day. Macey never mentioned her attempt at a normal conversation with me, and I didn't tell him about my conversation with Stella.

Some things were better left unsaid.

Chapter Twenty-One

"Lo?" Dad's voice filtered into my room and I stopped writing. "Loretta said you're here."

I closed the notebook and went out into the main room. "Hey."

He smiled as if that small gesture would fix everything. "Hey, Dad, what's up?"

"I have great news, sweetheart. The agent called, and the house is finally ready. We should get the keys by the end of next week. I brought some boxes to start packing." He flicked his head over to the pile of cardboard propped up against the wall.

"Are you planning on doing a Ross?" I joked but his eyebrows knitted together and I knew my *Friends* reference was lost on him. "I don't think we need boxes, Dad. It's not like we have much more than we arrived with."

"Well, just in case." He looked sheepish, and I hated it. Hated it made me feel guilty—like I was the reason for the distance between us. "Stella said yesterday was fun."

"Fun, yeah."

"Lo, please. I know you're still coming to terms with this, but she's important to me."

"So you keep saying."

Dad ran a brisk hand over his head and I could sense his frustration. But I couldn't just get past it, I couldn't.

"I want the truth," I stated flatly.

"The truth?" Confusion clouded his eyes.

I nodded. "You still haven't told me when this started, *how* it started. In fact, you haven't told me anything, Dad. You just dropped her on me and expected me to smile and welcome her with open arms. I'll remind you that you're the adult here, not me. I shouldn't have to tell you, you screwed up. People keep telling me how much you love me, how you only want the best for me, but all I can see is how this worked out excellently for you. So, tell me the truth. How long?"

"Eloise," his voice cracked, and I knew there was more to it—so much more. Things I didn't really want to know. But I'd asked. I'd given him permission to lay it all on me, so I had to suck it up.

He walked to the sofa and sat down, but I remained standing. "Stella and I were high school sweethearts."

"You're fucking kidding me?" The words flew out causing Dad's eyes to widen to saucers, but he didn't scold me. How could he when he'd just confirmed my worst fears?

"We dated for almost six years."

"She was your first love?"

"Stella was my first everything."

"I need a drink." I scrambled to the sink and grabbed a glass just as Dad said, "Lo, really?"

"Water, Dad, I need water." I filled the glass and held it up for him to see. "What happened?"

"Your mother happened."

It was my turn to stare in disbelief. "Mum?"

"The summer after junior year at college, I volunteered at a summer camp in Monteverde…"

I knew this story. Two young kids who wanted to change the world, spent the summer helping disadvantaged kids in Monteverde. Mum loved to tell me and Elliot the story. How they fell in love in the suffocating heat and mosquito infested forests. Supposedly Dad rescued her from being eaten alive, lending her his net. But never once did she mention the fact that Dad was already in love with someone else.

"What happened?"

He smiled fondly as if he was remembering. "The summer ended, and I had to return to UCLA for my senior year and your mother had to return to England. Watching her leave, saying goodbye, it was one of the hardest things I've ever had to do. When I got back to college, to Stella, I was different."

"You went back to her?" I gasped feeling my chest tighten.

"It was complicated. Love is always complicated. I loved Stella with all my heart. She was my first love, my first everything, but what I felt with your mother… it was magical. But her life was in England and my life was here, in California.

"I let her go. I came clean to Stella and told her there had been someone over the summer but that it was a mistake. Stella was my future. And for the next year, she was. I often thought about your mother, about what she was doing, where she was. And then one day, I was running errands for your grandma in town and I saw her. Standing there, like a mirage. I knew then, it was fate. I've never been a religious man, Lo, but seeing your mother standing there, it was a sign."

"She came for you."

He nodded, unshed tears glistening in his eyes. "I was engaged to marry Stella but in that moment, when I pictured my wife—the future mother to my children—I saw your mother's face. I broke things off with Stella and made plans to move to England. It wasn't an easy decision. Your grandparents reacted badly. They already considered Stella part of the family—by hurting her I also hurt them, deeply. It took a long time for me to repair that."

So much made sense now. Why they never visited. Rarely called. It wasn't until we were older that Dad talked about his family more. When he'd suggested visiting them last summer, Mum hadn't been keen. I'd overheard an argument but put it down to Mum's reluctance to leave Elliot, even though he was off doing his own thing most of the time.

"She didn't want to come, last summer," I said. "Mum didn't want to come, did she?"

"No. Your grandparents blamed her. I left for her, Lo. I was young. I gave up so much. But I'd do it again in a heartbeat. Marrying your mother was the best decision of my life. It gave me two wonderful children." He swallowed as if the words we painful. "And I loved my life in Surrey very much."

"What changed?"

"Excuse me?" Dad's voice wasn't defensive, just confused.

"You said you *loved* your life, what changed?"

"The accident, how you dealt with things, you know—"

"Don't lie to me, Dad. There's something you're not telling me. I can see it in your eyes."

He released a heavy sigh, and I braced myself. "When Elliot left for Oxford University and you started making plans for your future, I realised how much time had gone by. You would soon be off having families of your own and I'd barely spoken to mine in twenty years. It was time to make amends. That's why I wanted to make the trip."

There was more. Even now, he wasn't telling me everything. I don't know how I knew, but I did. The real reason—the truth behind all of this.

"You wanted to move back here, didn't you?"

Sadness washed over his face and I had my answer. "Yes. There was an opportunity at Stone and Associates and Gentry wanted me to come on board. It was time."

"And Stella?"

"I promise, Stella wasn't in the picture then. I wanted to make the move with your mother, and you and Elliot, if you wanted to come."

"And if we didn't?

His face blanched until he was as white as a sheet.

"You were coming anyway," I whispered, the words punctuating the air.

"Lo."

I held up my hand to silence him, trying to digest everything. "You were going to leave us?"

"Eloise, please. It isn't like that."

"Did she know?" The words spewed out of me. "Did Mum know?"

"She knew I wanted to move back, yes, but she didn't know—"

"Oh my God, she didn't know. She didn't know you were leaving. She died, and she didn't know. You bastard, get out. GET OUT!" My voice was no longer my own as I heaved ragged breaths, my hold on reality slipping.

"Lo, please, let's talk abou—"

"GET OUT!" I yelled over and over, tears flowing down my face as I pressed my palms into my thighs.

Dad left, but not before silently pleading with me to let him explain. I sank to the floor, rocking forward and backward. Mum didn't know. She didn't know Dad wanted to leave—with or without us. That he woke up one day and decided his life in Surrey was no longer enough. Maybe it should have brought me comfort that she didn't know, that her last breaths in this life were full of love. But it was a lie.

It was all a lie.

Dad hadn't brought me here out of desperation, to save me from a path of self-destruction. He'd brought me out of guilt because I had no one else in Surrey. I had no other grandparents or aunts or uncles to take me in if I didn't want to move halfway across the world. And although when we first arrived at the Stone-Prince house, I couldn't wait to leave, now it felt like he was taking me away from the only other people I had. I'd forged a strange bond with Kyle, and with time, I knew me and Summer could become good friends, but once we moved out how would that work? Would I be out of sight, out of mind? Would they all be as happy to see us go as I once originally felt about the day we'd leave here?

The urge to drown out the storm raging inside of me with whatever I could find in Gentry's liquor cabinet was strong. So strong I almost leapt up and ran into the house. But that would get me nowhere besides an unwanted hangover tomorrow. I wanted to scream. To throw my arms wide and yell until my lungs hurt and every last ounce of breath left my body.

My life was built on a lie.

Everything I believed about my parents fairy tale now tainted by the truth.

"Hey."

I met Summer's concerned gaze. I hadn't heard her slip inside the pool house. She came and sat on the floor beside me. "That bad, huh?"

"You could say that." I swiped my tears with my arm, sniffling back another sob.

"Want to talk about it?"

"Not really."

"Okay." She smiled. "We can just sit."

Seconds turned into minutes, but she didn't push. And I was grateful. I needed time to process. The stream of tears slowed and dried on my cheeks making the skin feel sticky.

"How are you?" I asked, rolling my head to her.

"You're the one sitting in a pool of your own tears and you want to know how I am?" Summer chuckled softly. "I'm okay. Thanks to you."

"And Nick?"

"He's good. We're taking it slow. Thank you," she paused, chewing her bottom lip in between her teeth. "For not telling them."

"It was your secret to tell."

"Macey hates you for it."

"She hated me anyway."

The youngest Stone-Prince shook her head, blonde wisps of hair blowing across her face. "She doesn't hate you. She just doesn't let people get close. Especially ones that look like you."

My eyebrows quirked up, and she smiled again. "Oh, come on, Lo, you're gorgeous. Which makes you competition." Summer winked.

"Competition, are you serious?"

"Who knows with my sister, but I can see why she'd feel threatened by you. You're so normal and nice and pretty. You don't care what anyone thinks of you and you're not out to win a popularity contest."

"Neither are you," I said, a little taken aback. It was the most I'd ever heard Summer speak.

"No, but I'm Summer Stone-Prince. People will expect me to follow in their footsteps."

"Popularity is overrated."

"So is sitting on a tile floor in a pool of your own tears." I heard the amusement in her voice and nudged her in the side with my elbow. "Come on," she said. "Your dad left and Loretta baked a bunch of stuff."

"Cookies?"

"I think so."

I followed Summer up and used a towel to dry my face. "Lead the way, oh young one."

We made our way to the main house. Kyle's head snapped up. "Thank God, I was about to send a rescue party."

I flipped him off and slid onto a stool, helping myself to a cookie. "No Laurie tonight?"

"Homework calls. So, what did your dad want?"

"The house is ready."

"No, you can't leave us." His face paled, and it reassured me a little that things wouldn't change between us just because I no longer lived here. "Things just got interest—"

The sound of raised voices silenced Kyle, and the three of us looked at the door leading to the hallway.

"Fuck that, Mom, I don't need…" Maverick's voice trailed off as Rebecca tried to reason with her son in hushed tones.

"Maybe we should…" I started, but they were already in the doorway, Rebecca's face ashen as a man I didn't recognise pushed past them and entered the kitchen taking the air with him.

"Kyle, good to see you again," the man said in a measured tone. Kyle stiffened and mumbled a reply. "And you must be Robert's daughter, Louise, was it?" He rounded the island and held out his hand. In a charcoal suit, pristine white shirt, and shiny silver cufflinks, he oozed money. But his eyes were the giveaway.

I glanced over his imposing figure to Maverick. His eyes were hard. Cold. And a shiver worked its way through my body.

"Hello." I took Alec Prince's hand. "I'm Eloise Stone."

He tilted his head slightly and narrowed his eyes. "The pleasure is mine, Eloise. I trust Maverick and Macey have made you welcome?"

"They have."

Kyle choked on something and we all looked over at him. He slammed a hand to his chest and waved us off murmuring something about a, "Chocolate chip got stuck."

"Well, excuse me. Maverick and I have some business to take care of. Kyle, Summer, it was nice to see you both again."

He turned on his heels and marched out of the room, his gaze boring into his son's as he went. Maverick scrubbed a hand down his face, gave Rebecca a pointed look and went after his father.

"I'm sorry about that." Rebecca came over to us, the colour slowly returning. "He wasn't supposed to come here."

He wasn't?

"Your father." She looked to Kyle. "He's not…"

"Don't fret it, Momma P, Dad is still at the office."

The tension on Rebecca's face seemed to lift. It didn't totally evaporate, but she seemed lighter knowing my uncle wasn't yet home.

Something crashed, like the sound of glass against a wall, and Rebecca dashed out of the room muttering under her breath. Kyle tore his eyes from the doorway and looked at me. "I'd better go help. You two, stay here, got it?"

"Kyle, don't you think—"

"Stay here, Lo." He warned.

Then he was gone.

A door slammed somewhere in the house, reverberating off the walls, and then the screech of tyres could be heard outside.

"Here we go again," Summer sighed under her breath and I wanted to ask her what she meant, but Kyle appeared in the doorway and his face said it all.

l. a. cotton

Something was wrong.
Very wrong.

Chapter Twenty-Two

"Oh my God." Bile rushed up my throat, burning my insides, as I raked my sleepy gaze over Maverick. "What did you do?"

His head turned slowly, and he smirked despite the split in his lip, which was still dripping blood. "You should see the other guy."

"Maverick," his name fell from my lips like a curse. He hadn't talked to me since the kiss—the one we'd both pretended never happened. There had been nothing except for the odd heated stare or elusive text message. I thought we were done, yet here he was standing bloody and beaten in the pool house. His eyes darted to the boxes Dad left, and he swallowed hard. "When do you leave?"

I shrugged, unable to tear my eyes from the devastation that literally was his face. "Dad thinks it'll be the end of next week."

The muscle in his jaw ticked again.

"You should let me look at that." I motioned to his face, expecting him to refuse my offer. Instead, Maverick perched on one of the stools and dropped his head in a nod. Maybe he was just too exhausted to argue.

I didn't dwell on it as I hurried to the bathroom and

retrieved the small first aid kit I knew was in the cabinet. When I returned, I ground to a halt. Seeing his face, his shredded knuckles, hurt me far more than it should have. But I'd come to accept that where Maverick was concerned, I didn't have a choice.

I never had.

Not since that very first night. I couldn't just switch off my irrational feelings for him. Something happened that night, something that imprinted him on my soul.

My heart.

Or maybe I was just a foolish girl that thought— hoped—she could tame the bad boy. After all, wasn't it most young girl's fantasy to be to the one who could?

Maverick sensed me watching him and his hooded gaze slid down my body, as I stood there in nothing but Elliot's oversized Oxford University t-shirt, clutching the small bag as if it was a life raft.

And Maverick was the storm threatening to wreck me.

"Got any pain meds in there?"

Nodding, I retrieved some tablets and handed him a glass of water. Our fingers brushed as he took it from me, sparks of electricity dancing across my skin. Maverick's eyes widened with surprise, focused on where our hands joined, then slowly he lifted his face to mine.

God, I couldn't breathe.

When he looked at me like that I wanted to melt into a puddle on the floor.

I *did* melt.

I wanted him to touch me, taste me, anything to make the deep ache between my legs stop. The longing.

"Thank you," he whispered.

I blinked and, with a tiny shake of my head, sifted through the kit to find some wipes. "This will probably sting."

"I've felt worse."

Rounding the breakfast bar, I placed a hand on his

shoulder to steady myself. His face was a patchwork of grazes and cuts, but I started with the worse wounds, the ones trickling blood down his bronzed skin like a stream of fat crimson tears.

"Fuck," he hissed a breath as the wipe smoothed over his cheekbone.

"Sorry." I moved slower, barely touching the angry raised cut. "Why, Maverick? Why do you do this to yourself?"

"Don't," he said. There was no warning in his tone. No bitterness. He almost sounded defeated.

Broken.

And it only made my need to fix him—to help him—stronger.

But then I remembered Caitlin. Her lips on his. Her hands curled around him like she owned him.

My mouth soured as I croaked, "This one probably needs stitches." The skin across his left eyebrow was wide open, and I wasn't sure a plaster would do the job.

"No doctors, I'll live."

"Maverick..."

His hand smoothed over my hip and curved around my waist, anchoring me to him. Sliding me between his knees. It was too close and yet, not close enough. My eyes fluttered shut, assaulted with memories of that night. His lips on mine, his hands running over my untouched body.

My hand pressed his shoulder. "Stop."

Maverick pulled back slightly forcing me to look at him.

"What are you doing, Maverick?"

His darkened gaze made the butterflies intensify and my head swim with lust. "Don't you ever just want to forget?"

All the time.

But the thing about forgetting was that it was only temporary, and when reality came back, it came back like a bucket of ice cold water.

"Lo," my name fell from his lips. That single word touched something deep inside of me, and I knew that every look, every interaction we'd shared since I arrived in Wicked Bay wasn't some figment of my imagination—it was real. Maverick wanted me.

Craved me as much as I craved him.

But up until now, he'd refused to give into his needs. Something held him back. I suspected it was the same thing that drove him to step into that ring and draw blood. After today, meeting his father, part of me wondered if he was the reason. He certainly seemed to trigger Maverick's temper.

I forced myself to swallow the breath caught in my throat and continued cleaning his imperfectly perfect face. After the last plaster was applied, my fingers lingered over his eyebrow. I went to move away but Maverick captured my wrist. "Look at me, London." His voice slid over me like melted chocolate.

"I should—" My gaze landed on his and the words died on my tongue. He was looking at me with such intensity.

"You should what?"

"Go, I should go." *Far, far away from here. From you.*

I tried to move, to break free from his hold over me—both physical and emotional—but Maverick tugged me closer, opening his legs wider until I was nestled between them.

"Maverick, stop."

He arched an eyebrow, challenging me—daring me—only I didn't understand why. He was with Caitlin, wasn't he? He'd made it clear he wouldn't touch me. Yet he leaned in closer, his mouth ghosting over my shoulder. "You're saying one thing, but your body is saying another." His fingers slid to the hem of my t-shirt and he twisted his hand into the material dragging me closer and I sucked in a sharp breath when his knuckles brushed my thighs. Over the part of myself I never let anyone see. His lips curved against my skin igniting a full body shiver up my spine and my eyes fluttered shut.

"What about Caitlin?" The quiver in my voice showed how weak he made me. And part of me hated it.

Maverick went rigid, the air around us thick with tension. "She's no one to me."

I hadn't seen them together, not since that night at the dance. But Caitlin watched him at school, longing in her eyes. She wanted him. Had already laid claim to him. And they had been together once upon a time.

"And I am?"

There, I'd said it.

"You know you are." His lips lingered, almost kissing my neck.

"But?"

"But we can't be together." It was so final. My heart didn't just sink, it withered and died leaving me empty and hollow.

I nodded stiffly and yanked free of his hold, but Maverick was stronger and his arms looped around my waist drawing me back in. And then he was kissing me. Consuming me.

Breathing life back into me.

My hands slid around his shoulders and I clung onto him like he was air, letting his tongue explore my mouth.

Like I could have refused.

Maverick was a force to be reckoned with. I'd seen it in the hallways at school—the way people gravitated to him at the same time as falling in line. If Maverick said jump, everyone asked how high. Except he didn't have to say anything, he only had to nod his head or send

215

someone a single look.

He held the power, even if he didn't want it.

"I've wanted you since that first day in the kitchen," his words vibrated against my lips, echoing in my chest.

"Oh God," I breathed between kisses as his hand skimmed down to my bare legs and trailed around to the juncture of my thighs, dancing over the thin cotton material.

Oh. My. God.

What the hell was I doing? Maverick had been nothing but cold and distant with me. Sure, he gave me rare glimpses of the boy who stole more than just my first kiss that night, but the illusion was always ruined. Usually by something that came out of his mouth.

"Stop thinking, London." Greedy lips traced a path to my neck. Biting. Sucking. Teasing. While his thumb rubbed lazy circles over my centre. "One night. Give me one night."

There was that old bitch Reality dousing me with her ice-cold water.

One night.

This wasn't the beginning of something between us, it was the end.

It was goodbye.

Once I moved out of the Stone-Prince house, it was possible I would only see Maverick at school. There would be no passing in the kitchen at night. No late-night visits in the pool house. No more of *this*.

My chest constricted, and I clung tighter. Maverick responded to my desperation and in one swift movement, he slid off the stool and picked me up, our bodies flush against one another. Eyes locked on mine, he refused to let me catch my breath as he walked us into the bedroom.

This was happening.

And I wasn't going to do a thing to stop it.

I'd imagined this over and over since laying eyes on

him in the kitchen. Was Maverick a bastard? Yes. But it didn't outweigh how he'd brought me to life that night. I was just a shy quiet girl, and he made me soar. I wanted to feel that again.

I craved it.

He lowered me to the floor and my legs hit the edge of the bed. I dropped down, staring up at him, following his lead. Maverick peeled the black vest from his body, revealing taut muscles. Even through the bruises and tender spots he was gorgeous. Broad shoulders tapered into a lean defined waist, and although he wasn't big and burly like the football team, he oozed strength and power.

He fingered the button on his jeans, popping it open. His hooded gaze never leaving mine. "I walked away that night," he said. "I'm not walking away tonight. Got it?"

I swallowed.

"This changes nothing, Lo. But I can't go another second without feeling you. I need to feel you." His eyes dropped to my legs. He was the predator now, and I was the prey. But there would be no chase, no bloody fight. I was here. And I was in.

All in.

Maybe it was a huge mistake. Maybe tomorrow when the sun filtered in through the blinds, shining light on my truths, I'd realise what a stupid, stupid girl I was. But I couldn't find it in myself to care. Since the accident, I'd lived in darkness. Moved with the shadows. I was used to it. And part of me would always feel comfortable there. But at the back of my mind, I knew that unlike alcohol or drugs, Maverick was an addiction I would never fully recover from. The quiet, shy girl I used to be wanted to feel like a woman again, and the reckless, snarky girl I'd become wanted to forget.

Maverick could help me with both of those things.

I reached out, gliding my fingers up his smooth stomach, rejoicing when he hissed. My touch affected him. After all this time, I still affected him. But vulnerability wasn't a trait Maverick wore well, and he caught my wrist, shaking his head. "Come here."

He tugged me up, running his hands down my t-shirt until he found the hem and yanked it from my body. His hand cupped my breast while his mouth attacked mine, and I moaned. There wasn't another word for the way he devoured me. Hard. Demanding. I melted against him, breathless and unsteady.

Maverick's jeans pooled to his feet, I felt the denim rub against my legs. "Your dad will be gone all night?"

"He's never here," I croaked, overcome by the sensations coursing through me.

"Good," he growled, lifting me like I weighed nothing more than a feather, forcing my legs around his waist. Maverick moved us to the bed, lying me down gently. He was such a contradiction. Hot and cold. Hard and soft. Rough and smooth.

I wanted all of him. Every single damaged piece.

He covered my body, his weight pressing me into the mattress, stealing the air from my lungs in the best kind of way. "Did you let him touch you?" Dark eyes pinned me to the spot as he ground into me, showing me how much he wanted this.

Wanted me.

I mashed my lips together and shook my head.

"I will ruin you for any other guy, you know that, right? I'm a selfish bastard, London. I can't keep you for myself, but I don't want anyone else to have you either."

Oh, God.

I should have stopped him then, pushed him away, and told him to leave but I didn't. My body arched into him, desperate for relief. Maverick eased off me, slipping a hand down to my cotton pants, and dipped inside. A moan fell from my lips. One finger curled into me then another until my moans became pants.

"I want you, London. I want to bury myself in you." Maverick's warm breath licked the shell of my ear as he leaned back over me, and a shiver worked its way up my spine.

It was too much. His touch. His words. The unspoken promise of things to come.

"Oh my God," my voice quivered with desire as ripples of pleasure rushed through me forcing my eyes shut.

As I floated down from the clouds, Maverick rocked back on his knees and inched my pants down and off and then stood shucking out of his boxer briefs.

And then we were skin on skin. Scars on scars. Lust on lust.

Although we hadn't seen each other for over a year, that day, when he walked into the kitchen, it was as if everything had built up to this.

Us.

No snide comments or battle of the wills. Just a damaged boy, and a broken girl. We didn't need words or heartfelt declarations.

This was enough.

For tonight, this was everything.

Maverick tore open the foil wrapper and rolled it over himself, nestling back in between my legs, teasing me slowly.

"Maverick, please," I whimpered and a wicked grin cracked his usually serious face. He ground into me again but pulled back at the last second.

"I want to savor this," he rasped, his control slipping. "But I'm not sure I can." He leaned down, capturing my lips as he finally pushed inside, groaning into my mouth with every inch.

We both stilled, our eyes locked on one another. And then the walls came down. Maverick wasn't gentle or loving or tender, he was rough and hard and relentless. Just how I imagined how he was in the ring. He dominated me, hooking a hand under my thigh, dragging my body closer as he thrust into me over and over.

And I loved every second.

I didn't want to be treated like glass, like a girl walking a fine line between coping and falling apart. I wanted to feel, to live.

To remember that I survived.

"Fuck, Lo, you feel so good." He rasped and through the lust haze surrounding us, I smiled. Because I made him feel that way. For this moment in time, I made him forget whatever demons haunted him.

He didn't want to beat the shit out of something or get his pretty face bust wide open, he wanted this.

He wanted *me*.

As he pushed us higher and higher, and a slow tingle built in my stomach, I began to freefall. I knew then, I'd made a terrible mistake because there would be no coming back from this.

From him.

All I could do now, was hope I survived the landing.

Chapter Twenty-Three

"We should sleep." Maverick nudged my shoulder, tracing a path from my neck to the shell of my ear with his tongue. I shuddered, a soft moan slipping from my mouth.

"If you keep that up, I think we both know sleep isn't going to happen."

"You're right." He pulled me closer, his body curved around mine, spooning me from behind. "Tell me about him."

I tensed, caught off guard by his question. "Who?"

"Your brother."

"I—" The room spun and suddenly I felt like I couldn't breathe. But he was there, anchoring me, refusing to let me fall.

"It's just you and me, London," he murmured against my skin. "No one else. You think I didn't see what happened that night at the fight? You saw Lyndon and looked like you'd seen a ghost."

"For a split second, I thought it was Elliot. I panicked." My voice quivered with the memory.

"You ran."

"It's still raw, Maverick."

He hugged me closer, tucking his chin into the crook

221

of my neck, his warm breath dancing over my skin like a soothing balm to my grief. "Gentry said he was an artist. Did he design your tattoo?" His fingers traced the intricate vine curling around my arm.

"It was a present. He painted this exact design on a canvas for my sixteenth birthday. I've always loved roses. When he di..." The words lodged in my throat and I blinked back the tears forming. "After the accident, I was in a bad place. My ex was a tattoo artist. He kept bugging me to let him ink me, and I had this ugly scar, he said he could cover it up. It seemed fitting, you know. Now I carry a piece of Elliot with me, always."

Maverick was quiet, but I felt the tension in his body. I wanted to ask what was going on in that head of his. But I wasn't sure I was ready to hear the answer, so I kept silent.

"Gentry said you almost didn't make it." There was something in his voice, something unexpected, but I didn't allow myself to think about what it could mean. Because tonight was just that... tonight.

One night.

I had to remember that. Forgetting would be dangerous. Not only to my head, but my heart. Maverick had made me no promises after tonight, and I'd gone along willingly.

"I didn't. I was in intensive care for four weeks and then it was a long road to recovery."

"The scars?" His fingers swept lower down my waist and to the tops of my thighs.

I nodded, unable to hold back the silent tears rolling down my face.

"You're different from the girl I met on the beach last summer." Maverick pressed a kiss to my shoulder.

"You're different too," I replied, unable to hide the sadness in my voice.

We lay there in silence. The events of the night—of

the last fifteen months—weighing heavily on us both. I had my demons, Maverick had his. But lost in one another, everything had been forgotten. Pushed aside. Now, in the quiet of the dark, it was all back.

More real than ever.

Maverick's breathing evened out, and I knew he'd fallen asleep so I closed my eyes and let sleep take me.

~

When I woke up, Maverick was gone. If it wasn't for the ruffled bed sheets and the delicious ache in my body, I would have questioned if it was all a dream.

But it wasn't.

Maverick had been here. In the pool house. In my bed.

We hadn't said goodbye with words, and that was okay. He'd worshipped my body, telling me everything he felt, and weirdly an odd sense of peace settled over me.

When we'd met that night, all those months ago, I'd known we were different. I was the reserved British girl out of her league at a wild beach party with her free-spirited cousin. I'd slipped away along the Bay and stumbled across a boy leaning against a wooden railing. Hair as dark as the night tumbled over his eyes a little, as he hunched over, clutching a bottle of beer like it was his oxygen. I saw his sore bruised knuckles, the shadow around his eye. Felt his torment as I drew nearer. It rolled off him like the waves lapping at the shore. He was angry. Volatile. I should have turned and walked away but his pain called to me and before I could stop myself, I leaned against the railing beside him.

"It's beautiful out here," I said, my voice small.

He grunted, barely acknowledging my presence, so we stood in silence. Minutes ticked by before he spoke. His voice was ragged—raw—and I wondered if he'd been crying. But he didn't seem like the kind of boy to shed tears, he seemed like the kind of boy who would tear a room to shreds in a fit of blind rage rather than dealing with his true feelings.

"Why aren't you at the party?" he ground out, and I shrugged, aware that he had been staring at me.

"I wanted to catch my breath," I said, tipping my chin in defiance. I knew what he saw. First appearances spoke volumes, and I screamed goody-two-shoes in my modest knee-length sundress and sensible kitten heeled sandals. But when his eyes slid over me, I shivered. There was something else there, in the dark pools staring at me. Something I wasn't familiar with.

"You're not from around here?"

"Just visiting." My eyes flickered away from his but he noticed.

"Are you scared?" He teased, and I met his gaze again, his eyebrows quirking up and the faintest of smirks tipping the corner of his mouth.

"Should I be?" I gulped, confused about what was happening. Why my mouth was dry and my skin tingled with nerves. Why part of me wanted to stare at his face all night but the other part wanted to never look at him again because she knew she could lose herself forever in his roguish good looks.

"Maybe," he answered, the single word punctuating the air. Silence settled over us and we watched the tide roll in side by side. "Do you ever want to escape?" he asked me a few minutes later.

It seemed like an odd question to ask a stranger, but I went along with it. "Escape?" I said. "From what?"

"Life. School…" he paused, drawing in a long breath as if the next word was almost too painful to say. "Family."

"Not really, no. I like my life," I replied. "Where would you go?"

"Huh?" He turned to me and I smiled meekly. He was

so handsome, but there was an intensity about him that made me feel out of my depth. Nothing at all like Elliot's friends back home who always made me welcome, treating me like their annoying younger sister as much as my brother did.

"You said you wanted to escape, where would you go?"

He shrugged, taking a long pull on his beer. "I don't know. Anywhere but here. The city, maybe."

We stood there for what felt like all night. My body started to feel the effects of the cool sea breeze dancing around us. "I should go," I said.

"Wait." He placed down his bottle and stepped away from the railing. We stood, eyes locked on the other. My heart beat furiously against my chest. "Why did you come over here?"

"You looked like you could use a friend." My gaze slid to his knuckles. If he was embarrassed, he didn't show it as he flexed his fingers out and curled them back into a fist. "Does it hurt?"

"Not as much as it should. What's your name?"

"Does it matter?" The words flew out of my mouth before I could stop them.

He shrugged, but I caught a hint of surprise in his eyes. Then he reached for me, brushing my hair off my shoulder, curling his hand around my neck and holding me in place staring right into my eyes. Something passed between us. Something no words could describe.

"Do you feel it?" he asked and I nodded without hesitation, my head swimming with new and exciting sensations. A boy like *him* was looking at a girl like *me* in that way I'd only dreamed of. Elliot warned me about boys all the time. *'Wait until you're older'*, he'd say. *'There's plenty of time to give your heart away'*. But Elliot wasn't here, and I was in another country. Didn't that mean taking risks and throwing caution to the wind? Letting all my inhibitions go out of the window?

My eyes fluttered shut as I leaned into him, waiting. The boy I'd known for less than an hour brushed his lips over mine, so gentle and uncertain. It was nothing like I expected from him, but it left an impression, nonetheless.

My first real kiss.

He smiled against my mouth, letting out a smooth chuckle as he tucked me into his side and guided me to a rock where we spent the next hour talking, and kissing some more. He didn't ask my name, and I wasn't brave enough to ask his, unwilling to break the spell we were under.

A knock at the pool house door yanked me back to reality, and I shoved off the cover and pulled on some clothes. "Coming," I shouted.

Kyle stood in the doorway, his eyes narrowed with suspicion as they swept over me. "Are you sick?"

"Hmm, no, why?" I tried to tame my hair, aware that I probably looked a mess.

"You're late. We needed to leave ten minutes ago."

"Late for…"

"For school. It's Tuesday. Are you sure you're feeling okay?"

Fine. Except your stepbrother kept me up most of the night and I can't think straight. "School, right. I'll brush my teeth and grab my bag."

His eyes grew even narrower as he studied me. "I'll be in the Jeep. Hurry your ass, I don't need Coach on my back for tardiness."

"Ten minutes," I called, already jogging toward the bedroom.

Crap. I'd overslept and in my moment of Maverick weakness, completely failed to realise it was a school night.

Double crap.

I dashed into the bathroom, peeled out of my clothes and hopped into the cubicle. It was the quickest shower in history, and ten minutes later, I was climbing into Kyle's Jeep with towel-dried hair.

"New look?" He arched his eyebrows and Summer stifled a giggle.

"Piss off," I mumbled, sinking into the leather avoiding eye contact. He was sneaky. I didn't put it past him to suspect something. Or know something. I got the impression where Maverick and I were concerned, he was already starting to connect the dots.

"Late night?"

"Just drive."

As soon as Kyle pulled into the parking lot and found a spot, I muttered goodbye, slipped out of the Jeep, and disappeared into the stream of kids heading into the building. Still reeling from the previous night's events, I was oblivious to the person coming toward me and smacked straight into a solid chest.

"Hey, steady there," a deep voice rumbled as I rubbed my nose.

"JB, always a pleasure." I dodged left to go around him but he pre-empted my escape plan, blocking my path.

"The pleasure is mine. Eager to get your hands on me, I see." He brushed his jersey off and I rolled my eyes.

"It's early. I'm tired. I don't have time for this."

Whatever *this* was.

Unaffected by my snarky attitude, he ducked his head, leaning in closer. "You seem tense. Need a little help with that?"

"Fuck off." I flashed him a sickly-sweet smile.

"Ooh, touchy," laughter pealed from his lips. "You're something else, Stone."

"Late. I'm going to be late if you don't move."

"Holloway," a voice boomed across the hallway and my eyes—and everyone else's—snapped over to Maverick's. He looked scarier than usual, the bruises angry and sore. His eyes hard and flat.

"Prince," JB replied with a hint of amusement. "I was just telling your girl here that she should really watch where she's going."

I tried to remain unaffected by his words, but I saw the muscle in Maverick's jaw clench. The whole hallway fell silent. Anticipation crackled in the air. Everyone watched, waiting to see what would happen. But out of nowhere Kyle appeared at Maverick's side. He leaned in close, whispering something in his stepbrother's ear. Maverick's eyes softened for a brief second, his shoulders visibly relaxing. I used the moment to my advantage, barging past JB and hurrying to class. Behind me, the usual morning chatter resumed. As I headed inside the classroom, I reminded myself that Maverick and I were done. Last night was a one-time deal.

It was goodbye—a chance to exorcise this thing between us.

A chance to lay our unfinished business to rest.

But the way he'd looked at me across the hallway... it was almost impossible to remember our agreement. He looked at me with longing, with regret.

He'd looked at me like he wanted so much more than just one night.

And I didn't know what to do with that.

~

"He looks like a wounded puppy." Laurie glanced over to where Devon was with Liam and some other boys, and I shrugged.

"He only has himself to blame."

She shot me a knowing look, and I said, "What?"

"Oh, come on. I told you he wanted more, and you refused to buy it."

"I bought it, Laurie, but I also told him straight. If he couldn't accept it, that's on him, not me."

"I totally agree," Autumn pitched in but Laurie wasn't done.

"He's a guy," she said. "They think with their dicks, and only their dicks. Even the good ones."

"Amen, to that." Autumn said.

I kicked my legs over the bench and stretched. "What's done is done."

"But it's Devon. After what Caitlin did—" Laurie clapped her hand over her mouth, her eyes wide with regret.

"What about Caitlin?"

Laurie shook her head still clutching her mouth, and I looked to Autumn for back up but she just shrugged.

"Laurie." I gave her a pointed look. "What. About. Caitlin?"

Her eyes darted to Devon and his friends again as she slouched down on the bench. "You promise not to tell?"

"Cross my heart." I marked my chest.

"Before Caitlin and Maverick got together, she was seeing Devon."

"Caitlin and Devon? Are you sure?" I said, discreetly looking over at him. He was so… rough around the edges and Caitlin, well she was polished and put together. They were like chalk and cheese.

Laurie nodded. "It's true. It was over the summer, apparently, and she wanted to keep it on the DL. He confided in me one night at a party that he was in deep. He wanted to go public, she didn't. And then school started up and Maverick swooped in and stole her right out from under him."

It explained a lot, but it didn't make me feel any better. Somehow, I'd ended up between Devon and Maverick too. Did that make me the new Caitlin? The thought made my stomach churn.

"Lo?" Laurie noticed my silence. "Are you okay?"

"Yeah, yeah, I'm fine. Just tired." I waved her off, glancing back at Devon. That's why he'd said I couldn't trust Maverick, because he'd stolen his girl. But it didn't explain why he hadn't told me the truth.

What the hell was it with the people of Wicked Bay and their secrets?

"You can't tell anyone, Lo. He'll kill me if he finds out I told you."

"Who am I going to tell? Devon? I think that ship has sailed."

"Don't be so sure. He's not a bad guy, Lo, he's just misguided sometimes. Caitlin and Maverick really screwed him over. So cut him some slack. You're the first girl he's shown any interest in since her."

I couldn't help but wonder if that had anything to do with my name—my connection to Maverick. Did Devon think by pursuing me, he'd be getting back at Maverick somehow?

"Yeah, well." I pushed up off the bench and stood. "Maybe it's for the best we're not friends."

Laurie's jaw dropped open and Autumn's permanent smile slipped, but I didn't stick around to explain.

They wouldn't believe me if I tried.

Chapter Twenty-Four

"It's… nice."

I barged past Kyle and shuffled into the kitchen, dropping the bags of groceries Rebecca and Uncle Gentry insisted Loretta pick up for us, on the breakfast bar.

"Yeah, real nice." My lips pressed into a flat line as I turned, taking in my new home. Despite only being a five-minute ride from the Stone-Prince house, it didn't resemble the wealthy neighbourhood they lived in. Here, the houses were in neat lines with the same matching driveways and decked porches. It was cute. The kind of place a family would want to raise their kids. Quiet. Friendly… *Nice.*

"I like it." Kyle flopped down on the sofa, raking a hand over his sandy-blond hair. "Own bathroom?" he asked, and I nodded.

My room was one of the best parts of the house. It had a sloping ceiling that ran to a huge window that looked out onto the yard and the woods that separated our neighbourhood and the more affluent part of town. And it came with its own en suite. Dad had taken the master bedroom which adjoined the family bathroom, at the other end of the hallway. The third room, too small to act as a guest room, would eventually be Dad's office.

"Can I get some help?" Dad called and Kyle blew out an exhausted breath. We'd been moving and building furniture all day.

"That's all of it?" I asked, peering outside to Dad's truck. He'd picked it up yesterday since he didn't want to have to rely on Uncle Gentry any more.

"That's the lot. I thought we could call it a day and grill out tonight?"

"Grill out?" I laughed. "Who are you and what have you done with my father?"

The smile on his face caught me off guard, and I realised I'd made a joke with him. Something that hadn't happened in a while.

"We have a lot to celebrate, kiddo. The house, your birthday. It's not every day you turn eighteen, Lo. Kyle, you'll join us to celebrate?"

He looked to me and I shrugged. "Sure, Uncle Rob," he said. "Laurie can come, right?"

"Of course. I've already asked Gentry and Rebecca, my parents, Macey, Maverick and Summer, but perhaps the invitation would be better received coming from you." He gave Kyle a pointed look, but I was too busy waiting for his next words.

To my surprise, they never came.

"It's okay, Lo," Dad said, laying his hand on my shoulder. "Stella and Beth are out of town for the weekend."

"Okay."

Okay?

It was the lamest thing I could have said, but I didn't know what he wanted from me. Did he want me to say it was okay? That he should invite them? To celebrate the new house? My birthday? We'd just moved in. I was still getting my head around the idea, without worrying about Stella Drake turning up ready to play happy families.

"If you don't need me anymore, I'm going to head home. I need to get out of these clothes and then pick up Laurie." Kyle fumbled with his phone and then looked up again. "Summer's in. I'm not sure about Maverick and Macey."

Dad's smile slipped. "Okay, well, hopefully they'll be able to make it. I'd like for us all to be here." He clapped Kyle on the back. "Thanks for everything today, son. You were a great help."

"No problem. I'll see you both later."

I gave him a small wave, trying to ignore the tight knot in my stomach. When the door closed, Dad let out a long sigh. "This is it, Lo. Home sweet home."

Emotion swept through me, Dad's words sinking into my bones. At Uncle Gentry's it felt temporary. Surreal. But this was it—this was the start of life in Wicked Bay.

There was no going back.

"Eloise?" Dad's eyes shined with concern.

"Yeah," I choked out, realisation crippling me.

"Are you okay?"

Mashing my lips together, I forced myself to nod. Dad's expression lifted a fraction, but I still saw the doubt there. "I know things haven't gotten off to a great start, sweetheart, but this is going to be a good thing for us. More space. Your own room."

"Yeah, Dad. It's great."

"Well, okay then." He rubbed his hands together and then ran a hand over his head. "I will finish up here and then figure out what we need for the barbecue."

"Sounds good," I said. "I'll be in my room unpacking. Shout if you need me to help out, okay?"

"Sure thing, kiddo."

The walk to my room seemed never-ending, each step heavier than the one before. I was relieved to be here—in the new house—but it felt so final.

It felt like goodbye.

Goodbye to my old life. The life before everything changed. It hit me like a bullet to the chest. This was happening.

And there wasn't a damn thing I could do about it.

~

"Really, Robert, couldn't you have found something a little bigger?" Disapproval creased Beatrice's face, but Dad laughed her off.

"It's perfect for us, for now." He squeezed his mother's shoulder lovingly. "We'll make a good life for ourselves here."

"And what about Stel—"

"Rob, let me takeover and you can give Mom and Dad the grand tour." Uncle Gentry came to his brother's rescue, and I turned back to face the pool, if you could call the small kidney shape that.

"I like it here," Summer mused beside me. "It's nice and quiet."

"Yeah, it's okay," I said. "At least, I'm not too far away. We can still hang out hopefully."

Summer opened her mouth to reply but Kyle cut her off. "Of course, we'll still hang. You're family. Nothing's changed that. Although I'm not sure how I feel about you being older than me." He grinned as if my being older was a new thing, and I discreetly gave him the finger.

"Your room is so cool, Lo," Laurie chimed in. "I'd die to have my own bathroom."

"Babe, if you had your own bathroom, I'd never see you." Kyle swept his arm around her and started tickling, and Laurie's giggles filled the yard. I glanced behind me. Gentry was at the grill while Rebecca was speaking on her phone, her face strained with irritation.

Kyle caught me snooping and smirked. "They'll be here, you'll see."

I shrugged. "Whatever."

He murmured something under his breath but I ignored him, gazing out at the woods.

"Have you been down there yet?" Summer asked and I shook my head.

"Between unpacking and helping Dad build furniture, there hasn't been time to explore."

"Kyle, Laurie, grab plates and cutlery please. These steaks are almost done."

"Sure thing, Mr. Stone," Laurie said in a saccharine sweet voice that had Kyle rolling his eyes and calling her a kiss ass.

When they disappeared, Summer turned to me and whispered, "I'm really going to miss you, Lo."

I entwined our hands between us and smiled. "Me too. But I'm right around the corner. If you need anything, at any time, you can always come here, okay? And we'll still see each other at school."

She nodded but I could see the hesitation in her eyes. Summer found it hard to ask for help. Even after everything we'd been through together, she still didn't come to me for advice or to talk. I didn't take it personally. The youngest Stone-Prince sibling found it hard to open up. I got that—better than she knew. Living in the shadow of an older sibling who radiated success and popularity wasn't always easy. Only, I'd been all too happy to bask in my brother's light. For Summer, it wasn't that simple. She lived in the shadow of not one, but three domineering siblings.

"I mean it," I added. "I'm here, Summer. Always."

She didn't get time to reply as Dad and my grandparents reappeared. "Something smells good," he said going over to check on Gentry.

My grandparents sat at the table and Rebecca joined them. Kyle and Laurie came out with plates and cutlery and we all got settled in to eat just as the doorbell chimed.

Kyle shot me a knowing grin, but when Dad disappeared and returned with Macey at his side, it melted into a frown.

I suddenly didn't feel hungry, but Kyle wasted no time leaning over the table to nab the biggest steak. Rebecca slapped his hands away and laughter filled the air. Dad used the moment to clear his throat and stand.

"Before we eat, I'd just like to say a few words. Don't worry Kyle, I'll keep it brief." He flashed my cousin a wry smile. "The last few months haven't been easy. In fact, they've been some of the hardest of my life."

Dad's gaze collided with mine and what I saw left me breathless. "I lost two of the most important people in the world to me. I almost lost Lo. And it made me realise that life is short. It should be cherished. It shouldn't be spent holding grudges. Time is precious, and in the blink of an eye everything you thought you knew—that you loved—can be ripped away from you." His voice cracked with pain and I helped myself to a napkin to dab my eyes.

"Gentry, Rebecca, thank you for opening your home to us. For offering us somewhere to stay and the chance for a fresh start." Dad raised his glass and his brother and his wife did the same. "Mother, Father, for loving me unconditionally and teaching me that it's okay to make your own path in life, and for welcoming me back with open arms all these years later. Sorry will never be enough, but we have all the time in the world now."

Beatrice burst into tears and my grandpa placed his arm around her, comforting his wife.

"And to the young ones around the table. You have your whole lives ahead of you. Make mistakes. Learn by them. But don't forget that occasionally, we old folk might just know what we are talking about."

Everyone laughed.

Even Macey managed a smile.

But Dad wasn't done. His teary-eyed gaze settled on

236

me again and I felt everyone watching me, their heavy stares pushing me further into my seat. "Eloise, you are the most important thing in the world to me. I know things are changing. I know you need time. And I know that tomorrow you become an adult. But you will always be my little girl and I will always be here for you, sweetheart. Whenever you're ready, I'll be here. Happy birthday, Lo." He cleared his throat, held his glass high and declared, "To family."

"Family," everyone said chinking their glasses with one another.

A month ago, I would have pushed away from the table and ran. But not here, not today. Dad was right, things were changing. *I* was changing. And for the first time, in a very long time, part of me couldn't deny that this—being here, surrounded by my new family—felt right.

~

By the time the sun disappeared over the tree line, I knew Kyle and Laurie were up to something. They'd spent the last hour huddled close, talking in hushed voices. Plotting. My grandparents left earlier, pulling everyone in, one by one, for a hug. Gentry, Rebecca and Dad stayed in the yard, drinking wine, and sharing stories from their younger days while Summer and Macey hung out by the pool. I'd offered to make a start on the dishes, but really, I just needed some time alone. After Dad's speech, dinner had been fairly civilised. Even Macey managed to be polite. But my mind was elsewhere. On the future and what it held.

Now we were settled in the new house, I knew the questions would come soon enough. What did I plan on doing with my life? Where did I want to go to college? What did I want to be? Truth was, I didn't know anymore. There'd been a time when I'd had my whole life mapped out, but losing Mum and Elliot changed all that.

The kitchen door opened and someone came inside but I kept washing. Dip. Rub. Rinse. Repeat. I found comfort in the repetitive action.

"It's your birthday," Kyle said. "You can't do the dishes on your birthday."

I glanced over my shoulder. "Actually, it's not my birthday until tomorrow."

"I really thought he'd come."

My lungs expanded with a heavy breath and I shrugged.

"Lo—"

"Let's not, Kyle." I rinsed the plate and placed it on the rack and dried my hands. "I'm tired, we have school tomorrow and I have a growing pile of homework."

His face morphed into a mischievous grin. "No homework for you tonight. We have plans."

"But—"

Kyle slung his arm over my shoulder and started guiding me to the door. "No buts. It's your birthday. We have to celebrate. Besides, it's already arranged."

Of course it was.

"Does my dad know about this?"

He grinned down at me. "Why do you think he decided to throw an impromptu barbecue? Distraction, baby."

"Has anyone told you you're a bit weird?"

"Yeah, but you love me."

Yeah.

Yeah, I did.

Chapter Twenty-Five

"Okay, is anyone going to tell me where we're going?" I leaned forward, poking my head between the front seats.

"It's called a surprise for a reason," Kyle chuckled at the same time as Laurie said, "No."

I threw myself back into the seat and crossed my arms over my chest in a sulk. After dinner, I wasn't sure I could handle another surprise. But Kyle and Laurie were so excited, and Dad insisted I go, reminding me that turning eighteen was something to celebrate. He wanted me to have fun. To be happy.

The irony wasn't lost on me.

"Hey, come on." Laurie twisted to look at me. "It's your birthday, Lo. Don't you trust us?" She arched her eyebrow and smirked.

"Do you really want me to answer that?" I shot back, and she shared a look with Kyle and they laughed.

"Just relax," he said. "Tonight's supposed to be fun, Cous."

"Fine."

Kyle laughed again, but it was quieter this time. He was disappointed Maverick hadn't shown up at dinner. I was too. But Maverick Prince didn't owe me anything.

And maybe it was better this way.

When the Jeep pulled up outside Laurie's house, I smiled. I'd spent a lot of time here recently. It felt familiar. Safe. But then I heard the music and rumble of voices from the back yard.

"What did you two do?" I groaned as a frisson of energy vibrated through me.

"It's your birthday and you only turn eighteen once, Cous. Uncle Rob said back in England turning eighteen is a rite of passage or something." Kyle winked and climbed out of the Jeep.

I stumbled out after him and Laurie, my stomach knotted tight. Her house wasn't as big as Uncle Gentry's but it still made my home back in Surrey look small. We went around the side to the gate and my worst fears were confirmed. Kids from school swarmed the place. Autumn spotted us and jumped up from her spot on the sun lounger. "The birthday girl is here."

Cups were raised in the air and people cheered but I wanted nothing more than the ground to swallow me whole.

"Don't be shy, Cous." Kyle slung his arm around my shoulder and Laurie pressed close to my other side, forcing me forward. They played a sneaky game.

"Happy birthday, Lo." Autumn reached us and my captors let me go so she could pull me in for a hug. "Surprise."

Lips pressed in a flat line, I forced a smile, and the three of them laughed. "Don't look so worried. Everyone's here for you, to help you celebrate," Laurie said.

Any normal person would have lapped up the attention, but the limelight wasn't somewhere I enjoyed being. Still, I managed to force a smile to appease them. And I was flattered. They didn't have to go to all this effort. But they did. For me.

The party went on around us. I didn't miss the way Kyle kept checking his phone. He needed to accept what I already had—Maverick didn't care it was my birthday.

He didn't care at all.

A red cup was thrust into my hand and someone steered me over to a chair. I plopped down and swept my eyes over Laurie's yard. It wasn't as crazy as I'd first thought. There were a few kids from school but they were friends of Kyle and Laurie. People who I knew by association. Matty and Trent and a couple of the other boys from the football team were playing quarters on Laurie's mom's garden table and Liam was splashing in the pool with some boys from our class. It wasn't like the parties at JB's, or Brendon Palmer's, where most of the junior and senior classes turned up, and I relaxed a little.

"You need to think about getting your license. I could teach you." Kyle announced, mischief glittering in his eyes.

"I don't need to learn to drive when I have you to chauffeur me around."

Laurie stifled a snicker, earning her an eye-roll from her boyfriend. "It's not as difficult as you think. It'd be good for you to learn. Give you some freedom."

"We'll see," I muttered before sipping on my drink.

"Coming in, Lo?" Liam shouted across from the pool and I waved him off.

"No, I'm good."

He pouted, but it soon slipped away when his friend leapt at him and they began to wrestle one another under.

"I swear, they're like big kids," Autumn said as we watched Liam disappear under the water in a big splash. "How would you have celebrated back home, Lo?"

Silence fell over our school group and Autumn clapped a hand over her mouth. "Crap. I'm sorry, I didn't think." Her eyes flashed with regret but I smiled.

It hurt. It hurt so much I could barely form words, but I managed to say, "It's okay."

Autumn had asked a harmless question. I figured she knew about what happened. Laurie's best quality wasn't keeping a secret, and that was okay. It wasn't a secret—it just wasn't something I wanted to advertise either.

If things had been different, I imagined Mum and Dad would have thrown me a party. I was never the most popular girl in college but I had friends. And Elliot and his friends would have made sure I turned eighteen with a bang.

But things were different.

I had no Elliot.

No Mum.

But I did have people. I had Kyle and Laurie and Autumn and Summer. I had friends. Good ones.

~

At five minutes to midnight Laurie appeared with a cake. "It's time." She grinned with excitement as she made her way over.

Everyone stopped, gathering around us as I sat awkwardly in front of the giant cupcake while Kyle instigated a very out of tune version of Happy Birthday. When they were done I closed my eyes, made a wish, and blew out the candle.

Laurie cut the cake into small pieces and handed them around on napkins. "What did you wish for?" Matty asked, before stuffing his mouth full of sugary goodness.

"That's for me to know, and you to find out." I stuck out my tongue and got up, brushing my crumb coated hands down my jeans. "Now eat your cake and get out of here. I'm an old woman now, I need my beauty sleep."

"Really, Cous? You're like a year older than us, hardly ancient."

"Hold the phone, did you just admit I'm older?"

Kyle rolled his eyes with a groan. "Fuck," he

murmured under his breath. "I'm never going to hear the end of this, am I?"

"Nah-ah. Now get your friends out of here."

"Yeah," Laurie said. "We should probably call it a night. Babe, can you and the guys bag up the bottles before you head out?"

Matty and Trent protested but soon started cleaning up when Kyle shot them a stern glare. I helped Laurie and Autumn take the glasses and dishes inside.

"Thank you for tonight," I said when we were done.

"It was all Kyle," Laurie beamed. "He loves you like a sister."

"I know." My throat tightened and the familiar ache in my chest rippled through me. I was glad to have Kyle. He'd wormed his way into my life, become one of my closest friends. But he would never replace Elliot.

"Liam is waiting, I'd better go. But I'll see you both tomorrow." Autumn disappeared off after her boyfriend and we went back outside to the boys.

"Where did Matty and Trent go?"

"They escaped before you,"—he jabbed a finger at Laurie and then stalked toward her—"made us mow your lawn or something."

She slapped his chest. "Behave. You know Mom and Dad only leave me because they trust me."

Kyle shut her up with his lips and I left them to it. "I'll be waiting in the Jeep," I called over my shoulder. "Night, Laurie, and thanks again."

Her mumbled reply followed me as I made my way around the side of the house. Cloaked in darkness, shadows danced across the wall. I'd almost reached the gate when a figure stepped out in front of me.

"Maverick?" I gasped as my heart lurched into my throat. "What the hell are you doing?"

He didn't touch me. If he had, I might have broken

down right there. But his presence seeped into every crack inside of me until I could see nothing but him.

He raked a hand down his face. "I wanted to wish you a happy birthday."

"Well, thanks," I clipped out. "But you're a little late to the party." I moved to go around him desperate to get away from him. The momentary shock at seeing him faded into irritation. I didn't want to do this with him. Not here. Not now. But he blocked my path.

"I'm sorry, okay? I wanted to come, but I couldn't do it. I couldn't..." His voice was thick with emotion.

"You couldn't what, Maverick?" My voice cracked with frustration. "What is this? What are you doing?"

Silence filled the space between us and then he said, "The new house is okay?"

"Yeah, it's okay," I sighed, disappointed he'd chosen to ignore my question. But then why did I expect anything else. This is what he did best.

"Good, that's good. You can focus on the things which are important, move on."

Move on? Was he for real?

Lips mashed together, I tried to fight back the words forming on my tongue. When I didn't answer, Maverick added, "Everything will work out, London." His fingers brushed the stray wisps of hair out of my face, lingering there. On their retreat, he brushed the bare skin along my shoulder and a shiver worked its way through my body.

"Yeah." It came out shaky as my gaze dropped away.

I wanted to be angry—I *was* angry. But I couldn't deny the effect his presence had on me. It was confusing.

Annoying.

But despite how much I wanted to give him a piece of my mind, to tell him this—whatever *this* was—had to stop, I couldn't do it. Because Maverick was here. He was here, and he was reassuring me everything would be okay. And it meant more than it should. Because it didn't change anything. I understood that now.

Maverick cared.

He just didn't care enough.

He watched me. His darkened gaze searching my soul for what, I didn't know. My eyes slid to his, saying everything we never got the chance to say.

It was the wrong time.

The wrong place.

Everything about us was wrong.

We moved like magnets until our lips hovered over each other's. Maverick buried his hands in my hair, pushing backwards until I felt the wall behind me. Our bodies blended with the shadows and I couldn't help the smirk tugging at my lips when I realised he wanted to make sure no one could see us.

Then he kissed me.

And I let him.

My lips parted on a soft sigh as he swept his tongue into my mouth. Slow and deep. Something was different in his touch, but I didn't want to think about what it meant. I just wanted to cling to the sensations running through me. Imprinting every stroke, every lick, every taste into my mind.

"Happy birthday, Eloise." He pressed another kiss to my swollen lips, touched his head to mine and then let go. With one last lingering look, he melted into the darkness.

Like a whisper on the wind, Maverick was gone, and although I wanted to heed his words, to believe everything would fix itself, I couldn't get past the part where Maverick was here. He'd come to check on me. To wish me a happy birthday. Because sometimes, no matter how wrong you knew something to be, it was impossible to ignore how right it felt.

Chapter Twenty-Six

"Great seats." Dad beamed, and I offered a strained nod. Things were still tense between us. Since moving into our own place—and after his heartfelt speech in front of everyone—he was trying. At least three nights a week he made it home for dinner and we ate in awkwardness. He talked about work. I talked about classes. Avoiding the important things, like Mum, Elliot... Stella. It was weird, and I couldn't help but wonder if he was worried I would go off the deep end again or if he was just softening me up ready to drop another bombshell.

Either way, it sucked.

"Robert, Lo, sorry we're late." Rebecca looked elegant in her wide-legged trousers and matching blouse, her long glossy hair twisted into a slick bun. She was the most polished person in the gym, even if it seemed excessive for a basketball game. But that was Rebecca. She probably slept in full make-up and silk pyjamas that were worth more than my entire wardrobe.

I waved at Summer, motioning for her to squeeze in beside me. She slipped past Rebecca and Kyle and dropped onto the plastic seat.

"Hey, I wanted to sit there," Kyle protested, but Rebecca hushed him, nudging my cousin into the seat next to his sister.

"Robert, may I?" She looked at the spare seat beside Dad and he half stood letting her past.

No one mentioned Gentry's absence. Whatever was between him and Maverick apparently extended to his opening game.

"Are you excited?" Summer asked me and for a second, I panicked. But then I realised she meant about watching my first basketball game. She didn't know I was more excited about seeing the team's captain.

A month had passed since that night when Maverick turned up at the pool house. Just thinking about it set my body on fire. But as the weeks went on, so had Maverick's withdrawal. Since the birthday kiss, he'd barely said two words to me. And every day that ticked by, I wondered if I'd ever meant anything to him in the first place. He'd discarded me so easily. Cast me aside as he'd done at the beach last summer. It hurt my head—and my heart— thinking about it.

An eruption of cheers snapped me out of my thoughts. The cheer squad were front and centre. Caitlin ate up the crowd's approval, shaking her hips harder and swishing her pom-poms higher. She looked possessed, but they were good. Really good.

Even Dad—the man oblivious to everything lately— noticed. "Macey and the girls look good out there," he commented.

"She's a great dancer. I just wish she'd take things more seriously." Even in the deafening noise, I heard Rebecca sigh. "I don't know how to get through to her sometimes."

"She's just a kid. Give her time. She'll figure it out." Dad patted her knee, unaware I could hear their conversation as he angled himself more to my aunt.

"Maverick's just as bad, Robert. The older they get, the more they pull away. Things have been..." her voice trailed off when the teams entered the court and she sighed again. "He looks so at home out there."

My eyes landed on Maverick. I'd never seen him in team colours before, but the red and white jersey stood out against his tanned skin and dark hair.

"Rick's looking good," Kyle chortled leaning back to catch my attention behind Summer. I shot him a terse sideways glare. His head shook with laughter but it was drowned out by the crowd.

As if he heard his stepbrother, Maverick's head lifted to where we were sitting. His gaze moved over Kyle and Summer until his eyes found mine. He hadn't looked at me in so long, I felt it like a punch to the stomach, and I shuffled uncomfortably on the seat. But then he was gone, jogging to his team as they prepared for the game.

I knew nothing about basketball. Back home, it was football in the winter months and cricket in the summer. But seeing Maverick, being here, I wanted to know everything. Because Rebecca was right, Maverick was at home out there.

At peace.

He still had an air of hostility about him. As he pulled the team in, he reminded me of a General about to lead his army into war. But when the referee called the captains in for the coin toss and the first buzzer sounded, I saw a glimpse of a different Maverick.

A boy in love with a game.

He glided around the court, commanding the ball, his movements precise and sure as if he was born to play. And when he pushed off the floor, cutting through the air in a move that seemed to defy gravity, grabbed the hoop and slammed the ball through the metal, I stopped breathing. I wanted to leap up out of my seat and cheer right along with everyone else.

But I didn't.

I couldn't.

My eyes drank him in as his teammates tackled him and congratulated him. His head snapped over to our side of the room and part of me wanted to believe he was searching me out. That he felt whatever I was feeling. But his eyes never found mine.

Maverick's early slam dunk set the tone for the rest of the game. The Wicked Bay Wreckers dominated. Even someone as clueless as myself could see that. Blurs of red and white zipped up and down the court. Maverick scored another five points, securing their first win of the season.

"I've never seen anything like that," Dad said to no one in particular as we filed out of the gym.

"Rick's one of the best," Kyle replied. "He'll get a full ride for sure." His eyes lifted to Rebecca, and they shared a look.

"It would a crime if he didn't," Dad added. "He could go all the way."

"You must be so proud, Momma P," Kyle grinned, bouncing up and down on his feet, punching the air rapidly. "Rick's going to play for the NBA one day and I'm going pro. Just think what it'll do for your street cred."

He was joking, but there was an undertone to his words that made me wonder just how much Rebecca supported her sons' dreams. She let out a frustrated groan. "Kyle, please do not call me that in public."

"Boys will be boys," Dad muttered under his breath with a slight shake of his head. "Elliot used to—" He stopped mid-sentence, catching my eye. I gulped and turned away. He never talked about Elliot.

Ever.

Summer slipped her arm through mine and tugged me ahead of them. "Are you okay?" she whispered.

I shrugged. I didn't know what to feel anymore. Everything was so different now. I was eighteen. I had my whole life ahead of me, but I couldn't think past tomorrow. Or the next day. Being here, in Wicked Bay, it still didn't feel real.

Maybe it never would.

Kyle's head popped up between us and he wiggled in, slinging his arm around the two of us. "Are you partying with us?" He turned to Summer. "Not you, little sis, you go home with Mom."

"Kyle," she hissed, shucking him off. "You're so annoying."

He laughed, rustling her hair. "And you're cute, now go meet Mom and Uncle Rob at the car." His hold on me tightened.

"Bye, Lo." Summer lifted her hand in a small wave. "I guess I'll see you at school."

"Bye." I returned her wave and Kyle tapped his head to mine conspiratorially.

"Now we party."

~

"Whose house is this again?" I took in the brick house, lit up like a fairground with twinkle lights draped over the gated perimeter.

"Luke Taffia's. He's Rick's—"

"Best friend," I grumbled not realising I'd said it out loud. Kyle's head whipped around and he arched his eyebrow, flashing me a knowing smirk.

Rolling my eyes, I stomped past him slipping between the crowd huddled on the huge porch.

"Stone, didn't expect to see you here," someone called out, and I heard the telltale slap of fist bumping fist. I paused but didn't turn around, trying to remain incognito.

"Holloway doesn't own me, Aaron."

250

"Could have fooled me. It's good to see you show up to support Rick. He's around somewhere. Probably out back by the pool."

Kyle came around and motioned for me to follow him further into the house. Like I intended on leaving his side. I'd been in Wicked Bay for almost three months, but kept my circle small. Kyle. Summer. Laurie and Autumn. Devon before he ruined things. Still, I recognised more faces this time and a few people gave me a wave or tipped their head in my direction.

"Is Laurie coming?" I said over Kyle's shoulder. She hadn't made the game but said she'd try to meet us here.

"She said she'll try to escape her parents and drive over here. Don't worry, Cous, I won't throw you to the wolves." He glanced back and winked.

I pushed him forward. "Don't let me get too drunk." Even though the urge to grab the nearest drink and knock it back in one, was strong.

Kyle stopped and slipped his arm around my shoulder. "Stop worrying. We're here to kick back and have fun. Luke is good people. I think you'll like him," he teased, but I refused to take the bait. It was the elephant in the room—what Kyle thought he knew about me and Maverick, and what I did know. Neither of us were willing to come clean, and I preferred it that way.

It was a conversation I didn't want to have. Ever. Besides, what was the point? Maverick had made it clear where we stood. If it came out, Kyle would never let me live it down.

The long hallway gave way to a kitchen similar to the one in Kyle's house. Unlike the pristine bare counters at the Stone-Prince's, here every surface was crammed with bottles, and bowls of tortilla chips. I helped myself to a handful on the way past, leaving Kyle to get drinks. He unscrewed a beer and handed it to me. "Stick to beer. For now." He grinned.

"Kyle," I warned. "Dad's expecting me home in one piece. One sober piece."

"Sober smober. Sometimes it's good to let loose, and I wouldn't let anything happen to you. No one will touch you here."

"What do you—"

"Stone," another voice boomed. "Get the hell out here and bring a bottle of Jack. We want to show Rick our gratitude."

"Fuck off," someone grumbled. Was that Maverick? My hands grew slick, a ball of nerves bouncing in my stomach.

Kyle's shoulders heaved with laughter as he grabbed a bottle off the counter and made his way through the French doors. They opened onto a sprawling garden. A big kidney shaped pool was tucked away in the corner, already full of half-naked seniors. I lingered back, sipping my beer, taking in the scene before me.

"Stone, my man, bring it to daddy," a lanky boy with a shaved head approached Kyle, taking the bottle from him. I recognised him from school. From the game. They fist bumped and talked some more. I risked looking over at the group.

Maverick sat on a rattan chair, surrounded by his teammates and a couple of girls as they talked animatedly. If he felt my presence, he didn't let on, and my chest tightened. Luke noticed me and his lips tipped up in a discreet smile. I gave him a small nod in return and looked away. Focusing on anywhere but their group.

What was I doing? I didn't belong here with these people. It was a party for the team—for Maverick. He didn't want me here. I spun on my heels to get the hell out of there, but I wasn't quick enough. Kyle bounded over to me, grabbing my arm. "Hey, where are you going?"

"This was a bad idea," I rushed out, my eyes flickering to Maverick.

Kyle reared back and looked offended. "Huh? Did I miss something? You can't hang out with your cousin at a party now?"

"It's not you, Kyle, it's..."

His eyes dared me to say it. To confess. But I swallowed down the words, steeling myself. "I don't know anyone. I shouldn't be here."

"You're here because I asked you come." He scrubbed a hand down his face. "Okay, I didn't ask, I dragged, but semantics. You're family, Lo. I want you here."

"Kyle." My eyes widened, aware a couple of kids were watching our exchange.

But not Maverick.

He didn't even glance in our direction.

Twat.

"Seriously, these things are usually way more fun than the football team's parties. Just don't tell JB I said that, okay? I kind of like my head." His eyes glazed over. "And my ass. And my dick. Definitely my dick."

"Kyle," I hissed this time, and he finally released me, his eyes softening a fraction.

"Come on, Lo, we don't get to hang out much now you're gone. It sucks. One hour. Give me one hour and if you still hate it, I'll drive you home myself."

My gaze dropped to the beer in his hand and his chest rumbled with laughter. "Okay, *Mom*, I'll walk you home. Better?"

"Fine. One hour. But if I'm not having the time of my life by then, we're out of here." I couldn't help the smile tugging at my lips. Kyle made it so difficult to argue with him.

He held up two fingers. "Scouts honor. Now let me

introduce you to some people."

~

Two hours later, I wasn't quite having the time of my life, but I was having fun. My blood hummed with the effects of the steady stream of beer Kyle and Trey—the bald guy—kept supplying me with. Perched on the end of a long garden sofa next to Kyle, I couldn't help but feel envious of how easily he slipped into the group. They were Maverick's friends, his teammates, and yet, they gravitated to Kyle in equal measure. The two of them were like dark and light. They looked to Kyle to provide fun and entertainment, but they looked to Maverick for guidance and direction.

"So, Lo, how're you liking it now you're not having to put up with these two for housemates?" Trey asked me.

I shrugged unable to stop myself from meeting Maverick's eyes. This time he watched me. I didn't break our connection as I said, "I like my own space. No more boys thinking they can just barge in and make themselves comfortable at all hours and annoying the hell out of me."

The noise and chaos went on around us, but Maverick's friends grew quiet. Even the couple of drunken giggly girls curled up on the other end of the sofa stopped to hear our exchange. No doubt waiting for a reaction from either Kyle or Maverick. My comment was innocent enough, it meant nothing to anyone on the outside looking in. But there were three of us it meant more to. Kyle's stare burned into the side of my head but it wasn't him I cared about. I only had eyes for the eldest Prince. His gaze hardened—his walls slamming down. They'd been down ever since my birthday but this was different. He was warning me. I was annoyed with myself as much as I was with him, but it didn't stop my body craving his touch. No matter how much I tried to forget—to remind myself it was just one night—my body didn't get the memo. Maverick continually pushed me out, but it only drew me in more.

Trey broke the suffocating silence. "I wouldn't want that fucker anywhere near my space." He shot Kyle an amused look and my crazy cousin leaped up and launched in his direction. Trey yelled and the two of them started play fighting on the chair Maverick's friend occupied.

"Cut it out." His voice was so cold everyone's heads snapped up. Kyle paused, plastered against Trey's outstretched body, he craned his head to the side and said, "Come on, Rick, we're just goofing around."

"Whatever, I'm out of here." Maverick drained the rest of his beer and slammed it down and stormed off. The table rattled. Luke called after him but didn't seem as surprised as everyone else at his outburst. His gaze slid to mine, lips pressed into a flat line. He whispered something to Trey and Kyle and went after Maverick.

Okay, then.

I didn't even want to try to analyse what that was all about. What was the point? I turned to Trey and Kyle as they untangled from one another, shook my empty bottle at Kyle, and announced, "I need more beer."

Chapter Twenty-Seven

"You're so drunk," I slurred.

"You're drunker," Kyle hiccup-laughed. He held me up as we made our way through Luke's house. Or maybe it was me holding him up. Either way, our bodies moved clumsily as we tried to find our way out of the mini-mansion. It seemed unfair my new house was a modest two-bedroomed bungalow with a pool no bigger than the bathtub. I needed to talk to Uncle Gentry about getting Dad a pay rise. If I was going to be stuck in Wicked Bay for the foreseeable future, I might as well reap the benefits. Starting with a pool big enough to swim in.

"Shit, we drank way too much." Kyle hiccupped again. "I blame Trey and those shots. Laurie will kill me."

"Kill you? We,"—I stabbed the air with my pointer finger—"should kill her. She bailed on us."

Kyle nudged my side. "I was supposed to look out for you, Baby Cous."

"Baby Cous? I'm older than you, Kyle."

"Yeah, but you're a girl, it's different. Besides, we're both juniors."

I stopped, pulling him back into me ready to protest, but we collided, bouncing off one another. "Motherfucker," he groaned, rubbing his forehead.

The room spun, and I buried my face in my hands trying to make it stop. "Oh God, I think I'm going to throw up."

"Come on." He started tugging me again. "I called Uber."

"Uber?" My head snapped up. "That's a real thing? I thought it was one of those things made up for movies."

"You've been here almost three months. Uber is like Starbucks. Everyone has to try it once. Wait, that's not right. Uber is like beer, you can't live without it," he murmured to himself. "No, that's not it, that's sex. Uber is like…" Kyle paused, rubbing the back of his neck and then he frowned. "What the fuck was I saying?"

"Uber is like coffee and beer but you can't live without sex?"

Sloppy laughter erupted from him as he dragged me toward the door. I was drunk. Beyond toasted but, unlike the football party, I still had my bearings. Maybe I should have drunk more. Teetering on the edge of control and the inability to walk a straight line wasn't a fun place to be.

"Kyle, wait." I yanked on his arm. "Wait, I need to—"

"Are you fucking kidding me?"

"Kyle what the hell is your…" The words died on my lips when my cloudy gaze landed on Maverick. He was coming down the stairs, and I blinked to make sure I wasn't seeing things. Because… drunk.

"Hey, Rick and…" he blinked at the slim blonde tucked into Maverick's side, hand curled around his arm. I'd never hated a hand so much as I did in that moment. "Hello, I don't think we've met." Kyle stumbled forward, extending his hand, only to thrust it behind his back when Maverick sent him an icy glare.

"I'm Selina. You're in my sister Bianca's class."

"Bianca Framer?" He seemed surprised. "You're Selina Framer? Didn't you graduate like two years ago?"

"Yeah, I go to Cal State now."

"And you,"—his head motioned from Maverick to the girl and back again—"two know each other how?" Kyle seemed to sober and I waited for her to answer. Not that it wasn't obvious how they knew each other.

God. I wanted to throw up all over the expensive parquet floor.

"How are you guys getting home?" Maverick ignored Kyle's question but kept his focus on his stepbrother, not me.

Never me.

I was invisible.

Insignificant.

I was the drunk British girl.

Fuck my life.

"I called Uber."

"Cancel." It wasn't a question this time. "I'll drive you. I have to drive Selina, anyway."

Of course he did.

Jealousy burned through me as I followed them to the car. They stood too close. Close enough that Selina's arm kept brushing his. I wanted to hack it off with my hair clip. Maverick opened the passenger door for her and she climbed inside. He left me and Kyle to fend for ourselves so I yanked the door open and stumbled inside, slamming it behind me.

"Since Maverick is above introductions, I'm Kyle, his more handsome, more humorous stepbrother. And this here is our sister from another mister, Eloise Stone."

Selina twisted her body to Maverick and quietly said, "You didn't tell me she was your stepsister."

It wasn't quiet enough and her words hung in the Audi, filling the space. Kyle laughed while Maverick growled. "Stone," he warned.

"Come on, bro, that shit is hilarious. Could you imagine?" He tried to catch his breath. Finally composing himself, Kyle added, "I'm just messing, Selina. Lo's our cousin."

"Oh," she whispered.

Oh, I mimicked silently, letting my head roll back against the cool leather. Maybe if I pretended this wasn't happening... oh, who was I trying to kid? It was happening. I was trapped in a car with Maverick and his latest conquest.

First Caitlin. Then me. Now Selina.

Where was that bucket?

The car purred to life, and we sped out of the driveway. It was late. Past my curfew if Dad ever bothered to give me one like a normal concerned parent. I pushed my arse off the seat, fumbling in my jean pocket and slid my phone out. Everything was blurred, but not blurred enough to see I had no texts. No message reminding me to be home at a reasonable time. To watch my drinks and avoid dodgy boys.

Fuck. My. Life.

I sank back again, drifting in and out of consciousness. Kyle's voice refused to let me slip under. He wasn't talking to me; his attentions were firmly on Selina. But the masochist in me couldn't stop listening. *Did she like school? How long was she back in Wicked Bay for? Would we be seeing her again?* If I didn't know he was crazy about Laurie, I might have thought he wanted to hook up with her.

When the car rolled to a stop, I pressed my face against the tinted windows, sighing when I realised we weren't at my house or the Stone-Princes.

"It's been a pleasure, Selina." Kyle saluted her as she climbed out of the car. The relief I felt was instant, and I sucked in a deep breath. But she had to go and stick her head back inside. "Good night, Lo," she said. "It was nice to meet you."

Nice my arse. I murmured a garbled reply, and the door clicked shut. Maverick waited for a second, raking a hand through his hair. His eyes found mine in the rearview mirror but I looked away. He didn't deserve to see my face. To know what I was feeling. He climbed out and walked her to her door like the true gentleman I knew he wasn't.

I didn't watch the exchange. I wanted to forget this whole night ever happened, but Kyle had other ideas. "She seemed nice," he stifled a laugh, and I shot him an irritated look.

Maybe he wanted a reaction. Maybe this was all a game to him. But I was sick of it.

"Yeah, real nice," I whispered, the words bitter on my tongue.

He chuckled, but it tapered off into a sigh as he pulled down his baseball cap, folded his arms over his chest, and tipped his head back against the seat. When Maverick got back into the car, he didn't speak and we rode the rest of the way in silence.

"We're here," his voice pulled me from the darkness and I rubbed my heavy eyes. Kyle snored softly beside me apparently not as attuned to his stepbrother as I was.

"Thanks for the ride." I fumbled with the door handle desperate to get out of there. I needed to be away from him—far, far away before I said something I would no doubt regret in the morning.

Maverick's darkened gaze burned into the side of my head. "London," his voice was smooth.

Too. Fucking. Smooth.

Just open the door. Finally, it clicked open, and I breathed a sigh of relief.

"Lo, wait."

My eyes fluttered shut, his plea pressing down on me, sneaking under my skin and demanding I concede. But I couldn't.

I wouldn't.

Slowly, I turned and settled my narrowed gaze on his face. "Goodnight, Maverick." Then I slipped into the shadows.

~

Sometime between Maverick dropping me off at the house, and Kyle picking me up Monday morning, I decided.

Move on.

It was simple, really. I couldn't keep playing this game of cat and mouse with Maverick. I'd followed his rules. Stuck to his game plan. It wasn't me who'd turned up outside his bedroom door in the middle of the night or jumped out of Laurie's bushes to wish him a happy birthday. And I'd gone along with it because Maverick touched some place inside of me that needed soothing.

But after waking up and replaying the ride home over and over in my head, I realised something. Whatever reason he had for putting me at arm's length, there was a much more obvious one—he wasn't a one-girl kind of boy and I wasn't emotionally secure enough, or deluded, to be with someone like him.

We were a disaster waiting to happen.

So, when I said goodbye to Kyle and Summer, and headed into school, I made a beeline for Devon. But he beat me to it. "Lo," he said, his eyes darting anywhere but at my face. "Can we talk?"

"Sure." Maybe my luck was turning because this was already going much easier than I'd anticipated.

Surprise flashed across his face as he met my gaze. "Yeah?"

"Yeah. Lead the way."

I followed him around the side of the main building to the gym. He leaned his foot against the brick and tipped his head back with a heavy sigh. "I owe you an apology."

"How about we don't?"

His eyes landed on me and his eyebrows quirked up. "Don't what?"

"No apologies, no mushy heart-to-heart. You messed up. But so did I. I knew you liked me and I still went along with it telling myself it would be okay."

"Okay, then, I think." He looked hesitant, so I continued.

"But you should have told me about Caitlin and Maverick."

"You know?" Devon dragged a hand over his face. "Shit, I—"

"No apologies, remember? I want to be friends. I'm not exactly swimming in them and I like hanging out with you, Devon. So how about it? No more secrets? No more lies? Friends?" I extended my hand, and he searched my face.

"Friends?"

"Friends." I nodded.

His whole face lit up. "I can definitely do that. I missed you too. Does that make me a total girl?"

"Total girl," I flashed him a genuine smile. "Now come on, class calls."

We walked in comfortable silence until we rounded the main building and Caitlin noticed us. Her eyes hardened, burning with contempt. I tipped my chin at her and kept walking. Then I felt him.

Maverick.

He watched us—his eyes following me. I don't know how I knew, I just did. It was a feeling I'd become accustomed to. But this time, I didn't search him out. I didn't pause to find him. I kept walking, chatting to Devon about his weekend. Because while Maverick and I couldn't be anything to one another, Devon and I could.

We could be friends.
Maybe one day, we could be more.

Chapter Twenty-Eight

A paper ball landed on my desk and I slid my hand over it, carefully smoothing it out.

You have to come.

I won't take no for an answer...

I scribbled a reply, scrunched it back up, and inched my hand down to my side, keeping my eyes up front. When the teacher glanced down at the pile of papers he was grading, I dropped it on Kyle's table. His stifled laughter made me smile.

"Psst."

I glanced behind me and shot Kyle a glare. The girl one desk over tutted under her breath and then hushed us. We both glared at her.

"Mr. Stone," the teacher's voice boomed. "Please concentrate."

"Yes, Sir."

It was my turn to snigger, but I fell silent when Kyle kicked my chair and the teacher's suspicious gaze levelled me.

Laurie wanted us to go to Winter Formal. *All* of us. I didn't. I wanted the four of them to go while I stayed at home and washed my hair. Or any of the other excuses I'd given her. I finally thought she'd accepted my answer. She hadn't. The cunning wily girl who was Laurie Davison had passed the buck to Kyle. And he had the persistence of a mule. Dad and I had spent Thanksgiving at my grandparents with him, Uncle Gentry, Rebecca and Summer. Macey and Maverick were with their father so at least I didn't have to endure them too. I'm not sure I could have handled Macey's snarky comments and Maverick pretending I was invisible on top of Kyle's full-scale campaign to persuade me over to the dark side of high school dances. He was worse than a dog after a bone. Notes in class. Constant text messages. Not to mention planting the seed in Dad's head. *"It'd be good for you,"* he'd said more than once since.

When the bell rang, I was first out of the room, trying to avoid any more of his persuasion tactics.

"Lo, wait up."

"Busy," I yelled, slipping through the crowd. Laurie spotted me and started in my direction. Crap. They had me surrounded. I weaved a U-turn and tried to pass Kyle against the flow of traffic, but he was too quick. "Got you." He grabbed my arm and pulled me out of the crush.

"Come on, Lo, you have to come. Tell her she has to come." Laurie nudged her boyfriend and I let out a frustrated breath at being tag teamed.

"Individually, you two are sneaky, but together you're a force to be reckoned with," I mumbled. "Does it really matter if I come or not?"

"Yes," they responded together.

"Fine, fine." My hands flew up. "I'll think about it. But I make no promises."

"I knew you'd come around," Laurie beamed but my

gaze settled on Kyle. The bastard looked so smug and I shook my head incredulously at him. *You owe me,* I silently told him and he flashed me his trademark smirk.

"We can make plans at lunch." Laurie clapped her hands together. "Agh, I'm so excited."

"And that's me, leaving. I'll catch you guys later." I waved them off and headed to my next class trying to push out all thoughts of stretch limos and prom dresses.

~

When morning classes were done, I was relieved to see Devon at my locker instead of Laurie and Kyle. It wasn't unheard of for them to sneak off to an empty classroom during lunch… or to the janitor's closet… or to his Jeep. We got something to eat from the cafeteria and grabbed a table at the back of the room.

"So, rumor has it, they broke you." Devon slid in beside me and helped himself to a chip off my plate.

"*Rumour* needs to learn to keep her mouth shut. I said maybe. Just to shut them up. They're exhausting."

"You're really anti-school dances, huh?"

I shrugged. "It's not that I'm anti-anything, I just… I don't know. I'm not feeling it."

"It could be fun." He waggled his eyebrows.

"Like Homecoming was so much fun?" Devon tensed beside me and I clapped a hand over my mouth. "Shit, Devon, I'm sorry, I didn't mean—"

"Don't worry about it, you're right, Homecoming sucked. In more ways than one. But I hear Winter Formal is going to rooock." Devon stuck out his tongue and waved his finger horns at me.

"Never." I jabbed my fork at him. "Do that again."

"Too much?"

"I'm scarred for life."

Devon's amused gaze landed on his leather wristwatch. "Oh crap, I have to shoot. I forgot I have an appointment with the guidance counsellor." He was already up off his chair. "But think about it. It could be our do-over. And I promise to keep my hands firmly to myself." Devon winked and left me sitting there pondering his words.

A do-over.

It didn't sound awful. We'd spent more time together since clearing the air. And he'd been nothing but a friend lately. If I agreed to go with him, would it be a date?

More importantly, did I want it to be a date?

He was safe and comfortable and nice. Ugh. That word tainted things, but when I thought about, really thought about it, was nice such a bad thing?

"That looked cozy," Laurie said as she and Autumn found me and I rolled my eyes.

"Do you ever stop?"

"Who, me?" She faked surprise as she dropped onto a chair. "So, what did he want?"

"Nothing much." I popped a chip into my mouth.

"You can't leave me hanging. We're friends. Friends share. Did he ask you to the dance?"

"Laurie," Autumn came to my rescue, and I flashed her an appreciative smile.

"He didn't ask me as such," I said. Sometimes, with Laurie, it was just easier to give up.

"Tell us everything. Word for word." Laurie leaned over the table and I relented, relaying my conversation with Devon.

"So, what do you think?" I asked when I was finished.

"He totally wants it to be a date," Laurie said, unable to disguise her excitement. "I mean, he's playing it cool, in case you shoot him down, but he wants a do-over, Lo. He wants to do it right this time."

He did?

"I need to go pee." Autumn rose from the table. "Don't leave for Parker's class without me."

Laurie nodded, and I gave her a small wave as she left. "So." Laurie slipped into Autumn's chair and leaned in close. "What do you think? About Devon?"

"I don't know, I mean I like him, I do, but…"

"But…" She prompted, her eyes wide, demanding an answer.

"I don't know, okay. When I first arrived, it was too much, too soon." And I was hung up on a certain Prince.

"And now?"

"I like him, but…" Could I do nice? After everything?

Laurie took my hands in hers and stared me right in the eye. "He's a good guy, Lo. I know you're dealing with a lot of shit with your dad and the move and what happened, but this could be a good thing. I know you like him. He makes you laugh, you're relaxed around him."

"Why are you pushing this so much? Shouldn't you be siding with Kyle on this? You know he doesn't want me to date Devon."

The corners of her mouth lifted conspiratorially. "Actually, he's coming around to the idea."

"He is?" My eyes went wide. Kyle had warned me against it more than once. I guess something had changed—something to do with his brooding stepbrother. My heart sank, and I pushed my tray away, no longer hungry.

"Fine."

"Fine?" Laurie's feet danced on the floor beneath us, excitedly. "You'll say yes? To it being a date?"

"Maybe."

"Lo!"

"Yes, okay, satisfied? If Devon wants to make a bigger deal out of it, I'll go along with it. You're right, maybe it'll be a good thing. But no heels."

The corners of her mouth tugged into a smirk as she shook her head with laughter. "I'm so proud of you." Laurie wrapped me in a hug just as Autumn reappeared.

She stared down at us with a curious expression.

"What'd I miss?"

"Lo's coming to Winter Formal." Her lips pressed together as if she was trying to hold in the next part, but she couldn't do it. "And she's totally going with Devon, on a date."

I rolled my eyes, Autumn smiled, and Laurie clapped again. The girl was crazy, but I was glad to have her in my corner. We cleared away our trays and walked out of the lunch room. When we reached my locker bank, I stopped. "I need to change some textbooks. I'll catch you guys later."

"Sure thing." Laurie tugged Autumn away but paused at the last minute. "Oh, and Lo, we'll get you into heels one way or another." She winked and their laughter floated down the hallway after them.

~

When Devon appeared at my locker at the end of the day, looking sheepish, I should have known Laurie had been running her mouth. Hands jammed into dark jean pockets, his eyes darted everywhere but at me.

"Devon?" I said for the second time. His lunch looked ready to make a reappearance.

"Hmm, yeah, hey."

"Hey." I laughed, leaning back against the locker bank. From his inability to form words, I figured this could take a while. "Did you want something?"

"Yes." He pulled one of his hands free and clicked his fingers as if he'd had an epiphany. "Winter Formal."

"What about it?" There was no harm in making him suffer, just a little. He was kind of cute when he was nervous.

"Well, Laurie said…" He scratched his head. "You might be up for, hmm, well, she said that…"

"Devon," I cut him off. "Are you asking me to the

dance?"

Relief flashed over his face. "Yes. Yes, I am." He smiled tentatively. "So, what do you think? Can I get a do-over, for real?"

"Devon, I would love to go to the dance with you."

His eyes widened with surprise. "Really?"

"Yeah. I meant what I said before though. I don't want any of that crap. No flowers, no awkward moments with my dad on the doorstep. Okay?"

"Got it. I think Liam mentioned a limo if you want to tag along with them? Or we can meet here? Whatever you're comfortable with."

"We can ride with the others."

"Cool."

I don't know how it happened, but we'd moved closer, only inches between us. Devon stared down at me and, for the first time since Homecoming, I saw the longing in his eyes again. But, unlike the times before, it didn't make my stomach twist with dread. It felt nice to be desired and my pulse quickened a little.

There was just one problem—the giant annoying thorn in my side I felt every time I stepped into a room or walked the length of the hallway.

My eyes darted around Devon and there he was, watching us. He was rigid, his gaze cold.

"Lo?"

I blinked up at Devon and smiled, "Yeah?"

"I asked if you needed a ride home?"

"Yeah, sure. Kyle has practise today, I think." I followed Devon down the hallway, but couldn't resist the urge to look back. But when I did, Maverick was gone.

~

By the time the weekend rolled around, my stomach danced with excitement. I hadn't expected it, but in a way, I was glad Laurie pushed me to say yes to Devon. I'd been in Wicked Bay for three and a half months. It was time to move on, or at least, try.

And Devon was nice. He made me laugh and smile. I could be myself around him

Checking my hair one final time, I tugged the loose tendrils falling around my face. They sprang back into place. Deep red gloss made my lips pop, contrasting against my smoky eyes. The full length black dress hugged my delicate curves, grazing the floor. It swished around the silver sequin kitten heels. They were a compromise when Laurie and Autumn had tried to force me into skyscraper heels. I'd wobbled like Bambi and rushed to pick out a safer, less risky pair that still matched the dress.

"Lo, they're here." Dad's voice filtered up the stairs, and I blotted my lips together one last time before grabbing my matching sequin clutch bag.

"I'm ready."

"Eloise," Dad swallowed. "My God, you look beautiful. When did my baby get so grown up?" He leaned in and pressed a kiss to my cheek, and I blushed at his words.

"Thanks, Dad." I put some distance between us. I knew why things were so awkward between us but in that moment, guilt coiled around my heart. "Well, I guess I should get going."

"Have fun, sweetheart. I know things haven't been easy, but I'm trying. I want our life here to work, I want you to be happy."

Lips mashed together, I offered him a small nod. I didn't want to lie to him and tell him we'd get through it—because honestly, I didn't know if we would—but we'd found a routine over the last few weeks. Some kind of normal.

When he realised I wasn't going to reply, he forced a smile and said, "Kyle has promised to get you home in one piece, but I trust you, Lo. I want you to know that."

"Okay, Dad. I'll see you tomorrow."

When I opened the door, Kyle stood there with a single rose in his hand. "Oh, hell, no." His eyes narrowed, sweeping over my dress. "Get back in there and change. Right now."

"Shut up." I shook my head with amusement, accepting the flower. "Thank you. Now come on before Dad wants another heart to heart."

"That bad, huh?" He offered me his arm, and I slid my hand through the gap.

"Wow, Laurie's dad went all out." The pristine stretch limo sparkled in the moonlight.

"He even filled the ice bucket with the good stuff. Come on." Kyle opened the door and waited for me to get in.

"Hey guys," I said to Laurie, Autumn, and Liam as they sat on the long leather seats, sipping flutes of something bubbly.

"Lo, you look so good. That is dress is… wow." Laurie gushed.

I complimented their dresses while Kyle slid inside, slamming the door behind him "We'll get Devon and then get this party started."

My bag vibrated, and I dug out my phone, reading the text message. "Change of plans," I said. "Devon is running late, he said he'll meet us there."

A low growl rumbled in Kyle's chest and I nudged him. "Hey, it's fine. No big deal." His heavy stare said otherwise, but I really didn't mind. Although I'd agreed to the date, this was all new to me. I was happy taking it slow. Autumn poured me a glass of champagne and I joined them in a toast.

Mr. Davison must have requested his money's worth since the driver took the scenic route, driving along the moonlit coast. Even from behind the tinted windows, it was beautiful. Twenty minutes later, we pulled up outside the hotel, a swanky place downtown. Kyle and Liam climbed out first, helping us out one by one. I searched for Devon in the stream of kids entering the hotel.

"Perhaps he went inside already," Laurie reassured me.

"Maybe." I checked my phone again, but there was nothing. "You guys go inside and I'll wait."

"No way," Kyle protested. "Not happening. We'll all wait and we'll all go in together."

"That's my man." Laurie snuggled into his side gazing up at him like he hung the moon.

When another ten minutes passed and there was still no sign of Devon, I called him. It went straight to voicemail. Shoving my phone back in my bag, I said, "Come on, let's go inside. He can find us when he gets there."

"Are you sure, Lo?" Laurie said, her eyes brimming with disappointment.

"It's fine."

"Well, I don't know about Liam," Kyle said puffing out his chest. "But I have enough to go around. Cous, get over here." He extended his arm as he'd done outside my house. Laurie shot me a wide smile and the two of us walked in with him.

The place was crazy; it put our occasional school disco back in Surrey to shame. It was easy to forget these were high school students. Boys wore complete tux's or tailored suits and most of the girls looked straight out of a beauty pageant.

"Isn't it exciting?" Laurie craned her head around Kyle and grinned at me.

"It's something, alright," I breathed out suddenly feeling out of my depth. "I'm going to go find the bathroom."

"Want me to come?" Laurie said, but I shook my head. "No, I'll be fine. I could use a drink though."

"Meet us at the bar." Kyle pointed to the long table at the other side of the room where waiters were serving what I assumed to be mocktails and non-alcoholic beers.

"Okay." I moved as fast as my feet could carry me, past the huddle of girls retouching their make-up and gossiping about their dates by the mirrors, and slipped into a stall. When I was done, I washed my hands and checked my hair and face. There had to be a good explanation for Devon being late and I hoped he was okay.

"Oh look, it's the princess," a voice said behind me. I glanced around, searching for the victim of the snide comment. When my eyes landed on Caitlin Holloway, I realised it was meant for me.

"Caitlin," I said touching up my lips. "You look nice."

Surprise flashed in her eyes as she folded her arms over her chest, staring at me through the mirror. "And you look… dateless."

Her friends sniggered under their breath but I didn't let their mean girl routine faze me. She was probably just pissed Maverick hadn't taken her back. And even though we weren't friends, I knew she hated that I had a link to him.

"I don't make a habit of sneaking my dates into the girls' bathroom." I stuffed the lipstick in my bag and turned to face them. "But if that's your thing then good for you."

Her smug smile faltered, replaced with irritation and I moved to leave, but she stuck her arm out to the wall, blocking my exit. "This will be so much fun."

Confused, I held her gaze for a second before knocking her arm away and leaving the bathroom. Her confrontation had thrown me for a loop. She'd barely said two words to me in weeks. I wasn't naïve—the girl hated me—but this was… unexpected. Refusing to let her dampen my mood, I checked my phone again and sent Devon another text before heading back inside.

Caitlin and her friends were ahead of me, just inside the main room draped over their dates like cheap scarves. Shaking my head, I searched for Kyle and Laurie across the room, but did a double take in Caitlin's direction.

No.

No.

Everything slowed down, the throb of my pulse beating against my skull. It made no sense. He wouldn't.

He wouldn't.

But as Caitlin turned to face me, tugging on her date's arm, her words made perfect sense. A rush of tears burned my throat as everything fell into place.

Chapter Twenty-Nine

"**D**evon?"

I stared at the guy I thought was my friend while Caitlin clung to him looking very pleased with herself. The dance went on around us. Apparently, a little drama wasn't enough to stop the party. But audience or not, she looked smug. Devon on the other hand looked like a wounded puppy, refusing to meet my disappointed stare. As far as I was concerned, he could go to hell. They both could.

They deserved each other.

"Cous, we good here?" Kyle was beside me in an instant, and I heard the coolness in his voice. He'd witnessed their little prank. The entire class had, but obviously no one else planned on coming to my rescue.

"Everything's fine, Kyle. Go back to Laurie, I'm going to head home."

"Like hell you ar..." His voice trailed off, and I turned my head to see what had silenced him. My eyes landed on Maverick across the room, standing in the doorway in dark jeans and a fitted black dress shirt. His eyes slid to mine, and I asked him a silent question.

What are you doing here?

His eyes seemed to hold the answer.

You know why I'm here.

I did? Or was I deluding myself?

Caitlin gasped, cursing under her breath. "I knew it. He—"

"Come on, Cat. I think we've done enough." Devon sounded dejected, but it was too late for that. I'd thought we'd cleared the air between us. I'd thought he was my friend, and he'd betrayed me. With Caitlin, no less.

"Hey." Kyle shouldered me and I blinked at him. "You good?"

I nodded over the lump in my throat.

"Okay, if you need me, I'll be right over there." He pointed to Laurie, and she gave me a small wave, shock glistening in her eyes. I lifted my hand in return, still stunned by the turn of events.

I wanted to leave, to put an end to the embarrassment burning through me. But leaving meant walking right by them. And besides, Maverick was still in the doorway. When I made no attempts to move, he closed the distance between us, ignoring the stares of our classmates.

When he reached me, I still hadn't moved, paralysed to the spot.

Could tonight get any weirder?

"You okay?"

"People keep asking me that," I laughed, but it came out strangled. People were watching. They weren't watching before when it was just me, Devon, and Caitlin. But this was Maverick Prince.

Now all heads were turned in our direction.

He was the main attraction, and they intended on watching the show.

"What are you doing here, Maverick?" My voice was small, defeated, and I hated it. Hated Caitlin and Devon had that kind of power over me. But no matter how strong I tried to be, it was exhausting, and at the end of the day, I was only human.

"It's my fault." His lips pressed together in a grim line.
"What's your fault?"

He glanced over at Caitlin and Devon. They had moved away, but she was still watching us. Anger blazing in her eyes, her body visibly shaking with rage. My gaze dropped to where Devon's arm was hooked around her waist, holding her back, and I couldn't help but think in the end he'd got what he'd wanted.

Her.

"Did you make her set me up and embarrass me in front of everyone?"

He rubbed a hand across the back of his neck. "No, but—"

"So, not your fault," I sighed blinking the tears away. "I just want to go home and get out of this bloody dress."

His eyes swept down my body and a shiver danced up my spine. When his gaze snapped back to mine, his irises had darkened to almost black. "You can't leave yet," he said.

"What? Why?" Was this another cruel joke?

But in a move that made my head swim even more, Maverick took my hand and led me to the dance floor. I didn't resist as he wrapped me into his arms and swayed us to the music. I couldn't have if I'd tried. Even under the disco lights, I felt their stares. Maverick Prince—the most popular guy in school—was dancing with me. Eloise Stone. His very British, very broken step cousin.

"What the hell are you doing?" I hissed through my teeth with a fake smile.

Maverick dipped his mouth to my ear, his breath eliciting another shiver. "I'm tired of playing games." His voice was measured—sure—as if his words made perfect sense, but there was an air of vulnerability that reminded me of the Maverick I'd met last summer.

Was it possible he was under there still? Locked away from the rest of the world? There had been moments when I'd thought I'd seen him, but they usually ended with him doing or saying something to ruin it and prove to me what an arsehole he'd become.

"Everyone's staring," I whispered, turning my head until our lips were almost brushing.

His eyes dropped to my mouth and every memory of being with him flooded my mind. I gulped, my heart racing in my chest like a runaway train. What was happening? What the hell was he thinking? As if he heard my words, he said, "Let them stare. I'm done pretending."

His grip on me tightened as if he needed to show me he meant what he was saying. Only I didn't really understand what he was saying. Hadn't he said we couldn't be together? For the last month, hadn't he treated me like I was nothing to him?

And part of me had hated him for it.

"Stop overthinking it," his voice caressed my cheek causing my eyes to flutter shut, and I snuggled closer trying to force out the shitstorm that wasn't only just tonight, but my life.

Maverick had always seen past the walls I built around myself and it terrified me. My hands twisted into his shirt as I pulled back to look at him. "What are you doing, Maverick?"

The corners of his mouth lifted in a smirk. "I thought it was pretty obvious, it's called dancing."

I narrowed my eyes. Waiting. Ignoring the wild flutters in my stomach. He leaned in, so close I thought he might kiss me, but he didn't. "Do we have to label it, London? I came here, to the fucking school dance, for you."

"I—"

Maverick pressed his forehead against mine, gathering me closer. "I have imagined that night over and over. Do you know how hard it was walking away from you? I was a mess, ready to do something really fucking stupid. But then you came and stood next to me. Fuck, you were so cute. So innocent. And I wanted to lose myself in you. But I could see you were nervous."

He wasn't talking about the night we spent together at the pool house. He was talking about that first night. Last summer.

"I couldn't do that. Corrupt the good girl. I am not him, Lo. I am not my father. But then I saw you standing in my kitchen. The angel who saved me that night. I thought I was seeing things. He warned me, you know? Gentry told me to stay away from you, to keep you out of trouble. He didn't want you to end up in trouble." He laughed bitterly. "Because that's me, right, trouble? So, I did it. And fuck knows I have tried to keep my distance. You were going to be living here. Going to school here. How the fuck was I supposed to be around you every day and not touch you?"

One of his hands danced up my back and around my shoulder, burying itself in my hair. His eyes shuttered as he drew in a deep breath. When he looked at me again, what I saw rendered me speechless.

"I told myself, one night. Fuck you and forget about you. That was the plan. It makes me a selfish bastard, I know that. But you were buried so far under my skin, I needed to do something. You were moving out. I wouldn't have to see you every day, lie in bed at night knowing you were just across the yard. I thought it'd be easier us not being so close. It wasn't."

"Maverick, I—"

"No, Lo, you need to hear this. I stayed away because I wanted to protect you. From me. From him. But I. Am. Done."

His lips barely touched mine when I noticed someone approaching us out of the corner of my eye.

"Hmm, I hate to be the one breaking up this beautiful moment, because let's face it, it's long overdue, but Rick, we got company." Kyle nodded over at the other door. JB stood there with a couple of his football friends, and Maverick cursed under his breath.

Kyle's hands shot straight up. "It wasn't me, I promise. I didn't know you would show up. But I bet I know who was banking on it." His gaze slid to Devon and Caitlin. She scowled, anger rolling off her in waves. If looks could kill, we would all be dead.

"Fuck," he murmured under his breath and I realised something bigger was happening here. Something that didn't just involve Caitlin and Devon getting back at me, but involved Maverick and JB, too.

"Go," Kyle said. "Slip out the back door, and I'll handle JB, okay?"

"Will someone tell me what's going on?"

"Ssh," they both snapped at me, the tension bouncing off them.

"Fine," I muttered, folding my arms over my chest. Maverick's dark eyes focused on my neckline sending a pulse of desire through me. He smirked, giving Kyle his attention again.

"Thank you. Don't do anything reckless. I owe you."

Kyle shot me a cocky smile. "You always owe me. Now get her out of here." He motioned to the door at the back of the room. Maverick slid his hand into mine and started moving just as Kyle called after us, "And don't do anything I wouldn't."

Maverick's shoulders shook with laughter as he guided us through the tables. Kids stared, whispering and pointing. But I ignored them. It was easy when Maverick was here. All I saw was him. The second I saw him standing there under the balloon-arch, everything paled into insignificance. Devon's betrayal. Caitlin's harsh words.

None of it mattered. Because he came.

He came for me.

I skipped closer to him, pressing into his side. "Maverick, what's going on?"

"Not here," he whispered, his eyes settled on the door. It was the same look I'd seen so many times, fierce determination.

He grabbed the bar, pushed, and shouldered open the door. We spilled out into the inky night. Maverick leaned around me to close it and then he was there, hands flat against the door, caging me in. I thought he was going to kiss me, but he didn't. Instead, his head touched mine, his body pressing me back until I hit the wall.

"Maverick?"

"Just give me a second." His voice trembled, and I realised he was barely in control. He wanted to fight.

To hurt.

To protect.

My hands slid up his shirt and over his shoulders, cradling him against me. What had happened for him to harbour this much rage and anger? Another second of silence passed, and then he pulled away, taking my hand. "Come on, let's get out of here."

~

Maverick didn't take me home. He shut off the engine and came around to open the door for me. I didn't fail to notice he'd parked at the point of the driveway furthest away from the house.

"Stealthy," I said as we walked up to the back gate. Maverick entered the code, and we slipped inside. The Stone-Prince's garden was bathed in soft light. I hadn't been back here since Dad and I left. Strangely, it felt more like home than the new house and I wondered if the boy beside me had anything to do with that.

We reached the pool house and my eyebrows

furrowed as Maverick pushed open the door, letting me enter first. It looked the same, only emptier. The sofa bed was fixed back as a sofa, and I walked around the small space while Maverick stood silent and stiff inside the door.

When I came full circle, and my eyes landed on his, I said, "What?"

"You." He pushed off the door and stalked toward me. "Look at you."

I swallowed, my mouth dry. His fingers danced over my neckline and across my shoulders. "You're beautiful, Lo. I could kill him for doing that to you." Anger flashed in his eyes.

"He's not worth it."

"No, but you are." Maverick kissed the corner of my mouth and my heart stopped. How had I ever considered settling for Devon when Maverick made me feel this way? It was intoxicating.

He took my hand and led me to the bedroom, and I gasped when I stepped inside. "Maverick?"

"When you left, I moved out here."

"You did?"

How did I not know this? More to the point, how had Kyle managed to keep it a secret?

"I wanted to feel close to you."

He'd changed the bedding. It was a dark cover, swirls of grey and black. Like a storm stirring on the horizon. I smiled to myself. It fit Maverick perfectly.

"Your mom and Gentry didn't mind?"

"I think they were relieved. Things have been…"

He didn't need to say the words. I'd seen it. We all had. Things were tense between the three of them. And Macey. But where she was a mean bitch, she wasn't angry or violent. Just misunderstood.

He came up behind me, wrapping his arms around my

waist and tucking his jaw onto my shoulder. "I missed you."

"You did, huh?" I turned into him. "Could've fooled me."

"Don't." Guilt swam in his eyes. "There are things you don't understand, Lo. Things I'm not sure I can tell you. But I want to try. I want…" the words died on his lips.

"Tell me, Maverick. What do you want?"

He squeezed me tighter, pressing a kiss to my shoulder. "You, Eloise Stone. I want you."

Chapter Thirty

Our lips connected, full of silent promise and understanding. Maverick's hands slid up my arms, eliciting a shiver along my spine, and buried themselves deep in my hair.

He was usually so cold and untouchable, but heat flowed between us. Something was different about him. He was gentle. Soft. Holding me as if he couldn't believe this was really happening. Handling me like fragile glass he didn't want to shatter. But as the kiss deepened, the Maverick I'd come to know resurfaced.

His hand curved around my neck holding me in place as he took control. He pulled me away slightly, enough for his mouth to hover over mine. "Maverick?" I whispered as he watched me. Obliterated me with his darkened gaze.

That wicked smile tugged at the corners of his mouth and he leaned in, sucking my bottom lip between his teeth, chasing the sting away with his tongue. A low growl rumbled in his chest and in one swift movement he scooped me against him until my soft curves fit against the hard ridges of his chest like two pieces of a puzzle.

"Do you know what you do to me?" His gaze travelled over my face, searching my eyes. "How fucking crazy you

make me? I can't think straight, London. You're in here."
Maverick clasped my fingers in his and tapped our joined
hands to his temple.

"The feeling's mutual." I admitted, earning me
another wicked grin.

"Enough talking." He gave me a lazy smirk as he
lowered me to the floor and unzipped my dress. It
tumbled down my body like warm butter and his hungry
gaze swept over me sending another shiver through me.
His irises were obsidian with lust. Maverick wasted no
time stripping out of his shirt. My eyes danced over his
tanned body. Drinking in every smooth dip and hard
plane. I reached out, desperate to touch him but he
caught my wrist and tugged me forward, capturing my
lips again. My hands went to his belt, pulling and
fumbling until we were nothing but skin on skin.
Maverick tilted my head, licking a path from the column
of my neck to my ear, drawing a soft moan from
me. God, this feeling would never get old. The way he
played my body like an instrument. Brought me to life
and made me fly. He was my addiction. I craved the high.
The escape. And I wanted to lose myself in him and never
come back.

Lust took over and before I knew what was
happening, Maverick pushed me down onto the bed,
covering me with his body. "I've waited too long for
this." His voice was raw with need as his fingers dipped
inside my lace pants and glided across my centre.

"Oh God," I panted, clinging to his shoulders.

"You're mine, Lo. Mine." Maverick devoured my
mouth, swirling his tongue with mine, owning me.
Claiming me.

And I gave him everything.

In a strange way, it had always been him; the
mysterious dark-eyed boy on the beach last summer.
He'd hurt me that night, but it hadn't stopped me

daydreaming about him when I returned to England. About his story. The secrets behind his dark indefinable expression.

I wanted to know him.

To uncover the story behind his cold exterior.

Maverick curled a finger inside of me, and another, working me faster until I was a blur of moans and sensations, and my world shattered around me. But he gave me no time to catch my breath as he shucked out of his boxer briefs, rolled on a condom, and pushed inside me. "Fuck," he groaned, but he didn't move.

"Maverick?" His name pierced the heavy silence.

"I just need a minute." His chest heaved with the force of his ragged breath, and then he rolled into me and we both groaned.

My legs pressed against his hips. I needed more. Maybe it was my need to escape—my addiction—or maybe this thing between us was real.

It didn't matter. It would later when the spell broke and reality came back. But right now, all that mattered was this.

Us.

"Lo?" Uncertainty filled Maverick's voice as he eased back to meet my gaze.

"Don't stop," I pleaded, arching my body up to his, fingers raking down his shoulders.

He searched my eyes, but I slammed my lips to his, pouring everything I felt—everything I needed—into the kiss. And relief washed over me when Maverick responded, kissing me deeper, harder. Each stroke of his tongue matching his thrusts.

Delicious heat spread through me, burning and deadly. Maverick sucked the salty skin along my jaw, whispering dirty words in my ear. How good I felt wrapped around him. How he wanted to hear me scream his name. I was so lost in him—in the way he felt stretching me, how his naked body felt pressed against mine—I was barely present. So far gone I almost missed him say, "I wanted you that night, so much. I wanted to lose myself in you. To make it stop."

But then stars exploded behind my eyes and waves of pleasure crashed over me, and Maverick's declaration melted away with my contented sighs and quivering limbs.

~

"What time is it?" I murmured.

"Past seven." Maverick's husky voice made my stomach flutter and my pulse quickened. Then it dawned on me.

"No one will come in here, right?" I could think of nothing more embarrassing than Rebecca or Macey... or even worse, Gentry, barging into the pool house and finding us wrapped up in each other.

"Don't worry, we're good." He pulled me closer, pressing a soft kiss to my hair.

Maverick... soft and gentle. It went against everything I knew about him, yet it felt completely normal. We lay in comfortable silence for a little longer, but I knew we couldn't stay here forever. There were things we needed to talk about.

"So..."

"So..." he laughed around his reply and I felt his lips curve against my skin. "It's too early to think, Lo."

"Can I ask you something?" Maverick let out a groan of frustration but I continued, anyway. "Kyle knows about us?"

He rolled me onto my back and hovered over me. "What do you think?"

"Did you—"

"Did I tell him?" He shook his head. "I didn't need to. He knew the second I laid eyes on you."

"He knew?" I whispered confused about what this meant.

Maverick grazed my lips with his own and the need for him built again. But I needed to hear this so I tamped down the urge to wrap my legs around him.

"We got drunk one night, right after I called things off with Caitlin, and I ended up telling him about the mysterious girl I met on the beach last summer. He didn't tell me it was you though. I guess he wanted me to find out the hard way."

Kyle knew.

He'd known all along.

Even though I suspected he knew *something*, I didn't realise he knew about last summer. I didn't know how to feel about it.

All this time, he'd known.

And he'd never said a word.

"What happened with Caitlin, Maverick? I saw you that night on the beach, at Brendon Palmer's party, and that night when you kiss… almost kissed me."

Maverick went rigid, a stony mask slamming over his face. "You don't need to worry about Caitlin. She won't pull that shit again. It was over way before you got here."

But I did worry. Maverick might not have wanted her, but she still wanted him. And the way she'd declared open season on me at the dance told me it was only the beginning.

Silence stretched out before us. Maverick tucked me into his side once more, drawing lazy circles along my ribcage, his lean body cocooning mine. There was so much I still wanted to know, to ask, but for now, I was happy to enjoy the moment.

If I didn't ask the question on the tip of my tongue, we could pretend everything was fine. But the longer we lay there the harder it became.

I wasn't that girl.

Maybe before the accident, I could have been. But not now.

Too much had happened, and I needed to know where I stood because for the last three months, Maverick said one thing and did another. He was here now, but what happened once I left?

"I can hear your thoughts from here," he pulled me closer.

"What happens now, Maverick?"

He shifted over me and caged my body with his. His eyes captured mine, holding me there, and then he lowered his face, touching his head to mine. "I need you, Lo." He breathed out, and I held my breath, waiting. "I don't know what tomorrow brings or the next day or the one after that but I need you."

"Maverick—"

"Don't ruin this. Not now. Not yet. Please." The plea in his voice surprised me. Maverick didn't beg—for anything. "Things are complicated, Lo. I'm complicated, but I'm done pretending. I meant what I said. I walked away once, I won't do it again."

There was a but in there somewhere—a pretty big one if I knew Maverick.

And I did.

But it was already too late. I was a goner the second he showed up at the dance. Maverick cared. He'd cared all along and it was enough.

For now, it was enough.

PLAYlist

Ocean Drive – Duke Dumont
High by the Beach – Lana Del Rey
To Belong – Daughter
New Americana – Halsey
Vicious Love – New Found Glory
Stay the Night -Zedd ft Hayley Williams
Calfornia Dreamin' – Sia
Running Up That Hill – Placebo
This Is What Makes Us Girls – Lana Del Rey
Cloud – Elias
Shine – Years and Years

AUTHOR'S note

Thank you so much for reading Lo and Maverick's story. Wicked Beginnings is my seventeenth published book. I can't quite believe that. When I set out writing this story, I wanted to create a world that left readers wanting more. More Lo and Maverick. More Kyle and Laurie. Even more Devon and Caitlin. I have so much more planned for these guys, I hope you'll stick around for the ride…

As usual there is a long list of people that I am indebted to for helping me hit publish. My alpha readers: Anna and Jenny. Without you both, I'm sure I'd go insane. Writing brought us together, but I consider you both my friends. My beta and proof readers: Samantha and Ginelle, thank you so much for helping me make this story shiny and polished. My Indie Girls, you are my safe place, my confidants, my go-to girls when I need to vent or talk strategy and plans. My British editor, Andrea. It was so much fun working with you on this project, I look forward to the next time. To Amber at Quirky Blind Date with a Book, I'm so honoured you ran Wicked Beginnings as one of your 'secret' titles. To each and every blog that has got behind the launch of this series, whether you've promoted, shared, or reviewed, it really is you guys that help get books out there – thank you! And lastly, to the readers who continue to get behind me and the stories I love to tell. A million thanks really aren't enough.

About The Author

ADDICTIVE ROMANCE

Author of mature young adult and new adult novels, L A is happiest writing the kind of books she loves to read: addictive stories full of teenage angst, tension, twists and turns.

Home is a small town in the middle of England where she currently juggles being a full-time writer with being a mother/referee to two little people. In her spare time (and when she's not camped out in front of the laptop) you'll most likely find L A immersed in a book, escaping the chaos that is life.

L A loves connecting with readers. The best places to find her are

www.lacotton.com

www.facebook.com/authorlacotton
www.instagram.com/authorlacotton